Surviving Chadwick

Surviving Chadwick

A Novel

Phillip Wilhite

Lucretia —
Thanks for your support.
Enjoy your input i
the bookclub
immensely.

iUniverse, Inc.
New York   Bloomington

Surviving Chadwick

Surviving Chadwick is a work of fiction. Names, characters, places, and incidents are the products of the author's imagination or are used fictitiously. Any resemblance to actual events, locales, or persons, living or dead, is entirely coincidental.

iUniverse books may be ordered through booksellers or by contacting:

iUniverse
1663 Liberty Drive
Bloomington, IN 47403
www.iuniverse.com
1-800-Authors (1-800-288-4677)

ISBN: 978-0-595-52094-7 (pbk)
ISBN:978-0-595-62158-3 (ebk)

Library of Congress Control Number: 2008939007

Printed in the United States of America

iUniverse rev. date: 4/23/2009

For Mom, Dad & Jim

Many thanks to the following: Mike Wilhite, Marian Wilhite, Paul Wilhite, John Wilhite, Mary Wilhite, Sylvia Wilhite, Akilah Wilhite, the entire Wilhite Family, Junot Diaz, Diem Jones, Elmaz Abinader, VONA, Joan Marie Wood, Temescal Writers, Clive Matson, Cheo Tyehimba, Jackie Luckett-Johnson, Pamela Shepard, Paula Payne, Sharline Chiang, Ly Nguyen, Sherri Moore, Anisha Moore-Johnson, Brandon Moore, Ron Davis, Anjuelle Floyd, Dera Williams, Yolanda Smith, The Marcus Bookstore Bookclub, Katherine Russell-Brown, Tamar Love, Coffee With A Beat, Kevin Ficklin, Kevin Singleton, Tracie Henry, Tashe Henry, Shelia Copeland, Jasmine Dawson

REUNION

As we begin another year at the Chadwick School, your donations are more important than ever ...

Junk mail. I had received so many of those green and white newsletters from the Chadwick School that I was in the habit of throwing them away after a brief glance at the front picture. Aside from the modern images, which showed that more women and students of color were enrolled, the newsletter never changed: the boring, pagelong message from the headmaster, followed by a list—by year—of alumni, documenting their significant achievements and current occupations. In the back was a tearaway envelope, which I was to use, ostensibly, to mail my donation to the school that had done so much for so many fine citizens, according to the brochure. I never understood why Chadwick sent me anything—I'd been kicked out after my first year. I guess after a while it didn't matter what you did while you were there, as long as you sent money. Howard Hughes had gone there and been kicked out; maybe Chadwick had begged for his money, too.

But I didn't automatically throw away this particular newsletter. From the smooth, round, mahogany dining room table in my home, I studied this newsletter—and the enclosed note—ignoring the stack of work invading my peripheral vision. It had been nearly fifteen years since I'd gotten the boot, but now I was going back. The reunion was a chance to set the record straight, but there was another, more important reason.

Jenaye.

* * *

1

June 20, 1989

Dear Isaiah:

Believe it or not, our fifteen-year reunion is approaching, and I'm hoping you can attend. I've taken on the task of getting in touch with as many "lost alumni" as possible, and you're the first one on my list. The reunion weekend will coincide with the Ojai Tennis Tournament, which should be fun. Plus I've got some good news to give to everybody. Don't forget to make your reservations and register now. You wouldn't want to miss it.

Jenaye

*   *   *

Fifteen years without seeing her was a long time. We'd kept in contact off and on, using letters and phone calls, each time agreeing to hook up in person at the next break in our schedules. Until now, that time had never come.

She was going to have a hard time recognizing me. Back in the day, I'd worn glasses, stood about six-four, weighed 185 pounds, and was cut. Lately, I'd ballooned up to 275 after a knee injury, and I was having difficulty buttoning the snaps on the elastic waistband in my pajamas. I wondered if she'd still look the same. Not that it mattered. Even if she'd cut her hair or gained weight, my feelings for her would be the same: strong. I was looking forward to this meeting, especially since she'd aggressively insisted on my appearance.

The reunion was coming at a good time, just on the heels of my recent promotion to chief financial officer at American Capital Corporation, a company that specializes in financing multimillion dollar construction projects. At thirty, I was the first black executive in the company's seventy-five-year history and responsible for all the major monetary decisions. And then there was the divorce. I'd finally put an end to my marriage to my college sweetheart. The papers were filed. Our relationship had been good at one time, but we'd never had any real chemistry. In the last year, Esther had started rationing our lovemaking to satisfy her growing religious belief that salvation would result from limiting the desires of the flesh, and I'd become too preoccupied with career matters to keep pressing the issue. When things had become unbearable, I'd grown depressed, using food as a substitute for my sexual appetite. Why make myself look more desirable? It was time to turn the page on a failed marriage. The divorce was final, and Jenaye sounded available.

When I was younger, Chadwick had meant a good education, privilege, upward mobility, and rich white folks, values I wasn't prepared to embrace back then. Now I was willing to explore things more deeply. In the corporate world, I was heading into "high cotton," as Mom would say, and I needed a guide, a compass. A visit to Chadwick and a reunion with my lost love just might provide me with the inspiration I needed for moving forward.

As I held the newsletter in my hands, its crisp, thick edges pushed against the lifelines that stretched along the center of my palms. The images of campus life contained a noticeable number of black faces now. Of course some of the family names inside were familiar: the Lavendars, the Chelseys, and the Bennetts. But the other last names—Washington, Wu, Tong, and Villa—signaled that much had changed, even if the newsletter itself remained the same year after year.

I wondered whether there were enough black students to form a student union and whether they had enough pull to play rap or R&B at school dances now. I wondered whether teaching the literary classics had been abandoned to include books containing black people and their perspectives. I wondered whether there was more than just token representation and whether the administration had felt compelled to hire a black faculty member. I wondered whether white students had embraced them and made them feel at home. I wondered just how much had really changed.

I put down the letter and sat against the high-back cherrywood dining chair, glancing up at the ceiling lights. A beam shot across the table at the empty space that my wife had once occupied. I certainly didn't want to think about her right now. She was gone, and that was good, but I was only half-glad to be alone.

Walking back to my bedroom, I reached under the bed and pulled out a heavy briefcase. I lugged it back to the dining room table, snapped the locks open, and slowly lifted the top open. I hadn't looked inside in years. Inside rested a notebook, a bundle of unsharpened pencils, dried-up ink pens, paper clips, old photos, calendars, and news clippings that I'd told myself I'd use to make a scrapbook one day. Jenaye's letters were neatly bound together, remarkably intact.

I had some time before I needed to leave for the airport. I took several deep breaths, leaned back, and steeled myself for a journey through the past, to my time at Chadwick as a fifteen-year-old high-school sophomore in the fall of 1973.

BOOT CAMP

Before Chadwick, there was boot camp.

I flew United to Minneapolis, Minnesota, because that was the easiest way to get to Northfield and to Carleton, a small liberal arts college about forty miles outside the city limits. Carleton College was the host of a two-week summer orientation session run by Rising Stars, a nationwide scholarship program for inner-city students who were planning to attend fancy prep schools. A counselor had told me about the Rising Stars Program when she noticed my high test scores. She raved about my academic potential and later handed me an application. I penned a glowing personal essay, passed a tough entrance exam, and was awarded a scholarship that included a full ride to Chadwick. The scholarship required me, along with the other black scholarship winners, to first attend a prep-school boot camp at Carleton, where, I'd been told by RSP representatives, I would learn some useful techniques for navigating the "insular" world of prep schools like Chadwick. I guess "insular" was another word for "white."

It's funny how you hear about things. Before I even knew I'd be spending two weeks at Carleton College, I heard about the school in a beauty shop, of all places. Tee, my running buddy whose mom owned the Getting Our Heads Together beauty parlor, had applied to Carleton and had already heard from the school's athletic department about a basketball scholarship. Mrs. Lassiter, Tee's wig-wearing, gold-toothed mother, who always grabbed my cheeks with her slippery, Afro Sheen-smelling fingers, bragged continually about her son's athletic prowess, especially when my mom made me meet her at the shop after school; if I wanted a ride home, I'd have to wait until she got her touch-up. Over time, I came to understand how important it was for me to do something good, like get good grades, so she too could have bragging rights at the beauty shop. Mrs. Lassiter was the same way about Tee.

"My son's been offered a basketball scholarship to Carleton College," Mrs. Lassiter said one afternoon. "Of course, it's not Cal or UCLA—it's somewhere near the Twin Cities—but he's going to be a star, and you'll be reading about him after he finishes high school."

She'd said it with a lot of conviction, but no matter what she said, knowing Tee the way I did, it was hard to picture him ever leaving the neighborhood. He followed the progress of the Black Panther Party religiously and said he wanted to be a full-fledged member one day. I liked the Black Panther Party, too, but I was still in an in-between stage. Before joining them wholeheartedly, I needed to see them do a few more things in the community—and figure out how I'd reconcile my love of the Party with my love of basketball, which the Party felt was just another way for the white man to marginalize blacks.

When Mrs. Lassiter talked, the patrons kept their faces focused on the ripped, outdated covers of *Jet* and *Ebony* sitting in their laps, their silence inevitably failing to subdue her enthusiasm. Sometimes I felt like Mrs. Lassiter rambled on about Tee because she believed he deserved a scholarship to private school, too.

I wasn't used to riding airplanes. Whenever I'd traveled, it had always been on a Southern Pacific train or in our Chevy Impala with my folks, taking trips to their hometowns in Rocky Mount, Louisiana, and Hernando, Mississippi. Dad didn't make much money in his job as a cook at the VA hospital, so he saved every penny. His idea of a vacation was to cram all of us into the car for a three-day, 2,500-mile trip with my brother and sister. Somehow, even with my long legs, I'd always end up in the middle, on the hump, with a sore butt, my legs rubbing against the back of the front seat, my shoulders smashed toward my head like bookends. There was nothing elegant about those crazy trips.

The trip to Carleton couldn't have been more different. I got to sport my blue blazer, a starched white shirt with cuff links, and my red and blue plaid pants with the gigantic cuffs. When Dad wasn't looking, I'd splashed on nearly half the bottle of his Old Spice and tried to keep my distance until takeoff so he wouldn't notice. But he found out anyway and scolded me, telling me I should have asked for his permission. My 'fro was starting to grow real long, about two inches, mainly on top, nothing on the sides. It looked funny, Mom said, as she had pulled the cake cutter through the kinks, so she made an appointment at Johnson's Barbershop before I left. Mom and Dad seemed determined that I make a good impression for the Rising Stars people, who we were already calling the "RSP folks." It was important to let them know Isaiah Issacson had class, even if he was only able to go to a fancy prep school because of some charity program for black students.

The pie-faced lady at the counter stamped my ticket, took a look at my large frame, and told me the plane was a Boeing 757 with a long, skinny aisle, loads of legroom, and a seat that reclined. The best seat for me, she said, would be the aisle. Her personal attention was just what I needed to help me contain my nervousness, confirming that even the airline attendants could tell I was on the verge of becoming a privileged black kid.

I should have stayed in my assigned seat, next to the aisle, but I decided to leave the middle seat open and sit next to the window, where I could check out the view and wouldn't be bothered by Richard Bonar, another black Oakland kid and a classmate who'd also been selected to attend Chadwick and its boot camp. Before takeoff, I glanced at Richard's smooth, reddish complexion, brown hair, and skinny frame. At the airport, before we left, he'd said he would need extra elbow room so he could draw pictures of Spider-Man and the Hulk. Before making the trip, I'd never even known he was an artist. It's strange how you can see a person almost every day and not know anything about them.

Across the aisle, an old white woman sat with her palms pressed together and eyes tightly shut, muttering something into the back of the seat in front of her. I quickly said my own Bible verse as the thin, miniskirted, blonde stewardess announced over the intercom the need to put our seats in a full upright position, stow our tray tables, sit back, and enjoy the flight.

In the air, I thought about leaving public school and my old West Oakland neighborhood. I wouldn't miss the fat lady's kids, better known as our thieving neighbors, who'd always managed to find a way to break into our garage and steal our baseballs, basketballs, and any other sporting equipment lying around. They'd even taken our black-and-white portable TV, the one that required pliers to change the channels. From our bedroom window, my brother, Melvin, and I could see them enjoying a show. I wouldn't miss our other neighbor, the man we called Papa Pete, whose voice was like a rooster's crow, snapping me from sweet NBA dreams after his late-night drinking binges. I wouldn't miss the smothering attitudes of my parents, who monitored my every move, but I'd miss my friend Tee, who'd not only tutored me in basketball, but whom I had, at ten years old, taken with me to our first Black Panther rally at DeFremery Park.

There had been many speakers that day, but the ones I remember best were the leaders, Eldridge Cleaver and Bobby Seale, who were dressed, like almost everyone else, in black leather jackets, white shirts, and tams. Dark shades covered their eyes as they demanded that Huey Newton, the Party's founder, be set free after allegedly killing a police officer. When Seale was finished, he led the throng of followers in a song: *"Time to pick up the gun/ off the pigs/No more police in my community/off the pigs/No more black men in jail/off the pigs."*

The rally days were long gone now, but the spirit of radicalism was still alive in Oakland, especially after Seale's recent attempt to become the city's first black mayor. I'd have to depend on Tee to keep me informed while I was away.

There were people I'd miss, including my teammates who played pickup basketball at DeFremery Park. They'd expressed their own opinions about my trip to boot camp, saying that the time there, even if it was only for two weeks, would hurt my game because I'd be spinning my wheels against weaker competition. I agreed with them. I didn't want to go.

The problem was that I didn't have a choice. Dad and Mom didn't care much about basketball. They had gone to segregated high schools in the South and were determined for me to get an integrated education—and they wanted me away from Tee's burgeoning radicalism, even if it meant sending me to a boot camp and, after that, an all-white boarding school.

The best thing about the plane was the bathroom. Even though I had to crawl over Richard to get to the tiny airplane bathroom, it was better than pissing in the mason jars that Dad carried underneath the seat for use during our family excursions. He was always in such a hurry to "get there" that he never stopped at a gas station or a rest stop. If I told him I needed to use the bathroom, he looked at his military watch, pulled over to the shoulder of the road, and reached under the seat, pretending we had a real deadline to meet and that we'd be irretrievably late if we didn't get to a certain city by the next hour. Joshua Issacson wasn't known for being flexible.

When the plane landed, Edgar Davidson, the pint-size founder of the Rising Stars Program, met Richard and me at the baggage claim area. The darkest man in a sea of white faces, Davidson stuck out, even without the red, black, and green dashiki, gold medallion, and mirrored shades he was sporting. Pudgy and barrel-chested, he moved toward us with his shoulders pushed back, wearing thigh-grabbing double-knit slacks, and two-toned earth shoes. His goatee was combed razor sharp, but the chest hair peeking through his V-neck was sparse and nappy.

"What's happenin', young brothers?" He looked us up and down, and I wanted to give him the black power salute I sometimes used to greet Tee, but Davidson was much older, and I didn't want to be too presumptuous.

Davidson's dress and greeting reminded me of the Party member who'd visited our junior high assemblies each year during Black Awareness Week. He'd talked about unity and brotherhood among black people and then passed out the Party newspaper, which invariably bore bold headlines about the next rally that would protest the killing of young black men by Oakland police officers or announced a fund-raiser for Bobby Seale's mayoral campaign.

As he moved closer, Davidson removed his glasses, and I noticed his bloodshot eyes. I thought about my grandfather, who'd stay up late sometimes, talking to me about the pain of segregation. That pain, evident in his eyes, never left my grandfather's face. Meeting Davidson made me hopeful that he'd take care of us while we attended boot camp and—like my grandfather—share the wisdom necessary for surviving in a world run by white people.

On the way to the car, Davidson talked a lot about RSP and the fact that Northfield, the town where we'd be staying, was the place where Jesse James's gang had been stopped, but he didn't really reveal much about himself. We got into the car, and he told us how he'd started the program because it was something he wished he'd had when he'd attended an all-white boarding school in the sixties. He said he wanted to help black people, something I could relate to from listening to my parents, my grandfather, and the members of the Panther Party.

The drive from the pristine-looking Minneapolis–St. Paul airport to Northfield took nearly an hour, much longer than I'd expected. Davidson had been a little vague about how far Northfield was from the airport, saying that it was somewhere close inside the city limits. What he really should have said was that he'd made the trip so many times he'd lost perspective. From my car window, the broad city highway changed from a multilane freeway to a winding country road, dotted with two-story homes, manicured lawns, and sprawling front porches. At home, these were the kinds of spacious houses the rich white people in Piedmont owned. I wondered what it would be like to live inside one of them.

Davidson drove with the failing air conditioner blasting, trying to counter the hot, sticky, humid August air. The dark gray clouds, the constant threat of thundershowers, and the ninety-degree temperature made that place seem like a different country, nothing like the cool Bay Area summer I'd left. I tried to keep my blazer on, but as soon as the sweat from my underarms soaked through my undershirt and onto my jacket, I knew I'd lost that battle. In the front seat, Richard was feeling the heat, too; he grabbed his extra wide tie in his right hand and started using it as a fan. I couldn't wait to get out of the car, and yet it seemed as though we were traveling to the middle of nowhere. It was not fun.

"You know they have thunderstorms here in the summer?" Davidson said, breaking the silence. We talked for a while after that, but when the conversation died down again, he changed focus, switching to the unity-and-brotherhood speech.

"It's gonna be real important for you two soul brothers to represent black folks in a favorable light when you get to your new school. You digging me?" After looking at Richard's baby face in the seat next to him, Davidson glanced back at me through his rearview mirror. "Boarding school is where the elite and very rich send their kids," he said. "You brothers are going to be like the Freedom Riders down South. You've read about them, right?"

"Freedom Riders?" Richard's high-pitched voice sounded surprised at the comparison. "Isn't that stretching it a bit?" He'd drawn pictures during the flight and didn't seem interested in any kind of freedom struggle. I was surprised he even knew who the Freedom Riders were. Based on what I knew of him, his heroes were the characters he found inside comic books and the ones he invented on his large sketch pad. They weren't at all like Malcolm X and other freedom fighters, folks who were mentioned in the pages of *Soul on Ice*, a book by the activist Eldridge Cleaver, which I'd tucked inside my suitcase to finish reading in my free time.

"Like I said," Davidson continued, ignoring Richard's comment, "the Freedom Riders went to a boot camp just like this to learn about racist white folks." He slowed the car, keeping one hand on the steering wheel, and pointed with his opposite hand to the sign spelling out the name of the campus. "Carleton will be *your* boot camp."

He drove slowly by a few historic-looking buildings and a big church, and he finally stopped in front of a cluster of dormitories sprinkled among the shade trees. "Make sure you get a good night's sleep while you're here. We're gonna be getting down to the real nitty-gritty, and there's not a lot of time."

*   *   *

The next day at our first group meeting in the dormitory common room, it was as if everyone—except Richard and me—was from down South or back East. One kid, who wore a fade haircut similar to the one I'd seen on the style wall in Johnson's Barbershop, stared me up and down, pausing at my name tag, which said my name and hometown of Oakland, California, and stopped at my shoes—white canvas, high-top Converse Chuck Taylors, which I'd washed for the occasion—and laughed.

"Yo," he said pointing downward. "They wear them sneaks in Hollywood?"

He'd misread my name tag, seeing the word "California," but not "Oakland." I'd heard it before from other kids, when I'd gone on those road trips with my folks back home. Everybody just guessed that because you were from California, you lived somewhere close to LA or Hollywood. Hadn't

Huey Newton, Angela Davis, and the Black Panther Party put Oakland on the map? Where had they been?

"I ain't from Hollywood," I said, looking down on the guy's closely cropped hair. The small nick in his crown made it look as though the barber had made several wrong moves. I grabbed at my T-shirt, straightened the name tag attached to the fabric, and pointed at my hometown with pride. "I'm from Oakland, nickhead." I bumped him with my chest.

"Yo, how far is that from Hollywood?" He started to hum the music to Kool & the Gang's "Hollywood Swinging," his comment seemingly intended as an added insult to my hometown, which didn't have a popular song named after it.

"Long way, man," I said, shaking my head in disbelief at his ignorance.

"So, is that what they still wear in Oak-Land?" He pointed to my shoes.

"You don't like my tennis shoes?"

"'Sneaks, man. *Sneaks.*" He took the back of his left hand and smacked it into his palm for emphasis. "They're not, as you say, 'tennis shoes.' Tennis shoes are for tennis playas."

First I'd noticed his word choices—*yo? sneaks?* The words sounded foreign to my Northern California sensibilities, yet they had a nice, cool ring—but now his accent was throwing me off. His speech wasn't slow and deliberate, like the Southern boys I knew, but faster-paced, and the emphasis on certain vowels and consonants made me smile.

"In Brooklyn, we wear Keds," he said. "We call 'em sneaks." He lifted his pants legs, so I could see his shoes, funny-looking black high-tops with a thick red and blue stripe near the toe, and then rested them on the floor as if he'd said the final word on the subject. "But we'll get you straightened out soon enough, Oak-Land. You'll be hip in no time." It seemed I had a new nickname, for better or worse.

"Yeah, yeah, yeah," I said, reading his name tag: Vince Beverly. But before I could go any further, I felt a tap on the shoulder. It was Davidson. He'd entered the room during my discussion and was ready to start the meeting.

"All right, all right, everybody, it's time to get down and get into it. Take your seats."

Davidson moved away from me and took a spot in the center of the room, which was encircled by folding chairs. I followed close behind him and then walked into the semicircle of metal chairs. I looked for a seat that was as far away as I could get from Davidson and the kid from Brooklyn. I had already heard too much from Davidson on our ride from the airport, and the kid from Brooklyn had made fun of my shoes.

Although I was trying to get away from Davidson and Brooklyn, I was hoping to attract the attention of the tall girl with the smooth caramel skin who'd just entered the room. She wasn't wearing a name tag. I envied her nerve for being late the first day and nodded my head in her direction to try to get her attention. She found a place on the other side of the room and ignored me. I tried to make eye contact during Davidson's opening words, but she kept looking away. She stroked her shoulder-length hair, whispered to the girl next to her, and tilted her head back to roll her light brown eyes toward the ceiling. I couldn't help staring at her.

To break the ice, Davidson made everyone tell a personal story.

I was first and eager to tell the story about how I'd recently won first place in a writing contest for an essay called, "Why the Black Panther Party Was Good for Oakland." I watched Davidson grow excited as I told him there were no crosswalks on my street before the Black Panther Party started to question the mayor and that party members were harassed for following the cops and reading aloud sections of the U.S. Constitution during arrests of other black people. Davidson removed his glasses when it looked like I was slowing down.

"Did you talk about the Black Panther Party's Ten-Point Program? Wasn't that great?" He beckoned me with his hands, encouraging me to say even more.

"Of course," I said, flashing back to my essay. "They demanded freedom, full employment, shelter, and exemption from military service, among other things."

He was shocked that I'd won. The Party had done some good things, but the reputations of some of its members, like Newton, who'd been arrested for allegedly killing a police officer, he said, were less than stellar. What I couldn't tell him, out of fear of bursting his bubble, was that my father had totally disagreed with the viewpoint I'd expressed. He thought the Panthers were confrontational and blamed too much on the system. "White folks would never give anything to a black man holding a gun to his head. The right way to advance in this society was through education and nonviolent protest," he'd said, mimicking Dr. King.

Davidson finally rushed me through the story so he could get to the next person. When I was done, he selected the girl I had been eyeing.

"I won a contest once, too," she said, crossing her legs. The wide pants leg of her frayed bell-bottoms swayed above her platforms as she rocked back and forth in her seat. "To win it, I had to make a big collage." She spread her arms, accordion-like, and then put them back at her sides to continue the story. While she talked, her shiny silver bracelets rested against the back of her hand and thumb. Her hair, bone straight and parted down the middle, lightly grazed her high cheekbones.

"Can you tell us more?" Davidson asked. Relieved my story was over, he seemed eager to pull the story out of her. "And can you tell us your name since you're not wearing your name tag? We'd all like to get to know you."

"I'm Jenaye Gardner from Camden, New Jersey," she said in a raspy, confident voice.

"Welcome, Jenaye." Davidson's voice sounded as if it had been prerecorded. "I didn't mean to interrupt you, but I'm sure everyone here wanted to meet you."

Davidson had read my mind. I couldn't believe how happy I was that I'd finally found out her name. *Jenaye*. It had the perfect ring.

"I've been in love with Michael Jackson and the Jackson 5 since 'Got To Be There.' One day, I saw this contest in *Right On!* magazine, offering the person who made the best collage a chance to meet 'em in person. Shoot, I pulled out all my pictures and everything. Nobody told me how to make a collage, but when I was done, I knew I'd won."

"Outta sight," Davidson said. He took the words right out of my mouth.

"I can't tell you how long it took me. All I know is one day someone called me from the magazine and told me I won. Me." She pointed at her chest. "Yeah, that's right."

"Sounds like you tapped into some of that soul power, Jenaye. I bet you could do anything if you set your mind to it, huh?" Davidson asked the question, but he wasn't waiting for an answer. He shot off his own response and took over.

"I'm glad you told us that story because going to boarding school for all of you will be like nothing you've ever done. It'll be like making that collage, you dig?" His voice was booming now. He was practically repeating every word he'd said to Richard and me on our drive from the airport. Had he done this to everybody?

"Some of you will be the only black kids in your class, and sometimes it'll feel like you're speaking for all black people." Changing from hip program director to a wise mentor and guide, he removed his glasses and circled the room carefully, using the opportunity to look us each in the eye. "The homework will be hard. Are you ready?"

His voice echoed against the walls.

None of us raised our hands. We just listened, and watched with fearful expressions, as he continued.

"In your English classes, you'll be asked to read the so-called classics. Don't be afraid. Read them, and be prepared to talk about them." He cleared his throat. "By the way, did you all receive a reading list yet from your schools?"

I raised my hand, not because I hadn't received the list, but because I wanted to talk about the one I'd received from Chadwick. It contained *The Adventures of Huckleberry Finn, Moby Dick,* and *The Old Man and the Sea.* There were tons more on the list, all of which I'd spotted in the library but had passed up to read books by black leaders like Eldridge Cleaver, Stokley Carmichael, or brothers doing something for the community . I'd even read *Sports Illustrated* before the ones on the Chadwick list.

He pointed to me. "Yes, Isaiah?"

I was concerned about the overwhelming list, and no one was saying anything. Trying to finish all of these books meant I'd have to abandon my consumption of black history and sports stories, and I didn't want to do that. "I haven't read most of these books, and I'm not sure I'll get to them now," I said. "What am I supposed to do?"

"Well, between now and the time you get to Chadwick, you'd better find the time to read them. Can you D-I-G I-T?" He spelled the last two words without hesitation and in doing so sounded a lot like my parents, who encouraged the impossible and didn't seem to care about the details or any obstacles. The only thing that mattered to them was getting the job done, which meant going to Chadwick and doing exceptionally well. It was a matter of racial pride and taking advantage of a onetime opportunity, but I was looking for an easy way out, and Davidson was scaring me all over again. Twenty books in a month and a half? No way.

The real truth was that I had done well on the admissions test to get into the Rising Stars Program and into Chadwick, never expecting I'd actually be forced to attend. I'd underestimated my parents' fervor for an integrated education. I might have done well on a few tests, but I never considered I was prep school material. Richard was the ideal candidate. In junior high, he'd been a member of the math club, the student council, and any other organization he thought would prepare him for white society. He was poised to move up and out of the neighborhood the moment he'd been accepted.

Me, on the other hand, I didn't care if I *ever* left my Oakland neighborhood. I had recurring dreams of becoming an NBA star like Bill Russell, who'd attended McClymonds High, too. Known as the "School of Champions," Mack, as we liked to call it, was famous for turning out professional athletes. The school had already turned out baseball stars like Vada Pinson and Frank Robinson, as well as track star Jim Hines. I was determined to become next on the list of stars. Of course, I'd also hang out with my boy, Tee, and I thought I'd join the black movement one day, also. I'd deal with real life and the responsibility of a career when the time came. The full scholarship to Chadwick was cool, but I wasn't fazed at all. I had other plans.

Up 'til now, I'd been treated with kid gloves in the classroom and given the benefit of the doubt on my schoolwork, just because I'd been given the most valuable player award in a city tournament and behaved myself on campus. Davidson gave me the ultimate reality check—my world was about to change. He looked and acted like a cool guy, but his message was serious.

I was beginning to feel a little nervous. What had I gotten myself into?

"Anyone else have any questions?" He looked around the room again, peering into each of our faces.

No one said a word.

"Good. It seems like you've got it. I know what I'm saying might sound like a lot of bunk to some of you, but you'll thank me one day. You'll be away from home, and you'll face racism from your classmates and teachers. Don't be surprised. Just deal with it like you would anything else. Confront it, but don't dwell on it. You hear?" He looked around the room again. "We've got a good reputation at RSP, and we want to keep it that way. While you're in this program and for the next few weeks here, I'll expect nothing less than your best. Ladies and gentleman, this meeting's adjourned. It's time for class."

*　*　*

I shared a math class with Jenaye. She had no idea of my growing infatuation, and I sat next to her so I could pick her brain. I'd been able to get a little information about her by asking around the campus, and instead of reviewing the assignment, like I should have been doing, I thought up questions for her, mumbling them to myself to try them out: *Hi, my name is … Where you from? What was meeting Michael like?*

Although I'd practiced my questions, I was still scared. What if she rejected me? It wasn't a far-off possibility. Back home, it had been my thick glasses and the white masking tape I used on the hinges to keep them from falling apart that scared girls away. Rejection and ridicule had been the story of my life with girls up to that point, and I was hoping to achieve a different result with Jenaye. As I waited for the instructor to enter the class, I folded my notes, shoved them inside my pocket, and mustered up some courage, surprising myself.

"Are you excited about going to boarding school?"

"I think so," she said. There was some hesitation in her voice.

I was surprised by the difference in her tone of voice. It wasn't the same one she'd used to tell her collage story. "You sound shaky." I played with the pencil between my fingers, trying to keep my cool. I guess it worked.

"You're not scared a little bit?" She was puzzled by my cool demeanor.

"When I really think about it," I shrugged.

"Shoot. It's going to be my first time away from home ... the first time ever that I'll be away from my mom."

"You'll be able to handle it," I said, smiling widely and imitating the encouraging words I received from my parents before I'd left.

"Well, I hope so." Her voice was raspy, but she was easier to talk to than I'd expected. Maybe she'd decided to talk to me because there was no one else sitting as close. "I'm going to Yarborough Academy in San Diego. It's a long way from Camden to San Diego." She paused for a minute to look toward the doorway to see if the teacher was coming. "It's going to be lonely out there."

I stole another glance at her beautiful face, berating myself for thinking she'd be rude because of her good looks. When she started talking again, her lips looked thin and her teeth crowded. She could have used braces, but aside from that, she was beautiful.

Seeing the coast was clear, she resumed our conversation. "What about you?" she asked. "You excited about going to ..."

"Chadwick." Still excited about my conversation with her, I wanted to downplay my attitude toward Chadwick and tell her about my basketball dream, about missing home, and the other stuff. Being too negative about Chadwick, especially since I hadn't even gone yet, would make a bad first impression, and I couldn't afford that, not with someone like Jenaye. I'd talk about the things I cared about until I could read her better.

"Yeah," she said.

"No," I answered faintly, "I'm not that excited."

She raised her eyebrows. "Why not?"

"Because," I said, jumping at an opportunity, "I wanna be the next Bill Russell, play at Mack just like he did, and maybe become a black militant."

She looked at me like I was crazy.

Everyone in my neighborhood knew that Bill Russell, Frank Robinson, and a host of famous professional athletes had attended McClymonds. If you loved sports and wanted to play in college or make the pros, you went to Mack; becoming militant or joining the Black Panthers was icing on the cake. The Black Panthers were appealing to me not only because Tee liked them so much, but also because they stood up for what they believed in. I envied their courage.

She smiled. "Mack? Bill Russell? You, a black militant?"

I nodded my head as she repeated each word, as if that would erase all doubt, but she wasn't satisfied. "The Panthers carry guns, right?" "And did Bill Russell play in glasses?" She looked puzzled. She touched the side of her face, near her eyes, nodding at my glasses.

"They used to carry guns, but they're doing a lot of good things now." I hoped I was maintaining my cool, echoing the story I'd told in front of the class earlier. I even told her about Bobby Seale's run for mayor of Oakland. A prominent member of the Party, Seale hadn't won the last election, but he'd come in second place behind the white incumbent, John Reading, getting everyone excited that Oakland was almost ready to elect its first black mayor.

"Sorry," she shrugged, "I've never heard anything good about the Panthers. You'll have to tell me more while we're here."

The teacher, a tall, clean-shaven black man with thinning hair and a flat nose, entered the room, carrying a thick blue notebook. Grabbing the desk, Jenaye turned to face the blackboard, but I wasn't finished talking.

"When I get a chance, I'm going to play basketball with some of the other guys in this program. Do you want to come see me play?"

Keeping her eyes on the teacher, she whispered back, "You any good?"

"Come see for yourself."

"If I have time ..."

The teacher finished writing a problem on the board. He looked around the room and then eyed our name tags.

"Je-naye?" He stumbled with the pronunciation. "I don't mean to interrupt your conversation with Isaiah, but would you come to the board and show the class how to work this problem?"

She winked at me and then walked to the board, reeking of confidence.

I was glad he hadn't called my name. Just like the reading list I'd been given by Chadwick, I hadn't even cracked open a book.

*   *   *

"Since you know math is one of my weak spots, maybe you can show me how to solve some of these geometry equations."

In study hall after class, I pushed a textbook and my partially completed assignment in Jenaye's direction, hoping she'd finish it.

She skimmed the textbook pages and thumbed through my homework. "This is going to be a piece of cake." She looked up, pushing the hair out of her eyes. "I just took geometry in summer school." She lifted her head slightly to show me her chin.

"You went to summer school before this?" I leaned in close, ostensibly to hear her answer. What I really wanted was an even better view of her.

"For a while," she nodded. "My mom said I needed to hit the ground running." She smacked her palms together, simulating an airplane hitting the runway.

"I heard the same thing from my parents, but they didn't send me to summer school." I was trying my best to sound a little disappointed.

"Maybe they should have," she said, looking down at my uncompleted homework.

"Don't rub it in." I wanted to snatch the paper away from her, but I knew I needed help.

"My summer school teacher told me that learning geometry is like being introduced to a foreign language. The key is memorizing terms." She turned to the beginning of the book. "Just remember postulates are statements you don't have to prove, and a theorem is a generalization which can be demonstrated to be true." She pointed an index finger at me for emphasis.

Getting excited, I moved a little closer to see if I could learn more shortcuts. "That sounds good. Tell me something else I need to know."

She was smiling like a proud teacher now. "The sum of the measure of three angles of a triangle is 180 degrees. That's a theorem."

"You sure?" I didn't care if she was right; I just wanted to remain in her presence.

She tilted her head to the side. "I got the answer right when I went up to the board, didn't I?"

"Yeah," I pictured her winking at me again.

"You'd better get this stuff down now. I won't be around long to help you," she said.

"That's exactly why we need to hang out together as much as possible while we're here. We don't have much time. Just keep showing me as much as you can. Is that a deal?" I stuck out my hand so she could shake it

She waved it off like it wasn't necessary. "All right, all right ... I'll help you out now, but the next time the teacher looks in our direction during class, I'm going to point at you. By the time we're finished, you'll be headed for the honors class."

That was what was so good about Jenaye. Unlike the girls I'd known at home who would have ignored me, she was perfectly willing to tutor me without any pretense.

And because she was beautiful, paying attention was easy.

*   *   *

As it turned out, I wasn't the only one interested in Jenaye. Brooklyn was, too. I can't say he was drawn to her with the same intensity as I had been, but he was giving me a run for my money. I marveled at Brooklyn's schoolboy haircut, his way with words, and the relaxed manner in which he and Jenaye strolled around campus. He always carried her books and walked real close to each other. I saw them enter the gym together while I was playing basketball, and that was enough to break my concentration on the game. As soon as I stopped playing, they headed toward me.

"Oak-Land!" he shouted. "You didn't tell me about this run."

"Run?" I was confused.

"Run, man ... you know. Translated, it means you didn't tell me you guys were gonna play ball today." He laughed and shook his head at me. "Pretty square, cuz."

"Oh," I shrugged, "I didn't know I was supposed to."

"Here." He reached underneath his arm and handed me a book. "Jenaye wanted to come see you play, and I came to give this to you."

The cover showed a picture of a gap-toothed black man leaning against a chain-link fence and holding a basketball. Above his uncombed head was the title, *Foul: The Connie Hawkins Story*. I knew a little about Connie Hawkins from reading *Sports Illustrated*, but not his entire life story. I flipped through the pages, my fingers stopping at the black-and-white photos in the middle. I glanced briefly at images of all the slender bodies on an asphalt court and then snapped the book shut.

"What's this for?" I'd already had my plate full of assigned reading, and getting another one was guaranteed to set me back even further.

"Read it," he said, "and then come talk to me."

I watched him walk away without any other explanation. I was glad he'd left because then I'd have another chance to talk to Jenaye.

"What was that all about?" she said, looking perplexed.

"I'm not sure." I covered my chest a little with my arms and wiped some of the sweat from my chest with my fingers. "Maybe he really wanted to play. Or maybe there's a message somewhere in here." I looked at the cover again and remembered that he'd been carrying her schoolbooks. "He kept your books, didn't he?"

"I'll catch up to him," she said. She looked through my arms, squarely at my bare chest, and then looked away. "Put your shirt on. I don't need to see you like that."

Blushing, I knelt on the floor and pulled on my T-shirt.

"Not bad," she said. Although I thought she meant my playing, I couldn't help but hope she meant my body, too. "If you keep that up, you really will be the next Bill Russell. Just don't act like some of the other b-ball players I know. All they care about is basketball."

"Don't worry." I said it with enough edge to put her concerns at ease. "I've got some other interests, too."

She placed her hand underneath her chin as if giving my statement some serious thought. "I guess you did say you wanted to become a militant one day. That shows a little ambition." She nodded her head in approval.

We walked to the nearby bleachers to pick up the rest of my clothes. "I'm glad you decided to give me a little credit." I was getting defensive, itching for a comeback. "So what do you want to be?"

"A doctor."

It seemed like everyone in the program wanted to be a doctor. Or maybe she said it because she thought that her wanting to be a doctor would impress me and make me think about becoming something other than a basketball star or a militant. Admittedly, I hadn't done much to alter her perception.

"Oh." I didn't want to hear anymore. It was getting too hot to talk, and I had remembered that there was a swimming pool on campus. I still hadn't gotten used to the Minnesota heat. "Do you swim?"

"What's that got to do with anything?" Jenaye asked, laughing a little.

"Nothing, really. Just asking."

"No. I don't swim."

"Will it mess up your hair?"

"Yeah." She touched her hand to the back of her smooth, sleek hair. "My mom would be mad. She paid a lot to have this done."

"That's too bad. It's too hot here for me. I need to cool down. You sure you don't want to go swimming, just to hang out with me?"

"I'm sure." Her voice was firm.

"Well, at least walk back to the dorms with me so I can pick up my trunks. We'll talk about school later."

"Deal."

*　　*　　*

For the remainder of my stay, I tried to avoid the hard-core questions about careers and academics, promising myself that I'd deal with them later. Connecting with Jenaye became my primary obsession.

Except for her brief wink at me during class, she fended off my attempts at intimacy like she was pushing away bad air. But that didn't stop me. I kept trying my best to learn all about her. At dinner, I discovered her weaknesses for German chocolate cake and vanilla ice cream. She'd never pass up either at the end of a meal. Her other weakness, besides Michael Jackson, was dancing. The big dance, the final event before the end of boot camp, was my last hope. Jenaye had gone on for hours about how she'd mastered dance steps by grabbing the doorknob in her room and imagining it was her dance partner. I couldn't wait to see her in action.

That night while getting ready, I could hear a stereo thumping through the wall. I put on a loose-fitting shirt, some slacks, and the pair of Buster Brown shoes that Mom and I had picked out for me to wear on the plane. They felt light on my feet as I stood up in them and tried to make some moves in front of the mirror. The slippery new soles glided against the thick, gray carpeting like skates on a clean roller rink floor. When I was ready, I reminded myself to walk carefully as I headed toward the dance.

The room was blue. Dark rays of light draped the roomful of bodies like a well-tailored suit. It was hard to find Jenaye in the dim light, but somehow, when the DJ played the Ohio Players' song, "I Wanna Be Free," a slow jam, we connected. She was standing near the wall, across from the turntable, mouthing the words to the song. Her bell-bottoms hung loosely around her thin legs, and her black platforms gave her slender body a few more inches.

I felt nervous approaching her. I was more comfortable when the music was faster, and I didn't have to worry about staying in sync with a partner. I had never really slow-danced, but after all our conversations, I decided to continue heading her way.

"You want to dance?" I asked.

"Why not?" She quickly volunteered her hand without any resistance.

I grabbed it, led her to the dance floor, and moved as close as I could to her body. She was at least an inch or two shorter than me, and I could feel her chest and stomach rubbing against my torso. My heart beat rapidly, almost out of control. I held her waist the way my cousin Daryl had taught me: "Move your hips slowly. Take your time. Don't fall. Be smooth. Watch your feet. Don't step on hers." His instructions suddenly made sense. I was feeling it. Once I'd relaxed, it was easy.

Just when things began to settle down, I saw something out of the corner of my eye. There was a dance move I wanted to try. Sexy. Fluid. Daring. Difficult. It was a move that could get you slapped with the wrong partner. I'd never seen it used before in Oakland at the few house parties I'd been to, but Brooklyn was doing it naturally. He and his partner moved their bodies toward the floor like a long rope being slowly dropped from a rooftop, until their kneecaps had scraped the edge of the carpet. I was hooked.

Jenaye caught me looking. "You want to try that?"

Before I knew it, I was saying, "Hell yeah. Let's do it." I took my time as I moved my knees back and forth against hers and pushed downward. Soon I was touching the ground and my face was closer than I'd ever been to hers. I wanted to plant a kiss, but I knew that wasn't going to fly. I paused simply to enjoy the music and the feeling. I didn't care who was looking. This was where I wanted to be, and Jenaye was the girl I wanted to be with forever.

As we started to rise again, I grasped the firmness of her waist, keeping her steady, moving her closer. She looked up and into my eyes, giggling nervously as if she'd witnessed something magical. She put her arms around my neck and held me tighter.

"Do they dance like this in Oakland, too?" she whispered.

"Sometimes." I didn't know what to say, so I lied out of fear of interrupting the moment and missing the beat. Jenaye was the first girl I'd ever held this close, but with each note, I was beginning to feel more confident and more attached, as if I could conquer the world.

Then it was over. Reality didn't hit me until the song ended. Soon I'd be leaving Carleton College, Jenaye, and the comfortable environment we were enjoying there. I had no idea what awaited me at Chadwick, and from the way Jenaye clung to my waist after the music ended, I knew she was afraid, too.

I tried to convince myself that I was ready.

GREAT EXPECTATIONS

September 20, 1973

Dear Jenaye:

Main Street, Ojai, looks like a John Wayne movie. As you ride through town to get to the school, there's a big supermarket, a few gift shops, a pizza parlor, and a record store. Outside of that, there's not much here. Just like Northfield, Minnesota, downtown is about one city block. It's quiet, dusty and hot …

Shortly after arriving home from boot camp, Dad and Mom drove me from Oakland to Ojai—six hours and nearly four hundred miles down the California coast—in our cramped, luggage-laden Chevy Impala. With all my stuff, there wasn't enough room for my brother or sister to ride, but parental attendance prior to my first day of school was required.

I spent the first few hours of the trip sitting on the spongy backseat, staring out the window at roadside eateries, abandoned farms, and miles of towering mountain ranges. During the second half of the trip, I thought about dancing with Jenaye and wondered what Chadwick would be like. Going to school with rich white boys was going to be different.

Mom and Dad, who had met singing in the church choir, practiced some new songs, Mom flipping through school brochures most of the time. She was excited by the whole idea of a boarding school education for me, and I was peppered with motivational speeches and biblical quotes almost every hour until the last exit.

As we entered the campus gate, I smelled manure. Holding my nose, I slid down in my seat, dreading the future. Boot camp was officially over, and now it was time to employ the techniques Davidson had taught us. After we parked, we got out of the car and strolled up a tree-lined path, looking for the headmaster's office. Forced into a slight detour around a big pile left by some four-legged creature, I pulled up the rear.

So, this was boarding school.

Mr. Breedlove, the headmaster, stood near a classroom door, shoulders back, chest full, cordially greeting students and parents like a newly elected politician. Even with a head of ear-clearing gray hair, he looked younger than the pictures in the application packet.

"Mr. Breedlove?" Dad switched the King James Bible he carried to his left hand and extended his right.

"Mr. and Mrs. Issacson, right?" The headmaster looked at my dressed-up parents, and then at me. "And this must be Isaiah."

I nodded my head, offering a weak smile as the headmaster kept staring.

"You're certainly much taller than I expected." He grabbed my shoulder and held it like he'd known me for years. "Welcome to Chadwick."

He invited us to his office, and as we walked with him, he pointed out the chapel, the computer center, and the observatory. The place seemed bigger than a college—it didn't even begin to compare to my dinky little high school back in Oakland. The headmaster's office was in the main administration building, off an opulent common room with a giant fireplace and walls lined with old photos and painted portraits of former headmasters. Closing his office door behind us, Mr. Breedlove took his seat behind a tall desk that held neatly framed pictures of his family, a marble pen holder, a coffee cup, a desk calendar, and a leather cup full of pencils. On the wall behind his head were color-coded flowcharts and graphs outlining the school's fund-raising goals. The box of empty white spaces near the top was a clear indication that he had a long way to go.

Straightening his Brooks Brothers jacket and red silk tie, he leaned back. "So, what do you think of our school?"

"Impressive," said Dad. He loosened his tie, which was wilted from the heat.

"Nice," added Mom, removing her sunglasses. "I can't wait to see more."

"Well, give it some time. You're going to absolutely love this place." Breedlove smiled. "You may have heard this already, but I'd be remiss if I didn't tell you that Chadwick has some unique aspects that you'll never forget. I didn't have time to show you the horses." Brows drawn, he swatted his hand at a pair of flies buzzing around his head. "Obviously our stables attract these creatures, but you'll get used to it, Isaiah. I'll take you up to our riding area later. Did you decide on the horse? It's part of the scholarship and a big school tradition." He grabbed a booklet off his desk and handed it to Mom. "Here's an explanation of the program."

She flipped through the pages until she found a story about Sherman Chadwick, the founder, who had started the school in 1887 after relocating here with his sick brother. The explanation about Sherman's love for education and animals, particularly horses, had endeared her to the place before she'd ever arrived.

"My grandfather loved animals, too," she said, pointing to the photo of Sherman Chadwick standing next to a horse. "I grew up on a farm in Louisiana, and we had everything. When I heard about the horses, I knew I wanted to send Isaiah here. He's really fortunate to get a scholarship. He said he didn't want a horse, but we'll see."

"There was no way we were going to pass up this opportunity," said Dad, looking around the office. The array of Breedlove's framed degrees seemed to have left him a little awestruck. "This is the chance of a lifetime. I wish I'd gotten this gift when I was Isaiah's age. There's no telling where I'd be now." Turning away from the plaques, he focused on me. "On the way down here, we couldn't keep him quiet. Right, Isaiah?"

I wanted to tell Breedlove the truth—that I'd never wanted come to Chadwick, that it was solely their idea. I wanted to tell him about McClymonds, my NBA dreams, and about never wanting to leave home, but I nodded my head and played along so I wouldn't get in trouble.

"I can't wait." I forced another smile.

"Don't sound so excited, Isaiah," said Breedlove, mocking the nonchalance that contrasted Dad's exuberance.

"He'll be okay," Dad said, trying to reassure Breedlove. Dad looked at me in disgust and shook his head, totally embarrassed by my weak response. "Did you hear that, Isaiah? Maybe we should just start unloading your stuff right now."

Breedlove furrowed his eyebrows. "You're not wasting time, are you, Mr. Issacson? You seem more anxious than Isaiah." His mouth was slightly open. I could tell there was more he wanted to say.

"We don't want to keep you. You've got other students to meet, I'm sure." Dad looked at me as if he wanted to kill me while Mom surveyed the room.

Moving quickly now, Davidson pulled a folder from his drawer and sat it on his desk. On the top, a small envelope was attached with a paper clip. "These are your keys," he said, handing everything to me. "You're staying in Middlebury Hall with the rest of the sophomores."

"I hope I didn't rush your presentation," said Dad with a fake laugh. "We're a little tired. It took us awhile to drive down here from Oakland, and we'd like to get back on the road before it gets too late. Plus Isaiah here can't wait to meet his new friends."

"I hope that's the case," said Breedlove, sounding disappointed that he'd have to cut his introduction short. "We've been waiting for him. Isaiah's roommate was a student here last year. He's from Massachusetts and has a very, let's say, *privileged* background. I gave this pairing very serious thought. In terms of their personalities, they'll be a perfect match."

"I'm sure," said Dad. "Isaiah can get along with anyone. He attended an orientation program a few weeks ago and didn't know a soul. There were lots of black students from all over the U.S. there. He fit right in."

"Speaking of black students, this is only the beginning for Chadwick." Breedlove pulled out another sheet of paper and scrolled down the list of names. "I'm just looking at the new class. We've started ramping up our numbers. It's not a lot, but Isaiah and Richard are at the tip of the iceberg. We're making some other big moves soon."

"You're bringing in more black kids?" Dad narrowed his eyes.

"We've got something big in the works. I'm not at liberty to reveal any details now without clearance from our governing board, but when you hear about it, you'll be pleased." Switching gears, he looked at me. "Isaiah, you haven't said very much. Do you have any questions? Maybe I can answer something about the teachers, your new roommate, or what our expectations are for you?"

"Well …" I swallowed the lump in my throat. "Do you have any black history classes?" For a moment, I avoided looking at the faces of my parents, staring out the window at the campus. I was sure they didn't appreciate me asking Breedlove this question at this particular time, but his answer would reveal a lot. Mr. Jones, my former American history teacher, had made sure that black people were more than just footnotes to historical events, and I was eager to find out if there was someone at Chadwick who would continue to keep me inspired.

Dad cleared his throat. "I think you should tell him about your expectations, Mr. Breedlove. That way we can all hear them. We want to avoid any misunderstandings, that's for certain … And if Isaiah gets out of line, well, we don't want you to hold anything back." He gave me a very clear look. "His mom and I don't believe in sparing the rod, as they say in this good book." He held up his Bible, and then passed it to Mom. Flipping through the pages, she found a familiar verse.

"'The rod of correction imparts wisdom, but a child left to himself disgraces his mother,'" said Mom, sounding like a preacher. "'He who spares his rod hates his son, but he who loves him disciplines him promptly.' That's from the book of Proverbs."

They performed this routine in front of school administrators at the beginning of every school year, and I hated it. I was fifteen years old, and I still got spankings for performing at less than my best. The last one had come right after we'd received the results of my admissions test. Mom, convinced that I should have scored even higher, had spanked me for my lackluster effort. Black people had to be twice as good as white people in everything, my parents often told me. No exceptions. Hearing them now, I wanted to crawl underneath the desk.

"Well, since you put it that way," Breedlove said as he straightened his silk tie, which was curling near the knot, "I expect only a few things from all the students." He swallowed. "They must study hard, dress neatly, and—above all—follow the rules."

"Sounds like you've had problems?" Mom leaned forward.

"Believe it or not, Mrs. Issacson, meeting those expectations is a tall order for some. Students failing to do so on a consistent basis have had a hard time surviving this place."

"2 Good 2 B 4Gotten"

My dorm room was tucked away inside the Middlebury maze. The interior was simple. The door opened to a bare picture window framing a grassy courtyard. Underneath the windowsill was an empty desk, and near the walls were two beds with bare mattresses sitting atop built-in dresser drawers. The shiny linoleum floor smelled like disinfectant.

The brown paneled walls held countless pinholes from previous residents. There'd be no problem hanging the poster of Tommie Smith and John Carlos giving the power salute on the victory platform at the 1968 Mexico City Olympics and the one of Huey P. Newton I'd concealed in my trunk. My parents, concerned with me fitting in and appearing too radical, would have opposed both photos. But no matter what, I was determined to stay in touch with and—when necessary—flaunt my blackness.

Dad carried in the new, all-in-one stereo component set he'd found at a Sears clearance sale, and Mom brought in the bedding. Setting it on the counter, Dad looked at me in the way he did when he meant business.

"Remember, don't play this too loud."

"I know." I looked for the wall outlet. I was anxious to plug in everything and see how the radio, record player, and the tiny speakers attached to it, sounded.

"White people think we can't play our music at a reasonable level," added Mom. "Just watch yourself."

"I'll keep it real low," I said.

"That's good," said Dad. "But I don't think you'll have too much time for music listening anyway. Especially the way Breedlove was talking. You're going to be pretty busy, I can feel it. Just do your work and make us proud."

He emphasized the word "proud," making sure I understood the magnitude of the undertaking. Not only was I representing the Issacson household, but I was supposed to be a role model for all the black kids in Oakland who hadn't been awarded a scholarship.

Mom, appearing oblivious, finished making my bed.

"You realize that leaving you here is much harder than we thought, don't you?" He'd been in a hurry in Breedlove's office, but now he was slowing down. Tears started to form in his eyes. Usually stoic, his voice cracked like a bad phone connection.

"I know," I said, thinking about how homesick I'd feel later. "I'll be okay. My new roommate will be here soon. I hope."

Dad delivered a long prayer, and then he and Mom broke down as we said our good-byes.

After they left, I sat on the bed, gazing at the ceiling as if it were a movie screen. Looking to fill the void, I found the Connie Hawkins book that Brooklyn had given me, intending to pick up where I'd left off. I was enjoying it. I'd already read the first two chapters, and parts of the story sounded a little like me. As a kid, Hawkins was the tallest in his class, and his friends called him Slim, Bones, and Long Tall Sally. Self-conscious about his height, he was sometimes quiet, but he was good at basketball, which ended up being his saving grace.

As I was getting ready to read the chapter about Hawkins making the All-New York City team, I heard laughter outside my window. How were other students making the transition so smoothly? Why weren't they holed up inside their rooms, reading, like I was? Thinking? Crying? Maybe it was because they were already familiar with the terrain?

Wanting to feel a little of the enthusiasm I was hearing outside, I put down the Hawkins book and reached my photo album, which contained pictures from boot camp. Searching for Jenaye's picture, I wondered how she was doing at Yarborough—was she like the students outside, laughing? Or was she feeling my same sense of trepidation? I flipped through the album, looking for her picture. She'd signed it before I left, writing big so that there was no way I'd miss the message: *2 Good 2 B 4Gotten*. That was the absolute truth.

The hard knock at the door jarred me from my reverie. I got up and opened the door, finding on the other side an older white man wearing short sleeves and a freckled-faced white boy in a Beatles T-shirt.

"Yes?"

Seconds passed before they responded. "I'm Eberhart," the young boy finally said. "I'm looking for Isaiah Issacson?"

"That's me." I touched my shirt.

"I didn't know …" He covered his mouth, turning bright red.

"You didn't know what? That I was black? Is that what you're trying to say?" I was amused by his reaction, not totally surprised. Considering my new surroundings, having a black roommate would have been virtually impossible. We'd been warned at boot camp that some white people would be shocked by our presence.

"Yeah …" he replied. "I mean, no."

The man accompanying him, who I assumed was Eberhart's father, adjusted his gold-framed glasses. His skin was beet red. "I'm Mr. Drake."

"How are you?" I shook hands first with Eberhart, and then his father.

"Not good," said Eberhart, who wiped his hands as if I'd left dirt on them and then turned away and stuck a finger down his throat as if he wanted to make himself puke.

"That's enough, E," said Mr. Drake.

I ignored my new roommate's statement. "You need any help with your stuff?"

"Not really." He turned around and walked outside, taking his time before returning with several large cardboard boxes containing stereo components. The pieces were brand-new, still in plastic.

"You won't need those." I gestured at my stereo. "I've already got the music set up. I hope you like James Brown."

He carried in the boxes anyway and set them next to my stereo. His system must have cost a small fortune. Wrapped inside were a black-on-black multichannel Marantz receiver, Bang and Olufson turntable, and a reel-to-reel tape deck. I'd seen pictures of his equipment in a copy of *Stereo Review* and dreamed of owning the set, but I knew my parents weren't going to be able to afford something like that. We weren't dirt poor, but we weren't anywhere near this rich.

Opening the boxes, he carefully began to remove the plastic wrapping paper.

"I don't want to hear any jungle music," he said. "I brought my own sounds." Even though he spoke loud enough for his father to hear, Mr. Drake left the room to get more of his son's things from the car.

As soon as the door closed behind his father, I stared Eberhart down. "Jungle music?" I raised my voice so that he knew I had heard him clearly. "You calling my stuff jungle music?"

"That's what I said, isn't it?" He nodded his head matter-of-factly, unfazed by my words.

"I got your jungle music." I rubbed my hands together in preparation for a fight.

"Like I said, I don't want to hear any of that jungle music on that piece-of-shit music box. This is quality." He jabbed his finger at his shiny receiver, which held more knobs than the dashboard on my dad's Impala. His speakers were big enough to sit on.

I moved in closer and grabbed his shirt near the collar. "Don't ever say that again about my music. You're lucky your father is still here."

"You aren't gonna do anything. Let me go," he said, trying to pull away. "I can say anything I want to say. This is a free country."

His father came back into the room carrying a tennis racket and an armful of posters and wall coverings. I reluctantly let go of his son's shirt.

"I think they may have made a mistake," said Mr. Drake, putting the rest of the stuff down. "Mr. Breedlove never said anything about this. I think I'll go and talk to him. Can you two keep things quiet while I'm gone?"

"Sure," I said, remembering that my father had warned me that it wasn't smart to lose my temper around white folks. As soon as they could, they'd use it against you, he'd said.

"I hope he gets me a new roommate," said Eberhart, walking toward the bed to pick up his tennis racket.

I wasn't sure how he was going to use it, so I stood behind him, close enough to make sure there wasn't enough room for him to pivot and swing it at me. "That ain't gonna happen. Breedlove's already told my parents about you. He worked really hard on pairing us up."

"So what? My dad is powerful." Feeling me behind him, he tossed the racket back on the bed and sorted through more of his belongings.

"That's what you think." I walked away laughing and then sat on the edge of my bed. I motioned for him to continue unpacking.

"You'll see."

An hour later, Mr. Drake came back from Breedlove's office. Without fanfare, he whispered something into Eberhart's ear before leaving. Anxious to hear the results, I followed the kid toward the dresser drawer on the other side of our small dormitory room as he carried a handful of T-shirts. I wondered if my prediction had come true.

He opened a drawer, dropped in his shirts, and slammed it shut. "Breedlove said I was stuck with you."

I bust out laughing. "I told you so!"

"That doesn't mean I have to talk to you, though. So for the time being, and until you unhook that piece-of-shit component set, we don't have anything to say to each other."

"I'll let Huey, John, and Tommie do my talking," I said. I unfurled a poster of Huey P. Newton posing in a fan-shaped wicker chair, wearing a black leather jacket, a starched, fully buttoned white shirt, and a cocked tam resting atop his Afro. Unsmiling, he held a rifle in one hand and a spear in the other. I thought about his message of black pride and self-defense as I tacked it on the back of the door. Then I opened the other poster, which showed John Carlos and Tommie Smith sporting their dark warm-up suits, victory medals, and black socks, standing on the podium while the national anthem played. Their gloved fists were raised in a silent protest of white America's treatment of black people. "They'll say everything I need to say."

*   *   *

September 20, 1973

Dear Isaiah:

How's the new school? We're expecting big things from you. You're the first one in this family to go to prep school, and if all goes well you'll be the first one to attend college. Have you changed your mind about getting the horse?

I've enclosed $20 so you can buy something the next time you go into town or to that snack bar on the campus. Spend it wisely. Money doesn't grow on trees.

Everyone's been asking about you. Dad sends his love. Melvin and Lenae can't wait until you come back for your first vacation.

I ran into your junior high counselor, Mrs. Jasper. We talked in the grocery store. She asked how that new set of luggage she bought you was holding up. Have you sent her a thank-you card? If it hadn't been for her connections to RSP, and that luggage, I don't know what we would have done. She's a wonderful lady.

What are the classes like? How are your grades?

Miss you …

Love,

Mom

THE JOURNAL

Mr. Hagman paced back and forth in front of the classroom, waiting for our chatter to die down. Grasping a small, leather-bound booklet, he lifted his head and stared at a clock near the rear of the classroom. After introducing himself as the English teacher, he said, "We're going to keep a journal in here. I want you to write about your new experiences at Chadwick."

From the back of the class, I heard something that sounded like a cheer from my Oakland counterpart, Richard. He was settling into the place much faster than I was.

"If you don't want to write about Chadwick, just pretend you're writing to a close friend. That'll get those writing juices flowing." He tapped the book in his left hand. "This little tome here is mine. I've been writing my thoughts in here for the last ten years." He placed the journal on his desk and kept moving. He was a small man, but he covered the area like he was much bigger.

"Is everybody in here going to read this?" I asked, feeling nervous.

"Just me," he said. "But I don't want you to censor yourselves. Write your deepest thoughts. Some of the world's best books started out as diaries. All the great writers kept them."

I felt a little better knowing my whole life and intimate thoughts wouldn't be broadcast around the campus, but I wondered if writers such as F. Scott Fitzgerald, D. H. Lawrence, and Mark Twain, whose books Hagman had placed on the reading list, had really kept journals. Even if they had, the boys I knew back home *didn't*. Was there a way out of this?

"Any more questions?" He waited for someone else to raise his hand, but nothing happened. "Good," he said. "Let's talk about something even more fun." He held up a newspaper article with a boldfaced headline about President Nixon. My mind raced over the impressions I'd formed of Nixon from talking to my dad, a staunch Democrat who had supported George McGovern in the previous election. Dad said that Nixon, a Republican, was lying about Watergate and had always been involved in political dirty tricks. "The other thing you'll do in here is follow current events. I know this is unusual for an English class, but you'll get my point later. Has anyone read about Watergate?"

My hand shot up fast; I longed for him to ask me something about Watergate. What could be fun about following the downward spiral of "Tricky Dick," as Dad called him? I'd be able to give Hagman my views on the presidency, lying, and the latest developments on the case—but he ignored me.

"Those of you who raised their hands will be ahead of everyone else when we start our news quiz," Hagman said, scanning the room, but refraining from calling on anyone. "For the rest, I suggest you get in the habit of reading the paper. I'm a firm believer that following this story will help you see how important it is to be honest and maintain your integrity. We hammer those values home at Chadwick. And if nothing else, reading it will help you improve your grammar and composition." He set the paper back down on his desk and went over the rest of the course syllabus.

In addition to the newspaper, we'd have to read *The Great Gatsby* and *The Adventures of Huckleberry Finn,* and there'd be lots of papers to write. He said he was determined to expose us to the best novels, but that wasn't all. He loved public television.

"You're all invited over to my house tonight to watch this new program."

I sat up straight in my chair, hoping the long drought I'd endured without seeing a movie had now come to an end. Aside from the dearth of black students, I still hadn't gotten used to the banning of television inside the dorms and the lack of movie theaters within walking distance. Black actors such as Fred Williamson, Richard Roundtree, and Ron O'Neal were starring in all kinds of movies, sticking it to white people. By attending Chadwick, I was missing *everything*.

"The show's called *Upstairs, Downstairs,* and it's hosted by the great Alistair Cooke. It's a wonderful series about the British upper class, which will give us the chance to learn about another culture. That's what life's all about, you know."

I slumped back down in my chair when I found out the program. I didn't really care if I learned about the British. All white folks were the same to me. Weren't there any black shows on public television?

He stared at my gangly frame. "We'll be discussing some of the episodes in class. Bring your notebook tonight. Write about what you see."

The assignment sounded boring, but to lessen the blow and make it bearable, I began thinking about using the time to compose a few letters to Jenaye. Thinking about her made me want to turn back the clock. I was looking forward to telling her about the drive here, my meeting with Breedlove, and the fact that I'd nearly kicked my roommate's butt for talking shit about my music. If I ever got the chance again, I'd hold her tighter, kiss her, and make sure she knew I really missed her.

"Isaiah, can you hear me?"

I'd been looking down, spacing out about Jenaye. "Yeah," I said, telling myself to concentrate on the here and now. "I'll bring my pen and notebook with me tonight."

*   *   *

Right after dinner, a nightly suit-and-tie affair requiring the attendance of everyone at Chadwick, the members of my English class met outside the dining hall. Hagman had stood up after dessert and announced what he'd already told us during class. His penchant for repetition was often annoying.

It felt like forever waiting for everyone to finish his dinner and for the student waiters to clear the tables. Outside the dining hall, near our meeting place, I tried passing the time by talking to my new classmates. I started with Dennis Pascal, an upperclassman from Santa Cruz, but all he wanted to talk about was his superior surfing ability, a subject in which I had very little interest. When I told him I didn't surf but loved basketball, he pointed in the direction of a tall, sunken-faced redhead standing by himself on the other side of the platform. "You want to talk to Frank Silverman," Dennis said, looking up at me. "He's the basketball star here."

I walked over to Frank slowly, thinking of a way to begin a conversation, eyeing his boxy shoulders, gangly arms, and the dark-colored sports jacket that covered his wrinkled white shirt.

We were nearly the same height. When our gazes met, I spoke up first. "Dennis Pascal told me you were the star basketball player here." I said it with a smile so he wouldn't think I was challenging him. I wanted him to think I was paying him a compliment.

"Yeah, I'm on the team."

At least he was modest.

"What about you? Are you coming out? You're tall enough." He tilted his head upward to look at the crown of my head.

"I play a little bit," I said, matching his demeanor.

He rubbed his palms together as if he'd found a treasure. "Really?" He moved a step closer, moving to see if our shoulders were the same height. Standing on his tiptoes, he asked, "How tall are you?"

"About six-four," I said, proudly tugging at the lapel of my suit jacket. I was clearly taller.

"We could use you." He brushed the hair from his eyes.

I found out all I could from him before it was time to go to Hagman's house for the movie, including the fact that his father was a stockbroker who could afford a black housekeeper. Frank talked about his close relationship with her, and I liked that. Since he was a senior, he told me a few important things about Chadwick, like what to expect from my teachers, particularly my history teacher, Mr. Negley. He said I needed to make sure I kept up with the reading assignments, but to keep some time open for working out with him when my homework was done. We shook hands afterward like old friends, and I walked away feeling like I'd found someone who had my back.

After my conversation with Frank, I left the platform and headed toward Hagman's house. His residence was on the other side of campus, away from the stables and the riding area and near the library. It was only fitting that Hagman, an English nerd, lived near the library. I pictured him making periodic stops to pick up one of those classics he talked about reading and burying himself in the stacks until dinner every night. I walked slowly past it now, trying to delay my arrival at Hagman's, but when I saw Richard walking along the same path ahead of me, I tried to catch up with him.

"So, are you ready for this?" As soon as I asked the question, he immediately flashed his notebook at me. I didn't want to carry mine to dinner so I'd folded up several sheets of lined paper and had stuffed them in my pocket. I'd enter my observations about the British in my notebook later.

"I think so," he said, without a hint of angst. "I've heard about *Upstairs, Downstairs,* but I can't wait to see it." He was at it again. First it was his flippant remarks about the Freedom Fighters in the South, and now he seemed unconcerned about the cultural impact of watching an obscure public television program explore British culture. He looked at my empty hands and developed a puzzled look. "Where's your notebook?"

"I'm going to write everything down later," I said, annoyed by his ambition. I wondered if he cared about *anything* black. Had he watched *Shaft* or *Come Back, Charleston Blue*? And if he had, what did he think of them? Did he like it when black people stuck it to the man, as I did?

"You're going to get in trouble for not having your notebook," he said, waving a finger at me.

"No, I won't." I pulled out the folded pieces of paper and ink pen lodged in my pocket.

He smiled and shook his head. "I hope that works."

"It will," I said, trying to stuff the paper and pen back in my pocket. My pen fell near Richard's shiny cowboy boots, and I reached down to pick it up. I followed the creases and the lines along his instep to the tip of his toes. "Are you wearing those now?" The pointed-toe boots were a deep maroon and black, the color of ripe plums.

"Something wrong with them?" he asked. All of the members of the class had finally gathered and were moving away from the dining hall and through the campus toward Hagman's residence.

"I've never seen a black boy from Oakland wearing cowboy boots," I said.

"That's what some of the white kids have been saying." Richard stopped in his tracks as if he couldn't believe what he'd just heard me say. "You've got to wear them if you're going to have a horse. It's dusty out there on those trails. If you had a horse, you'd understand."

"I know," I answered him without a trace of remorse. "I don't want the headache or the responsibility right now."

"You don't know what you're missing." Richard shook his head. "Those horses are really neat, man. Did I tell you about my first ride?" He was getting excited, but the other kids from our class weren't paying much attention. They were talking about the television program.

I looked up to see how far we were from our destination. We'd passed all the academic buildings, but there was still time for him to finish telling a short story before we'd got to Hagman's front door.

"You see how tall I am, don't you?" He lifted his arm to show me. "Well, I had to get on a tree stump to mount my horse and then my trainer had to keep telling me how to manipulate the reins to make the horse walk straight. You should have seen all the other kids. They laughed at me and rode their horses like they'd been doing it all of their lives. I fell off a couple of times along the trail, but I didn't care. I got back up on the saddle like a jockey and kept on going. I don't care what happens now—I'm determined to become one of the best riders ever."

I couldn't wait to get inside Hagman's house so we could stop talking about Richard's horse. I'd regretted dropping my pen and getting him started on this subject. With each turn in the conversation, I was becoming more incensed by his unquestioning willingness to fit into Chadwick's strange culture.

At the entrance to Hagman's residence, I pressed a finger against my lips as a signal to let Richard know that I'd had enough and then walked away to join the others. Inside Hagman's living room, the antique chairs were moved against the walls so that we could sit down, cross-legged, in front of a television set. I hadn't been inside the houses of very many white people, and I was curious to see just how they, in particular Hagman, lived. I wondered if their lives were really fuller than ours and if their accommodations were more comfortable.

"Sit anywhere you like," he said, as we landed on the carpet. "When everyone's ready, we'll turn on the show." Knowing I didn't have my journal, I sat behind some of my classmates and as far away from Hagman as possible and took out my paper and pen.

His bookshelves were filled with the classics, and on the wall was a picture of Mark Twain sitting on a couch and clutching a pen and notepad. I wanted to explore the other parts of the house to see what else made Hagman tick, but the program had started. I'd need more time to test out my theories or to confirm my suspicions about the lives of white people.

Alistair Cooke set the stage. His perfectly groomed hair and British accent pulled me in, but the show was a complete letdown. I wanted to go back to my room, turn on my stereo, and forget where I was, but I realized my roommate and I still hadn't resolved our musical differences. Maybe the key to my survival was yielding to the attempts at whitewashing. Dismayed, I blocked out the program and began writing.

September 20, 1973

Dear Jenaye:

It's been days since my arrival at Chadwick, but the reality of being at an all-boys school and miles away from you has me daydreaming about our first slow dance. You asked me while the music played if I'd moved that way before and I said yes. I lied. It really was my first time and I was real nervous dancing in front of everyone. I blocked the nervousness out of my mind and tried to relax because I didn't want to miss the opportunity to hold you closer, especially since I knew the time was running out. But, you probably could tell anyway. I wonder if you're thinking about me now ...

FOOTNOTES

The next day, my European history teacher started class with a pop quiz. Frank had been right about the reading assignment. His timely advice had made me reevaluate my distrust toward white people, which my initial encounter with my roommate, E, had only exacerbated. Maybe they could be trusted if you established some common ground.

Unfortunately, Negley had lifted his first question from the footnotes. Unaware of the consequences, I'd ignored the fine print in an attempt to get through an assignment about the French Revolution. Jenaye never would have done that. As with geometry class, she would have mastered all the terms and aced the exam. I could hear her admonishing me: "The key is memorizing the terms."

After class, Negley stopped me. "You heading to the lunchroom?"

"Yeah," I answered, wondering why he was asking.

"I'm going in that direction, too. Let's ride in my car. We need to talk."

The classrooms weren't a long way from the dining hall, but Negley, with his pudgy middle, looked like the kind of man who didn't enjoy exercise, even if it was just walking across campus.

My quiz rolled in one hand, he patted it repeatedly against his open palm. "These results were horrible. Did you study?"

"Of course," I replied.

"Well, you missed a lot of easy ones," he said. "If I didn't tell you before, I'm telling you now—you must read *everything*, even footnotes. Don't skim. You'll pay the price if you skip over the small stuff."

"But I didn't think those footnotes were important. I was just trying to get a general idea of what was going on. Isn't that enough?" I asked. I thought about telling Negley that I'd purposely neglected the footnotes out of respect for one of the Panther Party's educational goals: *We want education that exposes the true nature of this decadent American society. We want education that teaches us our true history ... We believe in an educational system that will give to our people a knowledge of self.*

"Just pay attention to the details." He continued the steady beat, quiz against palm. "And never begin an essay question with, 'The people ... ' Learn to be specific. This is not junior high."

"It's just the first test." I focused on his thick mustache. "Plus, I had to watch *Upstairs, Downstairs* last night. It lasted two hours, and then we had a discussion. There wasn't enough time to finish reading."

"That's an excuse," he said. "You knew about my assignment, too. At Chadwick, a different academic standard is expected."

"What do you mean?"

"Let's just say I read your admissions essay. Don't expect to get any special privileges. No one cares that your parents grew up under segregation and attended substandard schools. No one cares you went to an all-black school and that you feel black people have been the victims of an undue amount of discrimination. That's in the past now. Now that you're here, you've got to learn the material just like everyone else." He put the test in his back pocket.

"I wasn't looking for any favors," I said, recalling the essay. Of course I had written about some of those things, but he had misinterpreted the tone. I wasn't looking for special consideration.

"I'm just making you aware," he said. "I've heard some good things about you, but I'll have to reserve judgment for myself until I see more." He stopped in front of a canary yellow sports car and rubbed his hand gently over the body.

I'd only seen a car like this in a magazine. It was beautiful. "Wow. That's a nice car," I said. "What kind is it?"

"A Lamborghini," he said. "It's one of the fastest in the world and tops out at about 195 miles per hour." He continued stroking it like it was a pedigreed puppy. "You know, if I didn't pay attention to detail, this car wouldn't run very well," he said. "I read the owner's manual every chance I get. A little maintenance goes a long way. None at all is asking for trouble." He looked for signs of dust and dirt. "That should be a lesson to you for my class. If you don't do your routine maintenance—or study—you're going to have problems down the line."

"You don't need to worry about that," I said to Negley. "I've got everything under control now. You'll see."

"I hope you're right, Isaiah. Because from here on out, I'll be paying special attention." He opened the car door and slid into a seat that looked like the cockpit of an airplane. "Just don't screw up." He stuck the key in the ignition and started the powerful engine. "Now get in on the other side. Let's get a bite to eat before the food gets cold."

*   *   *

September 22, 1973

Dear Mom:

Everything is going real well. I just had a quiz in my history class and passed it with flying colors. You'd be proud of me. (smile).

Richard passed, too. He's made himself at home since getting a horse, but he's sounding more and more like a white boy. I thought I was becoming a nerd, but when I heard him say, "Far out man…that's really groovy," to the fact that I'd finally gotten a faint signal to a black music station on my radio, I had to wonder if we're really from the same neighborhood. If sounding like Richard is the price I'm going to have to pay for being here, you might not be able to understand me.

We're supposed to have a dance soon. That'll give me something to look forward to. The girls will be bused in from a nearby all-girls school. I wish it were Yarborough Academy. Seeing my friend Jenaye would be nice.

Love,
Isaiah

*   *   *

September 30, 1973

Dear Tee:

It seems strange not going to school with girls anymore. I never thought I would miss them, but I often think about this girl I met in Minnesota and wonder if I'll ever get to see her again. On our last day together, we made a deal to stay in touch.

I wish you or someone else from home could have seen me at dinner tonight. Everyone has to dress in a suit jacket and tie every night and our seats are assigned. Each table has about ten people with an even mix of freshmen, sophomores, juniors, and seniors. So far, the freshmen have been responsible for picking up the food trays and serving everyone. After dinner, they must make sure everyone gets dessert.

Pretty soon it'll be the sophomores' turn at waiting tables. I'm already nervous. One of the freshmen at my table dropped the food tray the other day and everyone in the dining hall stopped eating their dinner and clapped. The older students say it happens all the time, but what if that happens to me?

Dropping the food probably wouldn't be all bad because the food here is terrible. We had roast beef, mashed potatoes, and carrots tonight. It tasted like mush and I don't remember eating anything. I'm still starving. I hope breakfast is much better tomorrow. I've got some barbecue chips and some Fritos for snacks, but at this rate I'll run out in no time. I could use a good home-cooked meal.

Every night we have study hall. We're not allowed to watch TV or listen to the radio, so what else can you do? I haven't seen a good TV show since I've been here and it would really be nice to hear a black radio station without all the static. We're so far out in the boondocks that the black stations from L. A. fade in and out.

There have been some good things. I got to sleep in on my first weekend. That was a change from having to get up and do chores. Plus, I didn't have to endure the long, drawn-out arguments my mom was starting to have with my dad every Saturday morning about coming in at 3:00 AM.

There's no real church either, only something called vespers, a one-hour meeting in the chapel on Sunday evenings. It's not like the all-day Sunday church services at home with all the shouting and stuff like I'm used to. It's a quiet time and a lecture service. You really have to see this place to believe it.

    Isaiah

       *   *   *

October 8, 1973

Dear Isaiah:

Bonjour! It's me, Jenaye. Shunkers!! If you're not hip, bonjour is a new French word I learned that means hello and the other one is a dynamite word we've made up here for "what's happening?" It was good to hear from you. I guess I thought it would be sooner, especially after our talks and the dance at boot camp, but you must have had other things on your mind.

It's hard to believe that after all the preparation I've finally arrived at Yarborough Academy. The campus is full of beautiful stone buildings and contains a dance studio, a lab, and an observatory. The only things we don't have are horses.

The classes are hard here, too. Since the first day, I've had nightmares of flunking out. I'm taking French, geometry, history, biology, and public speaking. It's a heavy load, but my counselor here tells me that if I take the right mix and do well, I'd be able to go to Harvard or Yale. I'm not thinking about that now. I'm just trying, like you, to keep my head above water.

I never made it through my first biology lab. We had to dissect rats and identify the organs. I've seen enough of them in Camden, but these were the super-white kind and the insides were so gross, I gave up about halfway through the test and told the teacher I had a weak stomach. I know I said I wanted to be a doctor, but now I don't know. It sounded good at the time.

My favorite class is public speaking. Our first assignment was to give an impromptu speech about something that annoyed us about the school. I started to talk about the fact that aside from Judy, a black girl from Philadelphia whose father has a lot of money, there weren't many black students. Instead I talked about all the curse words scribbled in the stalls inside the bathroom. I thought I had left that kind of stuff behind in Camden. Mr. Matthews paid me a compliment after the presentation. He said I had the class riveted. Now after his class, I find a way to make conversation just so I can hear him talk. His handlebar mustache is so cute!

I think I'm developing a crush on him, but I've got to be careful about who I talk to about it. My classmates, the real jealous ones, have started to call me the teacher's pet and some of them have called me some other names behind my back. I've told my mom about it, but she's not taking it seriously. All she's said is, "Girls will be girls," and dismissed it.

Riding horses sounds fun. I love all animals, except rats, of course. I can't believe you're not going to get a horse. I wish they had them here.

By the way, I found that book Brooklyn gave you in our school library. I read a few pages to see just what his point was in handing it to you while we were at Carlton. Of course I think Brooklyn was jealous of you, but do you realize what happened to Connie? He was a good ballplayer, but at the end he got caught up in a gambling scandal and his whole life was ruined. Is that what you got out of it? The man sunk everything he had into his basketball dream and didn't have anything to fall back on. We both need to get busy and study. What else is there to do?

Unlike Chadwick, the food here is surprisingly good. We've got our choice every day of mashed potatoes and gravy, meatloaf, steak and all sorts of desserts. Sometimes all the good food makes being away from home feel like paradise.

I've got a white roommate, too. Her name is Rebecca Kauffman, but everyone calls her Becca for short. She asked more questions than your roommate when she found out I'd be staying with her. Her first question was about my long hair. If I get another question here about it I'm going to be ready to kill somebody. Don't these white girls know that black girls can grow long hair?

When she saw my pictures of Michael Jackson and the Jackson 5 plastered on the wall on my side of the room, she asked me why I liked them so much. I told her the whole story and she seemed to understand. We're slowly getting to know each other, but it's been hard making new friends. I never know what to say or do.

What happened to Richard and your roommate? Did you two ever resolve that stereo problem? Or did you end up fighting about it? You didn't mention it in your last letter? I can't wait to hear about it. Write me back soon. I've got to go.

Peace,

Jenaye

PEER PRESSURE

By the time I received Jenaye's letter, my roommate and I were on speaking terms. I never forgave him for making fun of my stereo and calling my music "jungle," but our disagreements grew less intense once we learned to coexist.

Talking about our parents seemed to thaw the ice. E's father was the second-generation owner of a multimillion-dollar vacuum cleaner company on the East Coast. At some point, E was scheduled to become a majority shareholder, so every month his father mailed him copies of the *Harvard Business Review* so he'd be aware of the latest financial news. In fact, Mr. Drake had already gone to all the Ivy League campuses to discuss the business programs with the deans of admission and let them know his son would one day be applying for the 1976 freshman class.

Chadwick was the first step toward what E's parents believed was a lock on maintaining his status among the very rich. However, becoming a wealthy businessman wasn't in E's plans. His parents didn't know it yet, but he'd grown his hair down to his shoulders and often dressed in wild colors, studded jeans, big-buckled rawhide belts, and cowboy boots. He always talked about becoming a movie star, like Clint Eastwood, and sailing, golf, and tennis, things his parents didn't think were practical.

My dad wanted me to be a lawyer. Because of segregation, he always said that if he'd been born in my time, there would have been no restrictions on his ambition. He dreamed of a life as the black Perry Mason but dropped out of school to join the Army so he could travel. He visited a lot of countries during World War II, but when it ended, he found a job as a cook at the V. A. hospital and never left. He badgered me constantly about law school, but I had no interest in becoming a lawyer. That profession was a far cry from the life I sought as a militant basketball star, and nothing was going to stop me.

The pressure to become professionals made smoking weed an act of rebellion; it took our minds off the expectations and made me feel as if I'd been accepted a bit by E. I'd started smoking a little before attending Chadwick, but I didn't tell E. I wasn't really used to talking to white people, and I'd been told they twisted what you said. The last thing I needed to be known as around campus was a burnout. Until I agreed to smoke with him, E assumed I was a full-fledged, white-boy-hating radical.

Tee had turned me on one day at the playground. He lit up a fat one next to the brown portable building that we leaned against after playing hoops.

"Come on, man, your mom ain't gonna find out. Just a little toke," he said.

Before I took a hit, I looked around, as if I expected my mother was somewhere close by, grabbed the joint, and inhaled slowly. I could see him watching me, smiling and laughing, glad I'd decided to risk it all and have some fun. I had a reputation as a good kid, a goody-two-shoes who never got in trouble. With that joint in my mouth, I'd given Tee and me something in common.

Mom and Dad had warned me about peer pressure, urging me to think for myself, but I knew they had no clue to what it was really like to say no to Tee. He could be relentless and quite persuasive when he wanted you to do something.

I didn't always enjoy smoking out. At first I'd inhale a little, while Tee watched, and then tell a story with a mouthful of smoke. The white cloud would seep through my nose and out from between my lips as I told him about the girl in our junior high that had a mad crush on me. He'd be thinking about my glasses, laughing so hard about the story, that he'd fail to notice that I'd blown out the smoke and was just trying my best not to get loaded.

My strategy worked fine for a while, except a few times when the weed was so strong I'd end up with a contact high. My eyes would get beet red, and I'd have to go home and sleep it off.

Sneaking past Mom was the hardest part. When she was in one of her investigative moods and I'd been out longer than normal, she'd wait by the front door so she could check my eyes and smell my clothes. I tried running to my room, but she knew something was up. She'd block my path, move up real close, and say stuff like, "Something sure smells funny. Are you smoking that stuff?" I'd look at her like I didn't know what she was talking about, and most times she'd back off and cast a skeptical eye in my direction. I answered her nearly the same way every time. When I got accepted to Chadwick, I think she was relieved because I was away from Tee, a person she considered a bad influence on me. She assumed that if I were away at prep school, it would be harder for me to get high, but in a lot of ways, it was much easier.

E raided his bank account often, using the cash to buy weed. I didn't have a bank account or much money, and he had no qualms about wanting to turn me on. He kept his stash in a clear, plastic baggie behind the math books above his desk. The Zig Zags were there, too. He was really good at rolling joints. I admired the way he moved his lips across the edges of the thin paper and slid his tongue against the sticky surface. When the paper had been assembled, he reached inside the clear bag and took out a handful of marijuana. He sprinkled it onto the paper, carefully leaving out the stems, and rolled the joint tight—but not too tight. He said he left out the stems because they made the joint burn unevenly. Details like that were important to E.

"You ready to go?" he mumbled one night after study hall, before our evening bed check. It was hard hearing him sometimes. He ran his words together like it hurt him to talk.

He had stopped smoking in our dorm room because lighting up in there had become too risky. One time, he'd placed a thick towel next to the small crack at the bottom of the door so the smoke wouldn't escape. The way he figured it, if he blocked the smoke from going out that crack, the only other escape route was the window. "Don't be scared, he said. "We'll be fine. Everything will go out over there." He pointed to the window. "You'll see." His plan worked perfectly until our next-door neighbor came up to us after breakfast one morning and said he smelled strange fumes coming through the walls. He'd reported it to the headmaster, and E, who had gotten busted while I was out practicing my jump shot, was put on probation. From that moment on, he found other places to smoke.

"Yeah, I'm ready." I got up from the bed, kicked a pair of his cowboy boots out of the way, and headed to the closet to look for my black turtleneck. I'd picked it out long ago because it matched my Shaft poster and made me look like a superhero. E let out a deep sigh. I pulled the thick material over my head and looked at him in his studded jean jacket. I wasn't sure where or how far we were headed, but I was gonna be warm.

We walked out of the dorms toward a zigzagging hiking path that led deep into the forest. The nearly full moon lit the cloudless sky and highlighted the squishy black and brown soil that stuck to my sneakers. Looking ahead, the hanging tree branches reminded me of the long-armed creatures inside the haunted houses of amusement parks, and the thick spiderwebs sticking to my cheeks felt like cotton candy. Rotting logs littered the ground. Crickets sang.

Crashing our way through the damp trail, we found a small clearing. The moss-covered rocks were our chairs, and a sawed tree stump was our table.

"Do you know where you're going?" I was nearly out of breath.

"I think so," he whispered.

"What kind of answer is that? We've got to get back to our rooms before bed check, you know?" I berated myself for giving in to him. Adjusting my glasses, I stared at his face in the dark. He wasn't ugly, but he wasn't handsome, either. Like his father, he had freckles underneath his eyes. The sweat glistened against his forehead, and his mouth, surrounded by peach fuzz, was barely open.

He pulled back the sleeve on his jacket and peered at his watch. The hands glowed. "We'll make it." He pulled down his sleeve and reached into his jeans to get the joint. He lit it, taking the first hit.

"Looks like someone's already been here," I said, looking around at the empty box of matches and the small gum wrapper lying in the dirt. It was hard to believe that anyone came this far. "You sure this is all right?"

"Positive. Don't worry, it's cool."

"Whatever." I was paranoid, and I hadn't even taken my first hit. I clasped my fingers together and rubbed my palms. Surviving Chadwick was on my mind. I watched as E took another hit, and then I blurted out a question. "Do you like it here?"

"It's all right," he exhaled. "I'll be glad when I get to be a junior or senior. They say it gets easier, but I don't see it. I'm supposed to go to business school, and the classes you need to take for admission are hard. That means I'll have to get straight A's." The weed hadn't relaxed him yet, and he was shaking his head.

"Don't worry, I'm not gonna make straight A's either. I failed my first quiz. It's hard to stay focused. I miss my old neighborhood, the fine girls, and good basketball. I just talked to a friend the other day, and he told me about all the basketball tournaments they're supposed to play in this year. He says everyone's been asking about me. They want to know when I'm coming back. If I left here, we'd be unstoppable."

"Yeah, right," E said. "You talk a good game."

He passed me the joint, and I took a long hit, the longest I could remember ever taking. The smoke passed through my mouth and lodged in my throat. I tried to hold it in this time and ended up letting out a heavy cough.

"Be careful, dude," said E as he watched me. "That's good stuff."

I took my time on the next hit, making sure I took a deep breath. I put the joint back against my lips, which were forming the shape of an O. It didn't take long to feel the smoke. I could feel the weed loosening my inhibitions, creating the sensation of intellectual insight. It's amazing how many exalted conversations you believe you can have while smoking weed. For the first time, I felt free.

"You ever thought about what it would be like to be me?" I asked.

"Once," he said. "If I were you, I wouldn't have to cut or comb my hair. Black people don't have to do that, right?"

"Where'd you hear that?"

"Nantucket. Where else?"

"Nantucket ain't the world," I said, growing upset that he'd started referring to his privileged upbringing again as if it were the center of the world. "I've got to comb my hair every day just like you."

"So much for that theory," he replied. "I guess I never gave it much thought."

"That figures ... Remember that first day you opened the door and found out I was gonna be your roommate? What about the expression on your face? What was that about?"

He looked embarrassed. "It was nothing, man."

"Really?"

There was an awkward pause. He'd answered my question too quickly. He tightened up.

"It had to be something. Your expression was too noticeable. Your dad had almost the same one. Would you tell me if it was?" I knew the answer to that question, but I wanted him to tell me.

"Actually, I don't remember what I did or how my dad looked at you. I wasn't sure who my roommate would be. I probably would have reacted the same way if it had been ..."

"Brad Zorbas?" I finished his sentence, knowing he was going to say that he would have reacted the same way if his roommate had been some goofy white kid at Chadwick. The weed had made me fearless. We both knew Brad Zorbas. He was smart and nerdy. Brad's father was the dean of academics, and in some respects he looked like the typical Chadwick student, if there was such a thing. Thick glasses. Izod shirt. Brown loafers. "I don't think so."

"Well, when you put it like that, I guess I was a little surprised that you were black." He let out a sigh as if he'd just found out he'd passed a difficult midterm. "I just didn't expect it. I saw the name Issacson, and I just automatically pictured a white kid. I didn't know there were rich black people." He realized he'd said more than he meant to, and he looked at my expression to see if he could determine if it was safe to proceed. "You're not going to get all mad, are you?"

"No," I said. "There are a lot of rich black people, but I'm not one of them." I held the joint away from my mouth and waited for another bombshell. He was dumber than I thought. I could have used the time to educate him, but I thought he was probably too far gone.

"I think you're getting mad."

"I'm just thinking, that's all." I took another hit.

"About what?" he asked.

"About all the rich black people."

"So there's a lot?"

"Yeah."

"Name 'em, then."

I hated myself for not being able to rattle off a list of names he might know. I started to mention some rich black doctors and lawyers in Oakland, professionals who sponsored the Links Cotillion and the Jack and Jill Club parties I'd attended at the invitation of my counselor. Mrs. Jaspar, a black woman, had been an active member of the club and had invited me to a black-tie scholarship dinner as a special guest to show her colleagues just what she had been doing to improve the lot of the less fortunate. As a bonus, I got an opportunity to rub shoulders with some of the richest black people in Oakland. I could have told E about all those people I'd met. He'd never believe it anyway.

"You haven't said anything."

"I'm thinking."

"Well, pass me the joint while you think," he said.

I handed him the joint and ran my hands through my hair. I opened my mouth to say "Muhammad Ali," but he had already moved on. As he took a hit, I weighed whether to tell him the truth—that I was on scholarship and in the Rising Stars Program. In boot camp, Davidson had cautioned us against saying anything, warning us that talking too much about our scholarships with the white kids would produce resentment. Now I weighed his advice carefully.

E passed the joint back to me. "Didn't you say your dad was somebody important at a hospital?"

"He's a dietitian," I said. I'd used the title because it sounded impressive and because I'd seen it used on a commemorative certificate he'd received for all his years at the same job.

"What's that?"

"He makes up the menus for all the sick people in a veteran's hospital."

"Does he make a lot of money?"

I shrugged. "I don't know."

"What about Richard's parents?"

"You'd have to ask Richard," I said, growing impatient at all the personal questions. Opening up had seemed like a good idea, but it was harder than I thought. I found myself holding back. "You finished?"

"You rushing me now?" He raised his eyebrows at me, joking.

"Nah. But we've been out here a long time, and it's getting late. I don't want to miss bed check."

"We're good, man. I'm the one on probation, remember?"

"I know, but if you hurry up, we can listen to some music. I've got the new Earth, Wind & Fire album."

"Which one?"

"*Head to the Sky*," I said. I'd purchased it at the only record store in town that sold black music. They carried only a few albums by the artists I liked, and so when they did arrive, I made sure I was there to purchase them. That was another problem with this place. It was hard to maintain your ties to music and black culture. Sometimes I felt like I was losing touch. "Come on. Let's go."

E took his time. He sucked harder, closing his eyes this time. I reached over to grab the joint from his mouth but was distracted by the crunching of dry pine needles. As the sound grew closer, I became nervous. For a brief moment there was silence, and then I saw bent, arthritic fingers tugging at the mustache before I saw the rest of his full body. Negley had obviously been in the forest with us for a while.

"Gentlemen?" The sound of his voice was precise and measured, like his class assignments.

I didn't reply right away. He had taken us by surprise. Out of the corner of my eye, I could see E palm the joint, and then insert it in his mouth as if he were shoving a stick of gum in there. He chewed a few times and swallowed it whole.

"Did you know it was past bed check?"

"Yeah." I answered. I'd been feeling a little buzz before Negley arrived, but I was quickly coming down.

"Then why are you out here?"

"We're just talking," I said, looking down and wondering if he could smell the weed.

"This is a strange place to talk. What's that I smell?" He took his fingers away from his mustache and expanded his nostrils to take in more air. We were silent. "You hear me, don't you?"

"We hear you." I replied for the both of us. "I can't smell anything."

"I hope it's not what I think it is. Maybe this is the real reason you can't pass any of your quizzes, Isaiah." He paused. "You know I've got to report the both of you to the headmaster for being out here, don't you?"

"What?" I wasn't ready for that revelation. I tapped my hands on my thigh.

"I'm required to tell the headmaster anytime someone misses bed check … and I'm sure he'd also want to know about anyone using drugs around here."

"We don't have any drugs," I pleaded.

"I smelled something," he said. "It certainly wasn't tobacco. I suggest the both of you head back to your room. We'll deal with this later."

I didn't want Negley to tell the headmaster—or anyone else—about our being out after bed check in the woods, smoking weed. If he told, we'd surely be punished. I looked at E, who motioned with his head that we should head back to the dorms. I wondered if he felt bad that he'd delayed taking my advice. Negley stood there, waiting. His fingers had found his mustache again, and he appeared firmly planted, waiting for us to make the next move.

E led the way out of forest, and I fell in behind him. Negley took up the rear. We moved quickly, retracing our steps toward the sound of the crickets, and yet the only noise I could hear now was that of Negley's footsteps, behind me.

FIRST OFFENSE

Breedlove cherished his deep blue Brooks Brothers suits, crisp white shirts, and red silk ties. He wore them daily, as if they were a uniform. My only visit to his office had been during the first week of classes. He'd seemed nice back then, but that was because I hadn't been in any trouble.

As I entered his spacious, well-lit office, the fish tank motor idled noisily atop the aquarium. A school of goldfish greeted me, and I imagined myself as one of them, blissfully swimming away to escape the scrutiny I was about to endure. I was not alone.

Breedlove entered, eating a cinnamon roll, the last of his lunch. He sat down in front of me, the lines on his forehead damp with tiny beads of sweat. A white button-down shirt and his signature red tie fit tightly around his neck. Pushing the roll aside, he wiped his fingers and mouth with a napkin and quickly got down to business.

"Hello, Isaiah." His voice soared above the noise of the fish tank, making him sound like he was speaking through a bullhorn. He looked down at the flashing red buttons on his phone, lifted the receiver, and told someone he'd be a minute.

"Hi," I mumbled back, ashamed that I had to appear before him.

He leaned back in a squeaking, high-back swivel chair, placed his hands behind his neatly coiffed hair, and looked straight into my eyes. "I heard some very disturbing information about you this morning, and frankly I'm surprised. Is everything all right?"

I wanted him to speak softer now, perhaps downplay the accusations in case someone was outside the door listening. I didn't want them to hear anything about me. I shook my head like there wasn't any problem and carefully thought about my response.

There wasn't much I wanted to say. I was becoming scared that I'd prematurely short-circuited my Chadwick experience before I was ready. I was beginning to wonder if I'd blown an opportunity to make something of myself. My classmates had rich families, trust funds, and parents with college degrees. If nothing else, they were more assured of a life of luxury than I was. I'd have to struggle for everything I got. I straightened up and put on my best face.

"Everything's fine," I said.

"Why were you out of your room after check-in? You know the rules." He wiped his forehead, which gave me time to think about how much I hated lectures. "Mr. Negley said your roommate was smoking marijuana. He didn't see *you* with anything. But you know smoking of any substance here is immediate grounds for dismissal, right?"

"Of course," I answered. The headmaster's direct manner forced quick responses. I clasped my hands together out of his view. "I wasn't smoking anything."

"Being the athlete you are, I didn't think so, but just in case, I need to warn you. You have anything else to add?" He looked down at his half-eaten roll.

I couldn't think of anything. My eyes focused on his lips. They were dry, and he could have used a glass of water or something. Then it hit me. "Will I be punished?"

"I'm thinking about it. You know I can't let this situation go without addressing it. It's like Coach Winstrom says, you've got to learn to take some responsibility. Actions have consequences."

Coach Winstrom, ex-baseball coach and chaplain, was always lecturing us about accountability. Dressed in his priestly collar, he wobbled his eighty-one-year-old body to the lecture hall podium each morning to deliver the same prayer before pushing us off to class: *God grant us the serenity to accept the things we cannot change, the courage to accept the things we can, and wisdom to know the difference.* I loved the sound of his voice. Distinct. Direct. Definitive.

"I hope the punishment won't be too hard. I promise not to be late or leave my dorm room after bed check ever again." I was laying it on thick, remembering that my parents had told me that for survival's sake, it was best not to question white people too closely.

"You say that now." He paused for a minute, unfolded his arms, and leaned forward. He pushed away the remaining bites of cinnamon roll and placed his palms flat on his desk.

I searched his eyes and the somber expression on his face for clues as to what he was thinking. He took in air and pulled his lips together tightly. I couldn't help wondering if this meant he would report the incident to my parents. They'd never understand what happened no matter how he told the story. Yeah, I was in high school, but somehow I knew that if the word ever got back to them about this, I'd be in deep trouble. I should have thought about the consequences earlier.

He sighed. "Since this is your first offense, I'm going to put you on work crew, Isaiah."

"Work crew?"

"Yes. I know you already have a morning job, but you'll work with Mr. McGuinness on special campus cleanup projects."

McGuinness, the baby-faced director of the outdoors program, had a reputation for pulling kids out of bed before sunlight to perform odd jobs or run laps around the school track. Everything depended on his mood. I had the impression he hated kids because he never smiled and frequently yelled at students for petty issues, like veering off the concrete walkways onto the neatly manicured grass. He took his other job—as the work crew and groundskeeping chief—much too seriously.

"Do you understand what I'm telling you?"

"Yes, sir," I replied. If that was the worst of it, I was in the clear, but I felt more was coming.

"One other thing. I'm putting you on probation and telling your parents."

My stomach churned as the news started to sink in. "Do you have to?" I sat up in the chair and begged him, adopting a pained expression designed to evoke some sympathy.

"I don't have a choice, Isaiah. I'm sure your parents won't be happy, but I've got to tell them."

"What about E?" Before I knew it, I was throwing his name into the mix.

"What about him?" Breedlove answered.

"Is he going to be on work crew? Are you going to tell his parents, too?"

"Don't worry about him. Just think about yourself. If things work out, you'll be off probation and work crew in no time. Be ready tomorrow."

"Is that all?"

"For now," he answered.

I pushed my chair back and got ready to leave. Breedlove picked up his roll and put it back down, gesturing with his hands as if he wanted to say something more. "Isaiah?"

"Yeah." I was standing now, and he was looking up at me with his head slightly tilted.

"I hope you know that in most situations like this, I usually dismiss the student. But since this is your first offense, and I like you, I'm willing to give you another chance." He swallowed in an attempt to slow himself down. "Coach Wilkerson told me you were doing well on the basketball court, and I'd like to see that continue." He pulled a tiny piece from the cinnamon roll and held it in his hand. "Apparently, you're everything they said about you, but you've got to work on your grades. When you get more time, we'll talk about that later."

I didn't know how to respond, so I nodded my head at his observation, turned back around, and continued out of his office. I'd been hearing compliments about my athletic ability a lot, but coming from Breedlove—at this point and in this context—made me wonder about his motivations, about why he'd selected this moment to mention basketball. Dad had told me about white folks not caring about you, only what you could do for them. He'd made his point.

"But, I don't want you to get the impression that just because you're a good athlete, you'll get special privileges. If you screw up again … let's just say that things won't be the same the next time this happens, so there'd better not be a next time, understand?"

"I understand," I said. "Anything else?"

"Be on time with Mr. McGuinness in the morning." He put a piece of the roll in his mouth, chewed, and then swallowed quickly. "It's important."

*　*　*

"Did you meet with him?"

E was peeking from underneath the covers in the middle of the afternoon when I came back to the room after the meeting. His mumble was unmistakable. He had called the infirmary that morning, faking an illness. Swallowing the joint had gotten him so high the night before that he didn't feel up to going to class.

"Yeah," I said, shoving the room key inside my pocket and walking toward him. He lifted the covers.

"So, what happened?"

"He put me on probation, and he's going to tell my parents."

"That's all?" He sat up, and his pajama top fell across his flat chest like a curtain. Each button was carefully fastened, which made him look as though he had the chills.

"I'm on work crew, too."

"Wow. You got off clean," he said. "Negley likes getting people in trouble. Did he say anything about me?"

"No. He didn't go into that. I asked him, but he said I needed to just think about myself."

"Hope I'm lucky like you." E ran his hands through his hair, raking it out of his eyes, and I turned around to remove the books I'd left on my bedspread. I needed to chill. "I knew you'd get off easy," he said. "There aren't many black kids here. Plus, you're good at sports."

"I don't think it had anything to do with that. You're the one Negley caught smoking, not me. I told you to hurry up." I wasn't expecting that response, especially since it felt like we were slowly breaking down our social and cultural barriers and becoming nicer to each other.

"I didn't hear you," he whined. I could tell he didn't like the fact that I'd reminded him that he was the reason we'd gotten caught. "What you gonna do when your parents find out?"

"Nothing." My voice trembled as I thought about the possibilities.

"You're scared, huh?"

"A little," I said.

"I'm not sure what's going to happen to me." He shook his head. "I'm already on shaky ground."

"We'll see," I said, lying down. "Whatever happens, I'm sure you'll make it through. Your family's got money. I wouldn't worry too much. If push came to shove, your father could give more money to the school. Isn't that how it works?" I was only half kidding, but I needed to get back at him for his comment that I'd gotten off easy because of my blackness.

"Shut up, man," he said.

"You know it's true," I continued, looking at the ceiling. "You don't have much to worry about."

"That's what you think," he said. He got out of the bed and stood over me. His shirt moved slowly with each breath. "Don't you have a class this afternoon?"

Mocking his nonchalant attitude from the previous night, I lifted my arm and pulled up my sleeve, the way he'd done while we were out in the forest. "I've got time. Wake me in a half hour."

DOUBLE STANDARD

E was right about me underestimating his fate. After visiting Breedlove's office, he came back with a long face and the announcement that he'd been expelled. Before leaving, he told me that his father was a jerk and had refused to donate money for Chadwick's new swimming pool unless the school named it after him, so that had sealed his fate. It didn't seem fair that he would get expelled after I got off so easily.

On the day E got the boot, I received a phone call from Mom telling me that she was on her way to Chadwick to see the headmaster about my situation. Dad, she said, wasn't going to make it because he had to work, so he was leaving everything up to her. If nothing else, she told me, it was important to maintain good conduct. I agreed with her to a point, but I just found it difficult to comply when measured against the lure of gaining acceptance from E.

Just as I had on my first day at Chadwick, I sat through another meeting with Breedlove and Mom, but this time when it ended, Mom and I went for a walk, ending up in the dormitory bathroom.

"Pull your pants down," she said after we had stepped inside. She carried her big black purse, the one with enough room for the condensed version of the Bible and the thick leather strap that, when doubled over, hurt when it hit you. "I'm going to whip your ass." She said it with such force that I was scared she'd get started on me and wouldn't know how to stop. The last time she'd spanked me was when she'd thought I performed less than my best on the entrance exam.

I pulled my pants down over my bare bottom, remembering the times she'd warned me that I'd never get too old for a beating and hoping that this would be over quickly. I didn't dare say anything to her out of fear that she'd blow my reaction out of proportion and later tell my dad. If he found out I'd resisted or talked back, he'd whip me, too. That was a pact they'd made between themselves—a house rule.

Behind me, she was belting out the Bible verse from the book of Proverbs she'd cited in Breedlove's office on the first day: "'The rod of correction imparts wisdom, but a child left to himself disgraces his mother.'"

There were more instructions, so I turned to look.

"Turn around," she ordered. "Don't look at me. Grab that." She pointed to the sink.

I grabbed the cold, smooth surface and stared straight ahead, my eyes focused on my reflection in the cracked mirror. I could also see my mother's eyeglasses sliding down her wide nose as she raised her hand to whack me with the belt. I tightened the muscles in my buttocks to absorb the first blow and closed my eyes, hoping she'd tire before the welts started to appear.

Each blow felt worse. After a few pops, I could feel my skin stinging from the leather smacking against my butt. I hated myself for smoking the weed. I hated Negley for finding us. I hated the headmaster for telling my folks. With each blow, I vowed not to smoke any more weed. I vowed to try to make decisions on my own from then on. I vowed to straighten up my act. I just wanted her to finish up before anyone saw me in there, getting my ass spanked by my mother, like I was four years old.

I could hear my mom talking to me as my eyes stayed closed. "I'm not going to hear any more bad reports, am I?"

"No, ma'am, you won't," I grunted. There was no way I could remain silent while the whipping continued. I tried not to say anything. I wanted to show her how tough I was, show her that things didn't hurt anymore, and that she was wasting her time now that I was fifteen years old. But my mom thought she could beat good conduct and discipline into me. I don't remember her ever beating me so hard or with such intensity.

"I want to make sure," she said, whipping me again. "You hear me?"

"Yes, ma'am," I said, opening my eyes.

By then, it had started to happen. My classmates appeared in the broken mirror, standing in the doorway, watching as I got one of the worst beatings of my life. I knew the use of this bathroom in the middle of the day would be a problem when she started whipping me, but I wasn't about to make it worse by saying anything. Mom didn't need privacy when it came to stuff like this. She still believed public humiliation was the best way to curb a kid's bad behavior. She'd embarrassed me before, but not by spanking.

The first time was in elementary school, after my first fight against Larry Staples, a boy who picked on all the younger kids. His insults became too much to bear, so we fought at recess. When Mom found out about the fight several days later, she came to the campus and made Larry and me walk around the entire school holding hands, while the other students trailed behind and ridiculed us. The incident taught me a lesson about fighting and about my mom's propensity for delivering punishment whenever and wherever she thought necessary.

The beating continued until her arm grew tired, but by then it was too late for me to save face. I tried holding back the tears, but they came streaming down my cheeks and onto my lips. I could taste the salt with the tip of my tongue.

"Pull your pants up," she finally said, straightening her clothes.

My classmates had watched in silence as the scene unfolded. I tried not to look at faces. All I could make out were Chadwick baseball caps, wrinkled T-shirts, and a bevy of eyes riveted in fascination. I wondered what they thought of me and what they thought of my mother. Did they think she was crazy for spanking me right there in the bathroom where she knew people would be able to see? Or did they feel sorry that a kid my age and size was still getting spanked?

The welts would heal, but I wasn't sure my ego would.

THE DANCE

The first school dance came right after my monumental ass-whipping. Watching the black and yellow bus packed with girls from St. Margaret's School make its way up the winding, tree-lined road to the center of the campus felt good, almost like the cold tap water I'd run over the burning welts on my ass after the spanking.

Richard stood with me. His narrow body stretched toward the drooping limbs of the pepper trees planted all over the pergola, the campus's central meeting place. By default, he'd become my roommate and buddy, now that E had been kicked out.

It was unfortunate that E was gone. Prompted by the letters and the weed, I'd started to open up to him and was slowly making him an ally. Now Richard, my homeboy, would have to hear more about what made me tick while I got over my fear of letting others know about the real me. He was probably tired of me by now.

Richard spotted my lips moving in silent conversation with myself, as I turned away from the bus and focused on the windblown leaves resting on the grass, and asked, "What are you daydreaming about?"

I guess it was obvious that the girls on the bus were only partially occupying my thoughts. "Nothing, really," I said, turning back toward him. He'd given his 'fro a blowout so that it was even all the way around, and he had put on a high-boy shirt for the occasion. "I'm pissed about that beating I got by my mom the other day. It seemed like everyone was there. Were you watching, too?"

"Yeah, I was there," he winced. "That was kinda rough. Are you feeling any better now?"

"A little." I shrugged. "My mom gets carried away."

"Forget about it. My grandfather beat me like that once. It could have been worse."

I had forgotten that Richard had told me he'd been raised by his grandfather after his own father had died of lung cancer. Too many cigarettes, he had said.

"I guess so." I took a breath. The embarrassment caused by the beating was still there.

"Definitely," he replied. "I mean, you could have gotten kicked out of here, like E. At least you got another chance. I think Breedlove likes you. I wouldn't blow it again, if I were you."

"That's what E said."

"He was right." He looked at my arms and winced. Some of the lashes intended for my butt had inadvertently landed on my arms. The marks were noticeable. "Your welts are starting to heal."

"Yeah. Don't remind me."

Our conversation was slowly being drowned out by giggles, as girls wearing pleated blue skirts, knee-high socks, and white blouses exited the bus. As they came closer, I overheard them talking about Steven Rusoni, the blond, broad-shouldered quarterback standing behind us, whose father, a big Central Valley dairy farmer, drove his Porsche faithfully to the campus every weekend to check on his son. Steve spoke in a Southern drawl—or something very close to it—and loved to wear white patent-leather dress shoes, just like his dad. Hearing them gush over Steve let me know that Richard and I were invisible to them.

"Looks like we're out of luck, dude," I said as the first crowd of white girls strolling up the walkway passed us by.

"What do you mean?"

"You know," I nodded at the group of white girls. "This dance won't be like our boot camp. I haven't seen any black girls. I guess I forgot where I was." I'd been looking forward to the first dance and had dreamed the night before that Jenaye was coming.

"Why'd you say that?" Richard continued to look at the bus while I watched that first group walk up the cobblestone stairway. "Look!" He grabbed at my arm and nodded in the bus's direction. "There's a sister for you."

I turned to look in the direction of the bus. My God, he wasn't lying! Standing alone, a short-haired black girl descended the steps of the bus, one hand clutching the leather handle of a small purse. Her dark, round face was anchored by a thin neck and narrow shoulders. She snatched a glance at several buildings before spotting us, and then ran, arms swinging, toward the rest of her classmates.

"No shit." Her appearance had taken me totally off guard.

Richard's face twisted into a frown. "You gonna dance with her?" He had spotted something that I'd missed. "Man, we can't win for losing. The last thing we need is some short-haired bear with chipped teeth. I'd rather study."

"I don't know. She's not that bad." In my mind I gave her more redeeming qualities, but to say she was beautiful would have been stretching it.

"You think she's fine?" He sounded dubious.

"Well, her hair's short, but there ain't nothing else wrong with her as far as I can tell. I didn't look inside her mouth."

"Except she's ugly," said Richard. "She doesn't look like Jenaye, that's for sure."

"Obviously," I said. "But she's probably got other things."

"What are you talking about?"

I didn't answer him. The girl headed toward Evans Hall, the multipurpose facility hosting the dance, and we abandoned the pergola and followed her inside to get another look. The band had started to play "Bad, Bad Leroy Brown," and everyone was dancing.

Listening to the music, I lost track of the black girl. She was impossible to spot among the sea of faces, even though the majority of them were white. I thought about how nice it would be to be back in Oakland, dancing to Stevie Wonder or the Temptations. Richard had stopped looking for the black girl, too, and was happily tapping his foot to the beat.

"Well, I don't know about you, but I'm going to try to dance with a white girl. You can have that ugly black girl," said Richard, spotting her and nodding me toward her. "I know you want to ask her, especially since you've been thinking about it so much. But I'm not."

"Go ahead," I said, waving at him. "My father told me it wasn't a good idea to get too friendly with white girls. They get you in trouble. I've already been in trouble, and I don't need to get in any more right now."

Then I thought about the things I'd heard from my father about white girls and black men and how he believed I should navigate that terrain. He never specifically said *not* to associate with them. He always talked around the issue, mentioning the lynching of a young boy in his Mississippi hometown during the 1950s for merely expressing an interest in a white girl. Deference to and fear of white women was expected back then. If he'd been caught walking on the same sidewalk with a white woman, and the wrong white folks had heard about it, he would have been in trouble. Even though it was

1973 and not 1953, and this was California and not Mississippi, I guess I carried some of his stories in the back of my mind.

Richard seemed to think I was crazy. "You *believe* that?"

"Yeah," I said, starting to wonder what I did believe.

He shook his head, looking like he pitied me. "You're crazier than I thought." He backed away from me and swiftly moved his lanky frame through the crowd of students in the direction of a petite white girl he then asked to dance.

Seeing Richard enjoy himself, I scanned the room and considered defying my dad by dancing with a white girl, too. After all, what difference did it make? We were all kids trying our best to fit in, and a simple dance wasn't going to hurt anyone.

The music was blasting, and the thrust of the speakers hanging from the paneled walls seemed to push me closer to a tall white girl standing by herself. Her long hair was pulled behind ears that sported small pearl earrings, and sandy brown locks curled against the nape of her neck, resting on her chest. Her cheeks were slightly rouged, and her lips were covered with a neutral gloss. Pretty and friendly looking, she moved her legs slightly to the beat.

"Wanna dance?" I made a move and extended my hand to see if she would follow, but she stood there staring at it. It was as if time stood still. Her eyes traveled from the tips of my fingers past the long sleeves of my gaucho, to my face. Her legs no longer moved; like a butterfly unprepared for spring, she retreated back into her cocoon.

"No, thank you."

She was polite, but I took the rejection personally. "You must like being a wallflower," I said.

"No. I just don't feel like dancing." She blushed slightly. "The music's too fast."

I could see her looking at my glasses. Embarrassed, I walked away without saying anything else and tried to determine if she thought I was too ugly, too black, or both. I looked around for other dance partners, but only the black girl seemed ready. This time I asked her to dance.

"You waited long enough." Her clipped phrase let me know that she'd watched as I tried to dance with the white girl. Her voice had a different ring, not the hip Oakland sound I was used to, but a choppy, foreign twang from a place I knew I'd never been.

"I'm shy," I said in my defense. I looked away from her round face and wondered if she noticed that I didn't know what to do with my hands. There was a long pause as I found the bottom half of her face again and peered at her deep dimples. My mind drew a blank, still stuck on being rejected by the white girl.

"What's your name, Mr. Shy?" The girl in front of me flashed a pleasant smile, showing a small, jagged-edged front tooth.

"Isaiah." I touched my glasses. "And yours?"

"Dofi." She said it quick, like I should have known it.

"Dofi?" I pronounced it phonetically to myself to get a better feel. Do-fee. "I love the way that sounds."

I stopped talking long enough to get her to the dance floor. Her waist and her hips rotated out of sync, and I tried to keep up, but I couldn't follow the beat. Dancing to "Leroy Brown," we were like fish out of water.

"I haven't heard many girls that sound like you or have a name like Dofi. Where you from?"

"Ghana."

"You mean Africa?" Before I knew it, I had blurted out the name of the continent like it was another planet. I'd never met anyone from Ghana or Africa, and my opinions about the continent had been tainted by the images of starving natives I'd seen in Tarzan movies. She looked nothing like them, and I found myself struggling even more to make conversation. "You're a long way from home. How'd you get here?"

"It's a long story," she said.

"Do you like St. Margaret's?"

"It's a lot different than my school in Ghana. Different, but good. My father's a diplomat, and he thought this was the best school for me. He travels a lot to LA. How'd you end up here? Your parents must be rich?" She said it like it was a question.

"Not really. I'm an RSP student."

She frowned. "What's that?"

"It's another long story." Before I knew it, I'd broken my own rule by telling her the truth about my background and the scholarship, but I didn't mind because, coming from Africa, she was an outsider to this environment, too. Talking to her didn't feel the same as telling E or my other classmates.

"Never heard of it," she said.

"You're not alone ... and speaking of that, where are the other black girls in your school? Are you the only one?"

"Only one more, but she didn't come. She went home for the weekend."

"My roommate and I thought there weren't gonna be any black girls."

"I don't think it matters to him." She looked at Richard, whose long arms stretched toward the ceiling as he danced with the white girl.

"That's Richard for you."

Like Jenaye, Dofi didn't have a fear of expressing herself and wasn't stuck up. At the end of the song, we walked off the dance floor, toward the stack of folding chairs near the wall.

"Has it been hard meeting boys?" I leaned against a cart full of chairs. The metal felt cold against my back.

"Sometimes. The white boys hardly ever dance with me. My friends never have a problem. Until you came up to me, I was beginning to think that something was wrong with me. I was starting to worry, lose faith."

"Lose faith? What do you mean by that?" I asked.

"You know. I was beginning to think that people didn't like me," she said, looking down at her shoes.

She had an odd way of saying things. I guessed that she meant she was starting to worry about her appearance, whether people perceived her as undesirable. Losing faith must have been another way of saying she was dangerously close to losing her self-confidence. So was I, but in a different way.

"I guess you're glad we met." I wanted to lift her head with my hands, but I knew it wasn't the time.

"Yeah," she said.

Another song ended, and I could see Richard's baby face approaching. "My roommate's on his way back. I know he'll have something crazy to say. I'd like to talk to you again, but not while he's around. How can I reach you?"

"I don't have a phone, but you can call the dorms. I stay in Benbow Hall. As long as you don't call after curfew, someone will pick up the phone and come and get me." Lifting her head, she was smiling from ear to ear.

"It's the same thing at Chadwick," I said. "We can't have phones or televisions in our rooms, but if you call the dorms, someone always finds me. My mom does it all the time."

"Where do you stay?" I hadn't noticed her small hoop earrings until she turned her face to see if she could see Richard coming. She was prettier from this angle.

"Middlebury Hall," I replied. "It's the sophomore dorm."

"I'll find you." She walked away.

Standing next to me, Richard put his hand on my shoulder. His chest heaved and his shirt clung to his body from the sweat he'd worked up on the dance floor. "Still afraid of your dad, aren't you?"

"I tried, but I got turned down."

"I didn't see you," he said. "You're probably lying and just using it as an excuse. I don't care how you twist it—your girl's ugly."

"She wasn't ugly, man. She was just different. She's not from America."

"I don't care. If you think that girl isn't ugly, then you've been here much too long."

Richard's comments made me think again about the conversation I'd had with Dofi. I'd noticed her chipped front tooth, and she'd probably noticed my glasses. What he didn't understand was that my regard for Dofi went beyond her looks.

"She might not be a beauty queen, but she's cool," I said, trying to cover myself.

"Whatever you say, man." He clearly didn't understand. "You got her number?"

I'd known that was coming. I weighed whether to tell him the truth, but since I'd found out where she was staying, I went with my gut. "Yeah, I got it."

He took his hand off my shoulder, slapped my palm, and then laughed out loud. "You ain't going to be calling her anyway."

He was starting to bug me. "How do you know?"

"You're still hooked on Jenaye, and she's miles away. I've seen those letters. What would she say?"

"Don't worry about it." I was angry that he'd been going through some of my personal belongings. "And stay outta my shit."

I hated to think about it, but Jenaye was so far away that it was hard not to become disillusioned about seeing her again. I kept my hopes up, but it felt like a pipe dream now. On the other hand, Dofi was close. She had caused me to forget about the beating temporarily and appeared to be experiencing the same things that I was going through at Chadwick. Richard said she was ugly, but he was stuck on white girls, anyway.

For the rest of the dance I walked around with a smile, wondering if Dofi's memory was as good as she said it was.

PASSAGES

Weeks later, I could barely remember Dofi as I opened the pages to *The Adventures of Huckleberry Finn*. I was well into the story but, feeling the pressure, I picked up the pace so I could finish the reading assignment before the next class. Sometimes I worked better under a deadline. Richard, who was sprawled across the bed, was rapidly flipping and highlighting pages too.

I tried concentrating, but I just couldn't focus. I picked up the book but quickly put it down again, distracted by the picture of Grover Washington's bearded face looking out at me from the *Inner City Blues* jazz album. Right now, listening to music seemed like a better and easier option. I turned on the stereo. The sweet sound of Grover's horn and the deep, pulsing bass made me forget about homework—and Richard, who was sprawled across the bed, rapidly flipping pages.

The next day, Hagman put me on the spot.

"Isaiah, would you read the passage at the top of page five for us?" The cigarette smoke escaped from between his lips. In junior high, teachers never smoked in class, but some of Chadwick's rules were unconventional. Most times, faculty members like Hagman did whatever they wanted.

I opened the book, cleared my throat, and selected the passage he was referring to:

> *We went tip toeing along a path amongst the trees back towards the end of the windows garden, stooping down so as the branches wouldn't scrape our heads. When we was passing by the kitchen I fell over a root and made a noise. We scrouched down and laid still. Miss Watson's big nigger, named Jim, was setting in the kitchen door; we could see him pretty clear, because*

there was light behind him. He got up and stretched his neck out
about a minute, listening. Then he says: "Who dah? Say-who is
you? Whar is you? Dog my cats ef I didn' hear sumf'n.

My classmates burst into laughter. I hadn't expected that. The scene
wasn't particularly funny, but the line I'd read had an immediate effect on
the kids in the classroom. I would have selected another passage, but I wasn't
given that option.

"Who dat ... you dat," said one of the students, imitating the sound of
my voice. The laughter grew louder as more students joined in.

I waited for Hagman to regain control of the classroom, but he ignored
the laughter and urged me to continue. As I stared at the page, images of
Stepin Fetchit and those Sunday afternoon Shirley Temple movies I watched
with my brother popped into my head. I hated them but watched anyway
because there were no other Sunday matinees featuring black actors. After my
beating, I'd been the object of put-downs and snide laughter from those who
had watched Mom wale on me; now the laughter felt similar. Was I making
too much of this? Maybe I was, and maybe I wasn't. Everything was mixing
together in my mind. Were classmates confusing me with Nigger Jim?

Anxious to finish, I kept reading.

After I was through, Hagman said, "Wow! What a lovely passage." He
always seemed to get carried away by the sound of words. "What do you
think about it?" He waited for my answer while holding the partially burned
cigarette by his side, the smoke curling against his body.

I'd known he was going to ask that question, but I was still stunned by
the laughter. In Mrs. Henderson's class at my old junior high school, we'd
read *The Best of Simple* and *Great Expectations*, stories with young characters
I'd liked. I didn't remember them using dialect, and if I read aloud, no one
laughed. In junior high, it had seemed as if everyone took it for granted that
in a novel, the black characters weren't real like the people you saw in the
neighborhood. Here, it was different.

"I haven't had time to absorb it," I answered.

"Well, just give me one impression," he said, pacing back and forth in
front of the classroom. He was bouncing on the tips of his toes as if he had
springs underneath them.

"Frankly, sir, I'm not sure you want to hear what's on my mind. I got to
bed late." I didn't really want to subject myself to any more laughter.

"That's not a good excuse, Isaiah. Are you trying to be smart?"

Sitting in the class now and hearing his question, I thought back to the
boot camp. Davidson, the program director, had told us that at boarding
school we had to be prepared to read everything, but I had no idea I'd be

reading while the other students laughed. He'd never said anything about that.

"Can I ask you a question?" I fired back. My classmates, sensing my anger and feeling the edge in my response, grew quiet.

"Go ahead," he replied.

"Why do I have to continue? I told you I didn't have a comment." We had read other passages in this class to get a flavor of an author's style, but those passages didn't involve black characters, slaves, or the use of the word "nigger." At that moment, I wondered why there weren't any books on our reading list with heroic black people who spoke good English.

"Well, Isaiah, it's a classic. Mark Twain is one of the great American writers of all time, and he's writing about a place and a time that we all need to better understand. Keep an open mind."

"I don't want to read any more passages or talk in front of everybody. Didn't you hear them laughing?" I looked around the room at the students whose laughs were now contained behind covered mouths. "Not only that. This book contains too many racial slurs."

"I think you're being a little too sensitive, Isaiah. We always read out loud in this class. You know that. Nigger Jim's a black character, and of course you're a black person. This story takes place in the late 1800s. Post-slavery. It's just the way they talked."

The laughter from my classmates picked up again.

"What's wrong with that?" Hagman continued. "Besides, I don't think any of the other students in this class, except Richard maybe, could have captured the rhythm of the language like you. Maybe I should have asked him to read. He looks like he's better prepared."

I glanced over at Richard's face. His brown eyes were riveted to Hagman's, and his long legs and knees were pressed against the bottom of the desk. The fingers of his big hands sat inside his book, which was open in front of him. Passages were highlighted, and the pages were dog-eared.

"What about you, Richard?" Hagman turned his back to me so that he was facing Richard on the other side of the classroom.

"Are you asking me what I think about the entire book or just the passage that Isaiah read?" Now Richard's elbows rested on the desk's smooth surface, his fist underneath his chin.

"I don't want your response just yet. Read something for us."

Richard opened his book and found something he had underlined:

After supper she got out her book and learned me about Moses and the Bulrushers; and I was in a sweat to find out all about him; but by and by she let out that Moses had been dead a considerable long time; so then I didn't care no more about him; because I don't take stock in dead people.

"That's a good stopping point," said Hagman, laughing. "So what do you think about what you read, Richard? You don't have to just talk about that passage you read. Give me your general impressions."

"I think it's a funny book. Huck and Nigger Jim use poor English, but that didn't bother me."

I looked at Richard in disbelief. I had hoped he'd say something about all the laughter or the racial slurs, but somehow I knew he'd respond that way or something like it. He had stopped reacting honestly to things when it came to white people, and that annoyed me. I couldn't wait until class was over, so we could get to the bottom of this.

"That's a good observation," said Hagman. "Tell us more."

"To be honest, I think once you get past the bad language, the book moves quickly. It seems like from the opening pages Huck wants to try new things. He's not afraid of adventure."

"Oh yeah?" Hagman moved a step closer to Richard's desk. He was absolutely eating this up. "First off, Richard, when you're speaking in front of an audience you don't have to say, 'I think.' We already know your thoughts because you're telling them to us. Just go ahead and say what you mean. But continue."

"I know Isaiah said the book contained too many racial slurs, but I kinda ignored them. I think Huck realizes that slavery wasn't a good thing. He can't pronounce things well, but he's really quite smart. I saw something entirely different."

"That's a good observation, Richard."

I was ready to take Richard outside and pummel him for making me look bad, but I knew that class was a long way from being over. My mind wandered until I thought of my father. I was absolutely sure that he'd object to the laughter and the use of the word "nigger." The Issacson household stressed proper English. Nigger Jim's diction was a poor example of how black folks should talk. Jim's dialect was something my parents wanted to forget. They'd grown up in the South, and poor grammar and blues music were forbidden. This book, and Hagman's request that I read out loud, was concrete evidence I could use to demonstrate that I should be studying elsewhere.

As the class dragged on, I scanned more pages, looking for passages that were devoid of dialect, but it was on every single page. I couldn't wait to tell my parents about this book.

"You did a really close reading of this book, Richard. I'm impressed. I think you really need to help your roommate along." Hagman turned around and looked at me again. "Isaiah?"

His voice snapped me out of my thoughts. "Yes," I said.

"I think you need to spend a lot more time focusing on your critical reading skills. In fact, I'll need to speak with you after this class. Is that understood?"

"Yes," I replied.

He had missed the boat in focusing on my reading skills, but what could I say? I couldn't just ignore Twain's use of "nigger" even if he wanted to. My classmates' reaction was only making things worse.

*   *   *

As the others left class, I stared at the assignment written on the blackboard and tried to prepare myself for a conversation with Hagman. He was near the classroom door now, making sure everyone had left.

Richard was the last to leave. As I looked up, our eyes met, and he shook his head as if to say, *Better you than me.* I'd deal with him later.

Hagman closed the door. Approaching my desk, the heels of his loafers gently tapped the hardwood floor. "I've had my eye on you from day one, Isaiah. It seems like you're a little too sensitive. If you keep on the same path, you'll make yourself crazy. I don't understand why you didn't want to read another passage. Well, let me say that I've got some ideas of why you didn't do it, but I want you to tell me. Do you want to talk to me about that?"

I shrugged. "I was thinking about our next game."

He sighed. "Speaking of games, you can't put all your eggs in the sports basket." He put his hand on my shoulder and continued. "Chadwick's a place where you focus on academics. I hear you're quite an athlete. You're trying to resist the pull of this environment, but you're going to have to give in. That's what's going to carry you through here and help you later in life. Have you thought about what will happen if you don't make it in basketball?"

He sounded too much like my parents. I ignored the question and looked away from him. What did he know?

"Probably not, huh?" he continued. "I've noticed your people focus on sports a lot. You're really built for that. Maybe you don't have the intelligence of the other kids, considering all of you come from such deprived backgrounds. To be honest, I never expected much from you."

I wanted the meeting to end, but without blinking, I glared back at him. If he was trying to get my attention, he had succeeded.

"But I don't intend to make things easy for you. Never have. Never will. I know what you're thinking about *Huck Finn*, that it's racist material, right? Well, I'm not buying it. I don't know what books you read at your last school, but here we read Twain, F. Scott Fitzgerald, and Hemingway. These writers are the best. They write about life, human nature, and man's inhumanity to man."

"They don't speak to me," I said.

"Well then, Isaiah, you've got a real problem. You'll have to find a way to let them speak to you so you can fully participate in my class, or you'll fail. Now tomorrow when you come here, I want you to have a better attitude. When class starts, you'll be the first one on my list again. Don't show up unless you're ready to join in the discussion."

He walked to the door and held it open without saying anything else.

*   *   *

I waited until after dinner to call my parents. I tried catching up with Richard to see how he really felt about what had gone on in class, but he wasn't at his usual hangout. I considered an all-out search, but I put it off while I thought about a discussion with my parents.

I needed an angle that would stir their passions. It was no use approaching things haphazardly. To get them to listen enough to talk about *Huck Finn* and what was happening at Chadwick would take more than a notion. Both of them were still upset over the weed-smoking incident, but I knew the word "nigger" would make Dad remember the time he'd nearly killed a man for calling him one.

He told the story often after dinner, about how he'd saved up enough money to buy a Buick, but a jealous supervisor, noticing his good fortune, had a fit, blurting out something like, "Where did a *nigger* get enough sense to save for a nice car like that?" Dad had said, "I got your nigger," but didn't do or say anything else to retaliate at the time. If Dad had responded physically to his verbal assault, he would have had to take extra precautions. After that incident, Dad vowed to leave Mississippi and never return.

He answered the phone. "Hello?"

"Dad? This is Isaiah. You busy?"

"Isaiah?" The high-pitched response let me know the call had caught him by surprise. "You ready to apologize?"

"I'm sorry," I said quickly.

"Are you taking care of business now? Did we make ourselves clear about the type of behavior we expect you to exhibit?"

I knew some of what he wanted to hear, and I said it to keep him engaged. "Yes, you did. I wasn't thinking. Things are different now."

"Doesn't your team have a big game coming up?"

"That's not what I called to talk about," I replied.

"It's something else?"

"It's this book we're reading in English class," I said.

"What's it called?"

"*The Adventures of Huckleberry Finn.*"

"I haven't read it, but I've heard a lot about it."

I hadn't expected him to have read it. Dad wasn't much of a reader. "It's an old book, but the real issue is my teacher and how he's teaching it."

"Oh?"

"Today in class he had me read aloud a passage from the book. All the passages are in dialect and the main character, Huck Finn, uses a lot of racial slurs. There's even a character named Nigger Jim."

"And you say he had you read a couple of passages out loud from the book?" His voice was still calm.

"Yeah. And while I read, the white kids laughed."

"What did your teacher do?" Dad raised his voice a notch.

"Nothing. I thought he was gonna say something, but he never did. He asked me what I thought, and when I told him I thought the book was insulting, he shifted over to my roommate, Richard. He liked it."

There was a long pause. I could hear Dad letting out air like he did whenever he finished telling the Buick story.

"Is that it?"

"No. My teacher made me stay after class and told me that if I don't participate enthusiastically, he'll fail me."

"Well, maybe I should call the headmaster. We seemed to hit it off quite well on my last visit. I'm sure he'll tell me what's going on. If need be, I'm not against making another visit. I can't say I like the fact that you were laughed at for reading racial slurs, but I'll get to the bottom of it." He paused. "I don't want you to get any ideas about being able to come back here because of that book. You let me take care of this. You got anything else you want to talk about?"

I knew there was no point in pressing the issue, so I changed the subject. "How's Mom?"

"She's concerned about you. Since that whipping, she's been asking me if Chadwick is the right environment for you. We can't keep beating you when you get outta line. You're getting too old for that, boy ... and now this. She may have a point. I certainly don't like what I'm hearing about your classroom."

Liking what I heard, I kept my mouth shut.

"She'll be home soon. Let me talk to her, and we'll call you back."

* * *

I was determined to find Richard. His attitude infuriated me. What did he think about the laughter? Had he become so comfortable with white people after the dance with St. Margaret's that he'd downplayed what had gone on inside the classroom? During breakfast, I'd missed an opportunity to ask him about his family, and now I wanted to fill in the gaps. Maybe I was being a little too hard on him.

I searched the vacant classrooms and the lobby near the dining hall, where he usually studied after dinner, but he wasn't there. I found him in the rare books room of the library, his back facing the door and his notepad open in front of him. He couldn't see me enter. I grabbed him around his neck playfully, but hard enough to make a point.

"Where have you been?" I maintained the choke hold and squeezed his mahogany flesh between my biceps. "Punk."

The eyes on his smooth face narrowed and the nostrils of his pug nose flared, as if he were irritated by my question. "How many times do I have to tell you that I don't look at things like you?" His high-pitched voice whined as he struggled to pull my arms away from his throat. He was much stronger than his skinny frame made him appear. He used his free hand to straighten the wrinkles I'd made in his green and white T-shirt.

"That's because you're looking at things through rose-colored glasses. *Huck Finn* is clearly racist. What's it gonna take for you to understand that? As I was reading it, I was thinking about that character Tom Buchanan in *The Great Gatsby.* He had these weird theories about race, and all I could think about was that Twain and Fitzgerald were getting it all wrong. I haven't seen one black character I could feel proud of or one who would talk about things like I would. All the books have focused on what *they* think, not what *I* think. I'm beginning to believe you're on their side," I moved around in front of him. His face was smoother than mine, and his mouth was slightly open, revealing crooked upper teeth.

Richard shook his head. "It's not that, man. I was just giving Hagman my impressions of the material. Maybe if you lightened up a little, you'd have something to say. You'd certainly enjoy it more while you're here." Richard stroked his T-shirt and straightened the logo on the front.

"Well, I didn't like Twain using the word 'nigger' all the time. He was too comfortable using it," I said. "Plus, everyone was laughing at me."

"If I'm not mistaken, you use it yourself sometimes, don't you?" Richard moved closer, so he could get in my face. It would be years before he developed any facial hair.

"But I know *how* to use it," I said, thinking of the stories I'd told him where it was someone else who had used the term, not me. "I use it with the right inflection, mostly as a figure of speech. You know what I mean.

Nothing negative. I'm usually telling a story about how someone else used the word. And I don't repeat it in mixed company. The white boys might get the wrong impression. After today, I'm thinking about changing, too. You know, just not using the word—period."

"I just think you're overreacting. Look at you." Richard reached out to put his fingers up against my loose-fitting jacket. "You're beginning to sound like Tom Buchanan yourself." He sat back and folded his arms against his chest.

"I'm not overreacting. Have you looked in our history textbook? We've started to read more about slavery in Negley's history class. The other day, I stared at pictures of the slaves and nearly cried. So many of them had welts on their backs after being beaten. Those pictures reminded me of that beating I got by my mother. You remember that day, don't you?" Trying to control my emotions, I pointed my fingers in his direction.

He nodded.

"I still think about that beating," I continued. "So it's hard for me to just read this book knowing what happened to me may have happened to Nigger Jim—except it wasn't his mother beating him, but some white man who owned him. Hearing the laughter from everybody as I read just made things worse. It's hard for me to think that Mark Twain can even begin to understand what it was like to be a black man during that time and express it with the right tone ... Yeah, I put the book down. After seeing those pictures, I'm not sure I can forgive white folks, Huck included. Sometimes it's hard for me to forgive my own mother for beating me in front of everyone. Now I know how the slaves must have felt." I took a deep breath and blew it out. "Tell me this, Richard, why would anyone have slaves? Can you answer that?"

"I don't know if I can," he said, unfolding his arms. "I wasn't thinking along those lines. I've never had a beating like that. My parents are gone, and the only person I've got left is my grandfather. He's never been that angry with me. I was just thinking about how happy he'd be if I finished up here with flying colors. That's all."

"I guess that explains your behavior." I nodded my head, but I wasn't totally convinced; his explanation sounded like an excuse. I just can't get beyond it when I hear that word around here or think about those slaves in my history book. I told my dad we were reading *Huck Finn* and about what happened in class."

"What'd he say?"

"He wasn't happy about it. He said he was going to talk to my mom. I'm not sure how that's going to turn out. They're strongly in favor of me being here, but that could change because of all this. I'm not even allowed to use the word 'nigger' in my own house."

"Well, I'm not going to get too bent out of shape about it." Richard leaned back in his chair enough to lift the legs off the carpet. "I read the book just like the others we've had to read." He put the legs of his chair back down on the ground and opened his notebook again. "How did your meeting with Hagman end up, anyway?" He flipped the pages, looking for the place where he'd left off.

"He said I'd better change my attitude by the next class or else."

"What are you gonna do?"

"I thought about studying, but it's too late to get started now. I'm just not going tomorrow."

"That's just going to get you in more trouble. You want that?"

"I'll take the F and deal with the consequences later. Besides, if my folks decide to come up here, I'll have an excuse. I just need a break."

"Whatever you say," said Richard. "You'd better find a hiding place other than our room. That's the first place Mr. Hagman will look."

"Don't worry, I'll figure something out."

*   *   *

The next morning, I skipped class by faking the flu. I hid in the infirmary and used the phone next to my bed to call home. My father answered.

"Son, I talked to your mother."

I grasped the phone tight, like an infant hugging his father's pants leg. My body grew weightless, and my lips suddenly became dry, anticipating the outcome.

"She suggested a face-to-face meeting with Mr. Breedlove. Frankly, I'd like to talk to Mr. Hagman to get a feel for why he didn't take better control of that classroom, but we'll see. Of course, I'm not too keen on interfering in school affairs, either, but this is something I'm a little concerned about. I'd like you to get a top-notch education, but not at any cost."

"Does that mean you're coming down here soon?" I held my breath.

"Yes it does, but we've got to rearrange our schedules. So, just sit tight."

Extra Credit

Dad called back later that same day to tell me that he and Mom were headed down for a scheduled meeting with Hagman. He told me to make sure I wore something nice, and I stayed up almost all night trying to select something that wouldn't embarrass them. The news of the meeting gave me some hope that they would reconsider their firm position on sending me to Chadwick. Yet I wasn't totally optimistic.

They arrived the following day after lunch, and I put on my only tie, a red clip-on, a clean white shirt, and my blue blazer. Dad wore his best gray suit and newly shined shoes. Mom stood nearby, sporting her dark blue turtleneck sweater and a double-knit pantsuit. She barely smiled when she saw me. Dad, who always gave me a bear hug, shook my hand.

"We've already checked in with Mr. Breedlove," said Dad, pacing in front of the academic building and checking his watch. "He said your teacher is waiting for us. Are you ready?"

As I led them toward Hagman's office, I thought about the book. I'd stolen a few moments during lunch to reread more pages, but even after cramming down more of the material, I still hated it.

"Have you stopped smoking that weed?" Mom asked as we walked past the building where she'd beaten me.

I remembered my classmates' curious stares, the stinging sensation of the belt, and the measured cadence of Mom's angry voice. The meeting with Hagman was the first time she'd stepped on campus since that day, and now I wanted her to rub her soft hands on my head, squeeze my shoulder, or place her arms around me, not remind me of something humiliating.

"No, Mom. I don't smoke anymore." It was the truth. I really had cut back on the weed. Peer pressure was the least of my worries now.

"I was just making sure. I didn't want to get into this meeting and be embarrassed. I didn't enjoy my last visit, and I don't want any more surprises."

"I know." I stuffed my hands in my pockets, wishing we'd taken another route. I walked faster, hoping we'd get to Hagman's before she decided to ask another pointed question.

Dad checked his watch again.

"So, do you want to tell me any more about this book you read and why you think the kids laughed at you?" said Mom.

I hesitated, trying to gauge the distance to Hagman's office. "We don't have enough time," I said, looking ahead. "There's plenty more, but we're almost there."

"I still don't get it." she said, shaking her head. "Did he make you forget your home training?"

"Something like that. You told me to always speak with the proper English. Reading this book out loud made me feel like I was going against my upbringing, and when some of the kids started mimicking me, I froze up."

"I see." She looked up at me and continued. "Well, I did say that, but I'm not sure yet if this situation fits. We'll find out. Isaiah, sometimes for the sake of education …" She stopped in mid-sentence. "Oh, son, we'll talk about it later."

We finally reached the entrance to Hagman's office, where he was sitting behind his desk, tugging at his thick mustache. As chairman of the English department, he was one of the only teachers with an office. He stood up and extended his hand. The sleeves of his suit jacket stopped just above his wrist. I hadn't seen him so dressed up since the first day of school, when he'd assigned the journal project. Everyone was looking good; it was just like church.

"Mr. and Mrs. Issacson, it's good to see the both of you. I see you brought Isaiah in with you. I'm glad he's here." He gestured to the chairs placed in front of his desk. "All of you, please, have a seat."

"Hello, Mr. Hagman," I said, echoing my folks. I looked down at his desk, at the neatly stacked homework papers and open textbook. A copy of Mark Twain's book sat in front of him.

"No doubt you've all come to talk about this book." He sat down and held up the copy. "I don't want to waste too much of your time, so let's get down to business. You all know it's an American classic, I take it?"

"I've heard as much," Dad said, leaning back in his chair and folding his arms. His long face was cleanly shaven, and his attention was focused on Hagman. "But what makes it such a classic?"

"As you know, Mr. Issacson, my purpose here is to give Isaiah a broad education. *The Adventures of Huckleberry Finn* is a classic because it has withstood the literary test of time and its themes are universal." He leaned forward and looked down at the cover. "Yes, there are some choice phrases in there. I've read it myself on several occasions, but the language is benign." He sat back. "Maybe you can tell me a little more about why this book upset Isaiah, about why it seems to be a little upsetting to the both of you, as well." He pointed his fingers at us with his hands clasped together.

"Benign?" Dad jumped on the word. Unfolding his arms, he started leaning forward in his seat. I had never seen Dad get so riled up at the sound of a word—unless maybe it was the word "nigger." The edge in Hagman's voice seemed to upset him, too, and the air of goodwill surrounding the meeting momentarily faded. "I'm not totally sure what 'benign' means, but I certainly know what the word 'nigger' means."

Hagman looked nonplussed, waiting for my father to continue.

"I've had a chance to talk a little about what happened in that classroom," Dad went on. "Isaiah told me about reading in front of the class and about the fact that you didn't do anything when the other kids laughed at him. You've used a fancy word, but do you care to address what actually happened in class?"

Hagman sighed. "There was only minor laughter at that time, as far as I'm concerned. The kids were just being kids."

"I grew up in the deep South, Mr. Hagman. Mississippi. Do you know anything about Mississippi?" Dad stared at my teacher.

"Only what I've seen on television and read in our book here." He picked the book up as if it were a prop and placed it down on the desk again.

"I know you don't want to hear this, but years ago in Mississippi, the white folks laughed and called us 'niggers' a lot." Dad moved closer to the desk, enough to rest his forearms on the edge. "The saying wasn't a term of endearment. As a matter of fact, I got out of Mississippi before I nearly killed a man for calling me one. I can remember the incident like it was yesterday."

He looked away from Hagman, gathering his thoughts, and for a moment, the gray hairs near his temple distracted me. I knew where the story was going. It was the one he told often. Dad caught his breath as Mr. Hagman straightened his back, positioning himself firmly against the chair. "I'm a man like any other," Dad said, touching his chest. "Mississippi left a bitter taste in my mouth. When white folks there used the word, it was always to remind us that we didn't belong. I sent my son here to get a broad education. I didn't intend for him to be laughed at or insulted."

He picked the book up from Hagman's desk and thumbed through the pages. "I haven't had a chance to read all this, but it seems like you lost control of your class, and that's inexcusable." He put the book down. "That's all I've got to say … I think my wife has something to add." He looked at her, eyebrows raised.

Mom clutched the handle of her purse—the strap was the same one she'd used to beat me—but let it go when she started talking. "Mr. Hagman," she said, adjusting her glasses. "We're not here to attack you, but the dialogue in this book *is* offensive. I know black people who still use dialect, but it's not something I sent my son here to imitate. The word 'nigger' doesn't have very good memories for me, either. Hearing it makes me think about those days when I walked to school while the white children were allowed to ride a bus. As I walked with my brothers and sisters, those children shouted 'nigger' out the window at us, over and over. It was infuriating. Of course, I didn't let it stop me from what I needed to do. Every time they passed the bus and shouted at us, I threw rocks back at them in retaliation." She grabbed the handle of her purse again, holding it with the same grip that let me know she meant business, and looked directly at Hagman. "I still think this is a good place, but I'd like to see the class read something else. Is that possible?"

He scratched his head and then patted the errant strands so that everything was in place. "I don't know. This was an assigned text, and it's been on the reading list here for years. We'd be breaking with tradition if it was substituted."

I put my head down with thoughts of my mom's suggestion swirling around in my head. Another book? How was I going to do that?

"Let me ask you one thing." Dad jumped in the conversation. "If you were Isaiah, and all the kids were laughing at you, how motivated would you be to read this book?" He folded his arms tightly after asking the question.

"I'd probably do it anyway," Hagman said. "If it were assigned, I'd know I had a responsibility to finish. It's that simple." He spread his hands, as if it really were that simple.

"Somehow, I doubt that," my father said.

"Let's not make *me* the issue," Hagman said. "I'd like to pick up the suggestion that Mrs. Issacson made a few minutes back. As a way to resolve this whole thing, maybe Isaiah can come up with a book he would be willing to read. If he read something else, maybe I could give him extra credit." He looked at my parents and then at me. "What do you think, Isaiah? You'll be the one doing the reading."

I was speechless. Hagman's sudden shift caught me by surprise. Finding something for extra credit sounded good, but it meant that I'd have to work a little bit more. I searched my brain to come up with the perfect rebuttal to *Huck Finn.* An immediate title escaped me.

"That suggestion sounds good … Can I think about it for a while before I pick a book?" I replied, looking down the row at Mom. She seemed pleased, but Dad was frowning.

"Why can't everyone else read the book *my* kid selects?" Dad asked.

Hagman sighed. "Well, Mr. Issacson, it's too late to change the syllabus. I don't do things haphazardly."

"I hope not," Dad replied. "It just seems like the perfect opportunity for you to correct a bad situation."

"Well, that might be true," said Mr. Hagman. "But I'd rather think a bit about letting the entire class read the book. I'm leaning more toward the extra credit idea." He turned the book over and adjusted his own glasses. "In case you haven't noticed, my eyesight is getting bad, and if I agree to this, I'll need plenty of time to get through the material. Right now we're in the middle of studying Mark Twain. I'll let everyone know when I'm ready. Who knows, if I fall in love with the idea of granting extra credit and I'm convinced the book won't create an uproar, I'll make sure that the whole class reads it."

*   *   *

The final decision from Hagman about the extra credit came days later as I lay on my bed, eyes closed, replaying fantastic images of me dribbling a basketball through my legs and lofting a last-second shot in front of a screaming mass of professional-basketball fans. The announcer was shouting: *All net! All net! All net!*

A math book was tented on my chest. It was after dinner, study hall time, and before I'd dozed off, I'd weighed the consequences of pretending to work. The knocking was loud and the voice familiar.

"Isaiah?"

"Yeah?"

"It's Mr. Hagman."

I grabbed the book and jumped up from the bed to get the door. I pulled it open and rested the math book against my pants, my fingers inside the pages to make it look like I'd been hard at work. "Yes, Mr. Hagman?"

He was dressed in a wrinkled shirt now and wasn't wearing a tie. I looked down at him, not knowing what to expect. He squinted at me through his glasses, then down at the book I was holding and smiled.

"I see you're studying."

"Yeah."

"I came by to tell you that I've finally agreed to let you select a book for extra credit. I hope it's not longer than five hundred pages. You've got two weeks, so I suggest you get started right away."

"Thanks," I said, standing in the doorway. I tried to remain calm, but my mind raced. This was the perfect opportunity. I'd finally gotten the chance to show what I could do. I was determined to perform well.

"You okay?" said Hagman measuring my expression.

"I'll be fine," I said. "I'm just thinking."

"Okay," he said. "It's up to you now."

I wasn't sure what I wanted to read. I racked my brain, trying to come up with a good book. I needed a novel that would hold my interest, please my parents, and catch Hagman's blinded vision enough to make him consider assigning the book to the entire class. I thought about *Soul on Ice.*

It wasn't a "literary masterpiece," as Hagman would say, but Eldridge Cleaver's ideas had captured my interest and influenced my thinking before I'd even attended Chadwick. Now, I fantasized about Hagman reading the perspective of a black man who wasn't afraid to call white people "crackers" and "ofays." How quickly the tables turned! In class, he insisted that Twain, Fitzgerald, and Hemmingway were the greats; I wanted him to sample Cleaver and then experience the sting of being called a name. If Cleaver's writing could make me feel good about the Black Panthers, would reading him in class erase the laughter from the lips of my classmates?

There was one central problem: Hagman would never give me extra credit for reading a book of essays containing volatile material, and Dad would object, too, because of his dislike for the Black Panther Party. I didn't want to accept it, but I would have to find something a little less political.

I left the room and headed to the library. The place was quiet, except for the sounds of students in the periodicals section turning newspaper pages. I walked quietly toward the fiction section and searched the stacks meticulously, eyeing the spines of numerous titles. I pulled out one book and then another, staring at them as if they were different shoe sizes. I found works by Melville and Faulkner, but I was determined to find something with black characters, written by a black writer I'd become familiar with in one of my junior high classes. The process was exhausting, but I finally found what I was looking for.

I pulled it from the shelf and stared at the cover. I felt its softness in my palms and rubbed the smooth surface over and over like it was a magic lantern. I'd read parts of *Invisible Man* before, but not entirely. The book touching my palm felt magnetic. The main character was a discontented black man, just like me, and the author, Ralph Ellison, was a writer intent on showing his readers just what it was like to be a man people refused to see. I couldn't wait to show Hagman what I'd selected. The book was long, but it was considered a literary classic. Dad would appreciate the choice of a novel about a young black college boy driven by circumstance to make hard decisions. He'd also like that I'd started, but was now going to finish, reading a book. Dad's angry outburst during the meeting with Hagman made me feel as if he'd get a vicarious thrill from my own and Hagman's reading of a black writer. After reading it, maybe Hagman would see my point and change his mind about the laughter.

I left the library and headed back to Hagman's house to show him what I'd found. I had no idea what time it was. It could have been midnight.

* * *

"What are you doing?" Richard asked days later, as he stood at the door, his green and white school jacket buttoned to the top. He was shocked that I still had my head in a book at 11:00 PM. His hands were full of them. "Is that what you're reading for extra credit?"

"Yeah," I said, attempting to sit up on the bed. "Hagman said that it was okay for me to read this."

"What is it?" Richard grabbed the top button of his jacket and pulled it apart.

"*Invisible Man*," I answered.

"Haven't you read that?" He placed his books on the desk nearby and then threw his coat on the bed near me.

"Not all the way through. There was a lot in there that I missed. You know how it is when you try to read something without a purpose? You lose your enthusiasm and move on to something else."

"I guess you've got a point, but I think that in the long run, you're really wasting your time trying to rock the boat. These folks here aren't interested in learning anything about that book, and I don't understand why your parents believe it's necessary for you to get extra credit, anyway."

"It's important to show these white boys that not all black people are dumb-sounding, like Nigger Jim. This book, written by a black man, will help balance things out. They won't be laughing when they read it. This will put them in the mind of a real black person for a change. I don't think I can stomach another one of those so-called classics." I put the book down and felt the *Huck Finn* book resting underneath me. For some reason, I'd kept it near me as motivation while I read Ralph Ellison's work. "They're bad for my psyche. I've already absorbed too much of this stuff. I think I'm losing my blackness, like you."

Richard laughed. "Forget you, man. I understand wanting to show these white boys that all blacks aren't dumb, but you've got to work at it their way. Why don't you just let that little incident go?" Richard walked across the room, pulled out the chair that sat underneath his desk, and sat down, facing me. His eyes were watery and bloodshot, another sign of how late it was getting.

His perspective seemed to echo the unspoken expectation at Chadwick that we integrate unconditionally and pretend like race was nonexistent. I still had not accepted those terms, but it seemed as though Richard had. At the fall dance, it had been obvious that he didn't care whether he danced with a black girl or not, but I did. With each passing day, he was becoming more assimilated.

"So if they apologize for laughing, would you consider forgiving them?" he asked. "You ought to seriously think about it."

"Forgive white folks?" I was dumbfounded.

"Yeah," said Richard.

"Not now," I replied. "It's just not going to happen."

"Whatever," said Richard, untying his shoelaces. "Good luck on your extra credit work. I don't think it's going to change Hagman's attitude about black people, but I'll let you test the waters. You're wasting your time trying to fight the power here."

He had managed to get his shoes off; his white socks, clearly soiled, needed washing. "I could care less what reading is assigned," he continued. "I've got one goal only at this place, and that's to get out of here. I don't have time to fight these folks, like you do. I'm looking to get myself a piece of the American pie, and if I have to read Mark Twain or any other white author, I'm going to do it."

"That's your problem, Richard," I said. "You're too accommodating. You've let these white folks off too easy. After I get through reading this, they'll know I've been here." I grasped the book even tighter, determined not to let it fall from my hands.

"Hey, suit yourself. Stay up as late as you want. I'm going to bed," he said, pulling off his socks. "My feet hurt, anyway."

*   *   *

Rereading the book was going well. I sat at my dormitory desk each night, poring over the material line by line until I felt the urge to talk. Needing feedback, I ignored Richard, who'd already let me know he wasn't interested. The only other person I could think of was Dofi. Sure, we had hit it off at the dance, but neither one of us had bothered calling. Seeking feedback from another black person, I finally took the initiative.

"I thought you said you had a good memory," I teased, as soon as she picked up the phone, but the line was silent for what seemed like an eternity—maybe because she hadn't yet identified my voice. "We haven't talked since the dance. Did you forget about me?"

"Isaiah?" She sounded as if she was trying to guess the name of a familiar song.

"Of course," I said.

She blew into the phone and sounded relieved. "I thought you'd forgotten my number and everything."

"Not at all." Pausing to check out the dial on the phone, I thought up something that I hoped would make her blush. "How could I forget those dimples and that moon face? I've been busy trying to finish a reading assignment. If I complete it, I'll get extra credit."

"Aren't you the smart one?" She laughed as if I were telling a joke. "I can't talk long—I've got to go to study hall soon—but what book is it?"

"*Invisible Man*," I waited to see if she recognized the book, but she didn't respond. "You should read it," I said, wondering if she hadn't read it because she'd come from Ghana.

"Why?" she asked. "I've already got enough homework."

"It's about this black kid that gets a scholarship to a black college, but he makes a mistake and gets kicked out. Of course, that's only the first part of the story. The rest is about what happens to him after he's expelled. He moves to New York, gets a job in a paint factory, joins a political organization, and ends up running for his life. He's living in a manhole." I swallowed to catch my breath. "When I'm finished, I'm supposed to talk to my teacher about it. I have to convince him that the whole class should read it."

"Pretend I'm the teacher," she said.

I thought it was really cool that she knew exactly what I wanted from her. I presented the argument in the manner that I'd use with Hagman.

"We haven't had to read it here," she said when I was finished, "but from the way you've described it, it sounds like something I should add to my list one day."

"Yeah." She couldn't see me, but inside the phone booth I was nodding my head.

"Maybe we can meet up at the next dance and you can tell me the rest of the story," she said, rushing me.

"If we meet up at the next dance, talking about *Invisible Man* would be way down on my list." I twirled the phone cord between my fingers.

"What do you mean by that?"

"You'd have to tell me more about you. We didn't finish at the dance because of Richard. Remember?"

"Like it was yesterday." Her quick response made me feel good and yet a little guilty for waiting so long to call her. "But I'd almost given up on you. You already know the story. I wasn't going to get my hopes up."

"When are you going to tell me about Africa?"

"Like I said, now is not a good time. But if you promise to call me later, I will."

"This time I promise to keep in touch," I said.

*   *   *

I tapped the smooth surface of Hagman's door with my knuckles and swayed to the sound of imaginary music as I waited for him to answer. It had taken me more than a few weeks to read the book, but when I finished, Hagman had invited me over to his campus residence to talk. That was a convenience of this place: the faculty members, as a condition of employment, were required to stay on the campus. If there were problems, they were easy to find.

He opened the door and invited me into a living room lined with bookshelves. A small television rested on a table in the corner of the room. At the beginning of the year, I'd watched episodes of *Upstairs, Downstairs* with my classmates in this same room. Entering the space again conjured up images of the insulated world of white people. Maybe that was why I loved basketball and sports so much. At least I got to see black people in a favorable light. The best thing about this visit so far was that the television was off and the room was silent.

"How did the reading go, Isaiah?" Hagman asked, resting comfortably in an antique chair. The armrests were carved into faces of lions. His short body looked even smaller as he stretched his legs until his heels barely touched the ottoman. Adjusting his torso, he relaxed his forearms so that his fingers covered the lions' mouths.

"Everything went well." I said. I stared down at the book sitting in my lap and then up at the laminated Harvard degree that he'd bragged about. It was tacked against the wall. The room was lit by the chandelier hanging above my head. "I was engaged by the reading," I said. I looked him right in his eyes and watched him move forward. I knew talking like this would excite him.

He looked down at his coffee table, at the pack of open Marlboros and the burning cigarette butt in the ashtray. The room was filled with smoke. He leaned forward and moved his chair closer, as if expecting me to say more.

I obliged him. "It was the first reading assignment I've gotten here that I've been excited about."

"That's an improvement," he replied, smiling. "I was beginning to wonder about you. You missed my class a lot last week. You know that's something I take personally. I started to look for you, but I decided it was a bad idea. I saw this as an opportunity for you to redeem yourself. Sometimes it's best to let things run their course. Anything else you want to add?"

"I learned so much," I said, not knowing where to start. "What did you think about the book?"

"That's a good question. I'm glad you asked. You seemed to object to Mark Twain's use of Negro dialect, but you selected a book with some very questionable passages. Let me read one for you." He reached out his hand to take the book from me and flipped through the pages until he found something:

> *I's big and black and I say 'Yes, suh' as loudly as any burrhead when it's convenient, but I'm still king down here. I don't care how much it appears otherwise. Power doesn't have to show off ... When you have it, you know it ... The only ones I even pretend to please are big white folk, and even those I control more than they control me. When you buck against me, you're bucking against power, rich white folk's power ... I'll have every Negro in the country hanging on tree limbs by morning if it means staying where I am ...*

"You heard that, didn't you?" He looked at me after he'd finished.

I remembered the passage and tried to remain calm while I gathered my thoughts. "Yeah."

"Well, do you care to explain this section?"

"The book has some flaws," I said. "But it does a good job of talking about what the main character and some of his contacts go through during the 1930s." I was determined to know my stuff this time, so I'd read the book thoroughly, like Richard would have done. There'd be no way he'd catch me off guard again. "That section you just read was a speech made by Dr. Bledsoe, a college president. Bledsoe was telling the invisible man how to exercise power. Of course, he starts out by using dialect, but it's totally different from that Nigger Jim character in *Huck Finn*."

"How so?" asked Hagman.

"Can't you see that Bledsoe is being sarcastic? He's letting us know that he'd sell his soul to keep his job." I smiled at Hagman, happy I'd gotten the chance to show him the intelligent side of me for a change.

"Not really," said Hagman. He glanced back at the passage and handed me the book. "No matter what, it's still dialect."

"But the book is still better than *Huck Finn.*" I sat up in my chair. "The main character is a black man. He wasn't a slave and had a scholarship, just like me."

"That may be true, but I'd have a hard time agreeing that this book is better than *Huck Finn.* The themes in *Huck Finn* are more, shall we say, universal." He unfolded his arms and coolly rubbed his face. "*Invisible Man* focuses too much on race. With all that's gone on here at Chadwick, it's an area that's too sensitive for an objective discussion."

I hadn't expected the conversation to take such a quick turn. I'd anticipated more questions about the book. "So is this your way of telling me that I shouldn't waste my time trying to convince you that the whole class should read this book? It's a classic, you know."

"That I'm not so sure about," he said. "I mean, this isn't a literary masterpiece in the way I'd define it."

"Exactly what do you mean by that?" I was having a hard time with this conversation.

"Well, Isaiah, I'm not convinced this is a book I'd like to teach. Like I said, there's a lot of stuff in here about race. It could cause too many arguments and disrupt my class. Ralph Ellison says that black culture and black people are largely invisible, but I don't really believe that. Look at you. You're not an invisible man at Chadwick. We just don't need that kind of controversy here." He leaned back and smiled. "Now that you've finished the extra credit work, I'll let your parents know that you've demonstrated that you've got the ability to do well academically and that this whole ordeal surrounding *Huck Finn* has been put to rest. Your focus, now that you've finished this extra reading, should be on getting things back to normal for yourself. I wouldn't worry too much about the reading assignments of the other students."

"But I'd like to hear what they think about this book. Can't we make a deal?" The words came from my mouth before I could censor them.

"No deals. I've tried to stick to books that everyone can relate to. Again, the issues brought up in *Invisible Man* would be a little dangerous for my class, not to mention that it's totally different from the rest of the books we've been reading. I think you should accept the fact that you were able to earn some extra credit and get on with things. I'll erase the F you earned with your performance on the Mark Twain book, but the next assigned reading is Ernest Hemingway's *The Old Man and the Sea.* It's short, so make sure you've read all the pages I've listed by the time you return from the Thanksgiving break."

My nostrils flared as my fingers flipped through the pages of the book. It had finally dawned on me that Hagman had no intention of introducing this book to the entire class. True, he hadn't committed to doing it in the first place, but now it was crystal clear to me that he only said he'd think about it in front of my parents to placate them. He'd never had any intention of having me share the book with the class.

I had dreamed of seeing my classmates' faces as they read the book and got into the mind of a black man. The novel, I was certain, would have inspired a dialogue about why my parents had sent me here and would have shed much light on why I didn't feel at home. Home. It was almost time to go back to Oakland, but now I felt as if I had a score to settle before leaving.

I stood up in front of Hagman, holding the spine of the book firmly in my right hand. I cocked my arm as if preparing to throw a baseball and moved it forward, letting the mound of paper sail in Hagman's direction. He moved out of the way and let the book sail past his ear. He straightened his clothes and looked at me through his glasses without saying a word.

HOME

As I rode Chadwick's yellow and black shuttle bus to the airport, I kept thinking about Hagman, the extra credit, leaving Chadwick for good, and Dofi. I couldn't wait to reveal to her the outcome of the assignment, see her at another dance, and learn more about Africa. Maybe she'd think that *Invisible Man* was better than *Huck Finn,* too.

Listening to the hum of the bus engine, I thought about what it would be like leaving Chadwick for good, wondering if I should ask my parents again if they'd consider the possibility. It was a long shot but worth a try. There had to be something I could say or do—I just didn't know what. The ninety-minute jaunt to LAX would give me some time to sort things out.

The Thanksgiving holiday was my first visit home. My brother, Melvin, and sister, Lenae, had laid bets that I'd quickly become some Oreo who'd forgotten where he came from, talking and acting differently, but when I got the chance, I'd tell them how I'd put up pictures of Huey and other militants in my dorm room and how I'd asked the headmaster about a black history class. The fact that I'd done those things would definitely prove them wrong.

On the night we sat down to eat Thanksgiving dinner, everything in the house seemed out of place, out of proportion. In my dormitory bed, I'd dreamed of our mahogany dining room table, surrounded by intricately carved wooden chairs. When I'd left for school, the image etched in my mind had been of this large surface, which had seemed big enough to seat several large families. Now when I sat down, I felt our legs and our elbows touching. The sweaty bowls of hot food barely left room for our plates and folded paper napkins. It would take awhile to get used to things again, probably until just before it would be time to head back to school.

Mom had made my favorite, a smothered-chicken dish she'd mixed with rice and sweet green peas, a meal she made on birthdays and holidays because she knew it made me feel special. She'd skipped the traditional turkey, dressing, and cranberry sauce and had spent the rest of the time making peach cobbler and homemade ice cream, things she knew I'd never get at Chadwick. It felt strange getting the royal treatment, considering the last time she'd seen me I'd been in trouble. It wasn't like her to just let things fade away, but maybe she sensed I'd learned my lesson since there hadn't been any more bad reports. When I looked at my arms now, the scars were barely visible against my dark skin, and the pain was gone.

I filled my plate until there was no more room. At Chadwick, I'd gotten used to eating my chicken, even fried chicken, with a fork. It was good table manners, my classmates told me. Eating chicken with a fork was foreign to the Issacson household. When the food was served and grace had been said, we just dove in, forks, fingers, and all. I wasn't prepared for the stares I received from Melvin and Lenae after I'd gotten my first forkfuls. I'd been away so long that I'd forgotten how to eat and how to relax. To them, my new habit was incomprehensible.

"I knew it," Melvin lowered the chicken wing from his lips, trying to talk before he had swallowed his food. His cheeks were full, his hair nappy, and his voice deeper than I remembered.

"Me, too," said Lenae. She'd moved the green peas and vegetables to one side of her plate while she watched me. Her Afro had started to grow long like the movie star Pam Grier.

"What?" Looking at Melvin's thick, wet fingers and at my sister's hair, I tried to pretend that I didn't know what they were talking about.

"You're eating chicken like white folks now." Melvin always ate fast and talked with his mouth full. "You been away at that school way too long."

"That's not it. I just don't want my fingers to look like yours. That's all." I quickly put some chicken in my mouth and sat the fork down next to my plate. "People stare at you funny at school when you eat with your fingers."

"That's better." Melvin would have waited forever for me to put the fork down. He was younger and looked up to me. "I was beginning to wonder about you." His rough skin was a shade darker than the soda bottle full of cream soda that sat in front of him. I was much darker, and it was sometimes hard to tell, if you didn't know us, that we were siblings.

"Leave him alone," Mom said in my defense. She protected me when she wasn't doling out punishment. "He'll be all right." She waited a few moments until the attacks subsided. "Tell us about Chadwick. How do you like it so far?"

I chewed slowly, using the time to think about all the things that had happened. I had been betrayed by Hagman, scored poorly on a history quiz, and been put on probation for smoking weed. My first few months had been a whirlwind of adjustments, and now everything ran together.

"I want to come back," I said finally, looking down at my plate. My reflection was barely visible near the edges. If I looked up and studied their reactions, I'd change my mind and become timid. The table grew silent. In the distance, I could hear the tap of Dad's utensils against the table.

He cleared his throat. "You want to do what?"

"I said I was ready to come home. I don't like being around all those white people. They make me sick."

"What?" There was an edge to Dad's voice that reminded me of how he'd sounded during his confrontation with Hagman.

"I just told you." I said.

"You don't have to like them," Mom said. "You've just got to apply yourself. That's what we've been trying to tell you since you left. We've got a lot riding on your education. We didn't show up on that campus to talk about *Huck Finn* just so you could decide to come back now."

The look of determination that had been on her face during the beating popped into my head again. The reason why she had humiliated me was becoming clearer. The "we" part of her statement meant that she'd told everyone, all her friends in the neighborhood and at the church, that I was doing well and that in a few years I'd be finishing up at an all-white prep school.

She'd embellished things considerably in the phone conversations I'd inadvertently overheard her have with friends since I'd been back. Usually by the time she finished talking about me, I was well on my way to some grand future. In her mind, and in the minds of her friends, I was already the class valedictorian. She had created an expectation I knew I'd never be able to live up to. It would embarrass her if I failed.

"Mr. Hagman lied about the extra credit." I tried being more specific.

"You got to read *Invisible Man*, right? And he's already explained why the entire class wasn't given the assignment," said Dad. "Of course I would have preferred that everyone read it, but we still got a small victory."

"It was an act," I said, thinking about the book I'd thrown at my teacher.

"Regardless, you ain't coming back here, that's for sure," said Dad, waving his crooked index finger in the air. He could be tough when he wanted to.

Going to public school and hanging out with Tee, two things he knew I wanted to do, were no longer an option.

"I told you when you got your acceptance letter that you'd have to stick this thing out all three years. That's the problem with your generation of black boys. Seems like you want to quit when something gets hard or things don't exactly go your way. You might as well just get ready to go back. Man, when I was your age …"

I tuned him out before he could finish. It was the beginning of another story I knew by heart—the long, hot days on the farm, the long walks to school, the small classrooms, the attempts at learning without books. We were fortunate, he'd said more times than I could remember, and me, I was super lucky. He told stories of the old South a lot, and just when you thought he was finished, he'd lean back, rub his face, and talk some more. As his jaws bounced, he focused on the ceiling as if he were peering into a time machine.

It had taken a lot for Dad to send me away to school, but the scholarship was too good to pass up. All expenses were paid except for spending money. He liked discussing political theories at mealtimes and believed the individual and not the environment determined where you ended up in life. For him, a private-school education was nice, but it wasn't a necessity for doing well. You had to perform, wherever you ended up, he often said.

And then there was the vision he'd had of me as a lawyer, which he'd seen while looking at my entrance-test results. He'd imagined me standing in front of a packed courtroom, delivering arguments in a major case. He had a thing about visions. Once he'd experienced one, he'd become determined to make it happen. At Chadwick, I'd make all the right connections.

"I don't care what you have to do to survive," he said. "All I've got to say is you're not leaving that place until you finish."

I knew Dad was taking a hard line about my return to Chadwick for other unspoken reasons. He had never finished high school, and my feelings now were probably reminding him that he'd given up too early in pursuing his own education. He was working on his GED, and his struggles with the coursework made him regret dropping out. He earned an honest living, of course, but he saw too much of his own former self in my statement, and he wasn't about to let a word like "quitting" enter my vocabulary.

"But what about Mr. Hagman?"

"Son, we had this talk." He picked up the light blue bottle of Maalox, which was always parked next to his dinner plate, twisted the top, and moved it up to his lips. I could tell by the pained look on his face that his ulcers were starting to act up. I watched his Adam's apple jump as he swallowed. Picking up a napkin, he dabbled at his lips, but the white, chalky film remained. "I told you from the get-go that if you got accepted to that school, you wouldn't be able to quit. I meant what I said."

"I know, but … I hate the food. I just want to come back. I promise if you let me out of there, I'll study hard."

"So, Hagman's not the only issue, huh? You just got down there and realized it wasn't going to be all fun and games, didn't you?" He paused. "Now you think you're just going to come back here and be able to run the streets with your buddies. Like I said, I've made my decision." He held the fork above his green peas. "Now let's eat."

"I ain't hungry anymore." I stared at the food on my plate until the steam stopped rising from the green peas. Not eating was a sure way to get my parents even more riled up.

Dad's firm stand took me back to that moment in the car after the admissions test, when we'd discussed this subject. The dialogue had been spirited. During the ride, he'd told me that if the test results came back positive and I got accepted, he'd send me to Chadwick. Then he said something negative about public schools. I don't remember what it was, only that he'd been so engrossed in the discussion that he'd run a red light. He insisted that blocking out any alternatives to Chadwick would teach me the importance of perseverance and single-minded decision-making.

"You're hungry, all right," he ordered. "Pick up that fork and finish that food."

Reluctantly, I grabbed my fork and tried to finish eating my chicken. I didn't care what Melvin and Lenae thought anymore. I figured that if I wasn't going to be able to get out of going, I might as well continue to eat the way I'd recently been taught.

"Besides, these Oakland schools are a mess now," Dad said. "Don't you follow the news down there?"

"Of course," I answered, thinking of Hagman's English class and how I was diligently keeping up with current events.

"Then you know that a bunch of radicals, the Symbionese Liberation Army, just took credit for killing Marcus Foster, the superintendent, and that the Oakland school system is not a great place to learn anything right now. Ain't that right, Melvin?"

Melvin nodded in agreement. He had finished eating and was watching me in amazement. We'd talked on the phone the day Foster was killed, but he knew when to disagree and now wasn't the time. Dad was on a roll.

"I really think you're trying to throw away a good opportunity. You might not appreciate it now, but down the road, it's gonna pay off. I know it."

I pushed the remainder of my meal around my plate to make it look as if there wasn't anything left. "Can I be excused?" I was losing not only my appetite, but also any hope of changing Dad's mind.

"Let's just have a nice dinner," Mom said.

"It's too late for that." I pushed away from the table, daring someone to challenge me, and headed back to my room. I needed an outlet for all the pressure of thinking about returning to Chadwick. I knew the only thing that would work would be playing basketball. It calmed my nerves and took my mind off my worries when I had initially been accepted. Getting in was supposed to have been a happy occasion, but I knew it meant my whole life was about to change. That day when the admissions packet arrived in the thick manila envelope, I'd played ball until my feet hurt.

I combed through the closet, looking underneath clothes and tennis shoes that were now too small, until I spotted the round surface of the ball peeking out from beneath a pair of pants. I pulled it out and felt its seams against my fingers. Its worn surface carried tales of unfulfilled hoop fantasies, buried emotions, and a rekindled soul. I bounced it hard against the wooden floor, transferring my anxiety from my fingertips to the basketball's smooth cover.

Maybe, I thought, *maybe one day they will understand.*

PLAYGROUND

The next day, I walked to the playground where I'd first learned to play hoops and where, if nothing had changed, my friends hung out.

I couldn't hear horseshoes clip-clopping along the dusty path, a sound that had grown familiar during my months at Chadwick. Replacing them was the hum of bus engines, the honking of car horns, and the howl of barking dogs. Small, one-story bungalows sat within earshot, needing paint, flowers, and lots of attention. I thought about what these houses lacked, comparing them with my new surroundings in Ojai, where lush green trees, carefully manicured lawns, rich kids, and mansions dotted the landscape. Yes, Oakland and Ojai were worlds apart.

I walked down the street and peered through the wire fence surrounding Lafayette Playground. I could see the shape of a male body, moving quickly across the asphalt, with an intensity that was uncommon among the athletes at Chadwick. It was a cold, windy, wet day, and he was shirtless. It was Tee.

I couldn't believe he was playing with his shirt off. He suffered from asthma, and playing without his shirt in this weather was a sure way for him to get sick, but that was Tee: he took risks, believing he was invincible. We'd met at this same playground as kids, when he'd challenged me to a game of one-on-one in front of some elementary school classmates. I'd bragged that he was too short to win and had bet him my lunch money that I'd trample him. That was all the incentive he'd needed. When money was on the line, he paid attention. That day, he'd ended up kicking my butt.

Tee's short frame, uncombed Afro, and scars that ran along both long arms were a welcoming sight. He lifted the orange ball and pointed it toward the basket, practicing his jumper—a sweet shot he helped me master one day when I'd asked him how he made it look so easy. He'd added a few more scars to his body since the last time I'd seen him, including a nasty gash underneath his right eye. It seemed like he was forever getting nicked and scraped, even in my absence. I'd nicknamed him "Crust" before departing because a visible part of his body always bore a flaky scab.

"Look who's back! Look who's back!" he shouted with his hard, raspy voice. I walked through the gate with my basketball. "You ready to ball?" He pounded his basketball against the pavement, pushing it from his left hand to his right as I moved closer.

"You know it," I said. He faked passing the ball to me. When we got close enough, we embraced and then moved to get a better look at each other.

"Your pants are fitting a bit different. Looks like you lost a lot of weight," he said, picking up his basketball and placing it snugly underneath his arm.

"Food's terrible," I said. "But what the hell happened to your eye?" I couldn't stop looking at it.

"You sound funny, too." He pointed to his eye. "It happened playing one-on-one with Baron." He ran his fingers along the swelling underneath his eye. "The boy is wild. His elbows are like razor blades." He paused. "So how is it?"

"How's what?"

"The new school."

There was so much to say. I wanted to tell him about the orientation program, the tests, the horses, E, Breedlove, Dofi, Jenaye, and the dance, but before I knew it, I'd blurted out something quick.

"Hate it, man."

It was a simple reply, but I realized that if I'd told him about everything, he would have been overwhelmed. That was the nature of prep school. It was hard to sum it all up. It changed you, even though you tried to resist its pull. For the first time in a conversation with Tee, I felt worlds apart.

"That was fast," he said.

"I know."

"What's the matter?"

"The work's hard, but that's not the only reason I hate it." I bounced the ball a few times. "I miss being here. The guys at school seem square. We've got nothing in common. And the hoops team sucks."

"They've got a gym, don't they?"

"Oh yeah. The gym is almost brand-new. The headmaster gave me a key. You'd love it. Problem is, there's not much competition. I run through those guys like water. Our biggest rival is Proctor, another prep school. We've got a game with them coming up, but I don't think it'll be that tough a game, especially if they're like all the other boarding schools we've played."

"So you're the star, right?"

"My friend, Frank, sometimes calls me 'Ice.' He said I was cool under pressure." I nodded my head slowly. "I'm the star now, but Frank's also pretty good. I've been working with him, trying to improve his game. If he gets better, we'll be awesome." I told Tee a little of the story of how Frank and I had met during the first week of classes after dinner and how he'd warned me about the reading assignments. I'd sensed then that he'd be a cool white boy, someone I needed to get to know better.

"That's a plus. Just make sure you don't give him all your secrets. He might overtake you. Man, if you're the star, that's what the college scouts will notice. If you keep it up, you'll start getting letters."

"I don't think any college scouts will be coming to see me there," my voice dropped off. "That's the other thing about that school. No one outside of that campus cares about its sports program. The school is only known for academics. It's not the school of champions, and that's been worrying me. I'm scared my dream of becoming the next Bill Russell is gonna die there."

"I coulda told you that. Did you tell your folks what's going on?"

"I just did."

"What'd they say?" Tee's concern was genuine. Considering our history together, he knew me better than anyone. I'd missed being with him. A starting guard on the McClymonds High basketball team, he was a year older than me, but it didn't matter. He'd taken me under his wing, just as if I were the younger brother he'd never had.

"My dad ain't happy. He wants me to stick it out. He doesn't care how bad I hate it."

"What are you going to do?"

"I don't know yet. I'm thinking about not going back. Got any suggestions how I can pull that off?"

Tee looked back at me with a raised eyebrow. The statement, coming from me, surprised him, but I could tell he liked the idea. "No, but let me think about this for a minute." He put his hand underneath his chin. "Man, if you came back, I think we could win the city championship. You'd definitely be the missing link. And when we're not playing, you can help me raise money for the Panthers. They've got a free breakfast, free grocery, and a free shoe program now. Bobby Seale's campaign was just the tip of the iceberg." He smiled as he pondered the possibilities. "If you ain't happy, I don't see why your folks won't let you come back home."

"I see the problem," Tee continued. "You've got to be more creative. If you want to come back, you can't just tell them you hate the place. You've got to raise the stakes a bit. You could tell them that they're preaching some crazy religion. You know how your folks are about going to church and about believing that man came from Adam and Eve. You could tell them that the teachers are really pushing that guy who believes in survival of the fittest. Yeah. That'll get your dad's and your mom's blood pumping. If they heard something like that, they'd probably try to pull you out of that place in a heartbeat."

"You talking about Charles Darwin?"

"That's his name." I wasn't surprised Tee knew about Darwin. He could have been a much better student and gone to Chadwick, too, if he weren't so radical and if he tried harder at getting good grades.

"I don't know, man. That's a little far-fetched." It was a crazy idea, one I hadn't thought about, but leave it to Tee to come up with something like that. He was crazy like a fox.

I thought about his suggestion for a minute, weighing whether I had the confidence to lie like to my parents. But knowing them, I'd need something stronger than that to convince them that I needed to come back. I held my basketball up against the sharp wind, the smooth surface resting against my left palm, fingers spread. I used my right hand as a guide and extended my elbow, pushing the ball skyward. I watched its rotation. The ball spun until it landed safely back on my fingertips. What the hell was I gonna do?

"You ready to play?" Tee interrupted my thinking. "I want to see if you've gotten any better."

I rolled my ball away and stepped onto the court, where he held his basketball in a ready-for-action position.

"Take the ball out," I commanded him. "You've got the ball first. Show me what you got." I got down in a defensive stance, pulled up my pants, and waited for him to make the first move.

"I'll show you I haven't lost a step. I know I can beat you now, even if I am a few pounds lighter."

BONES

After Tee had showed me he was still on top of his game by kicking my butt, we took the long way to my house to change clothes and listen to music, stopping at the liquor store to get some Gatorade. Playing records was our ritual after every workout, our chance to rap about personal stuff.

As we passed his house without stopping, he waved at his mom and dad, who were watching television on the other side of the big picture window. To hear him tell it, he didn't ever have to say anything to his folks about where he was going, which seemed like an ideal arrangement to me. At times, I wished his parents were mine, especially his dad, who smelled like the pickled pigs' feet he kept in the refrigerator and seemed more relaxed, less intense about rules and regulations.

As we trotted down the street toward my place, I could hear dice rattling in Tee's pocket. For some reason, I hadn't heard them while we'd been playing ball. I was a little worried—Tee was already on his way to becoming a big-time gambler. He'd picked up the habit of shooting dice from his father, who was known throughout the neighborhood for his turned-up Pittsburgh Pirates baseball cap—and for placing big bets. His father had won a lot of money gambling. Tee often bragged about how his father always gave his mother part of the winnings to keep the beauty shop going. Tee believed he'd have the same degree of good fortune, but unfortunately he had not inherited his father's gambling luck. It didn't stop Tee from trying, though. He came up with one scheme after another, hoping one day to strike it rich, and vowed to use the proceeds to help keep the Party and its community projects alive.

It seemed like everyone in the neighborhood knew the basics of shooting dice except for me. I always found something else to do when Tee and the other boys started to play. My folks were totally against gambling, too, which was probably why I didn't care about it. From the time we were all little, Mom and Dad had told us that gambling was a waste of money and a sin against God. To keep us from giving in to temptation, my dad had even removed the dice from the Monopoly game, so we could only play under his supervision.

Hearing the click in Tee's pocket, I knew that he'd soon start in on a tale of gambling woes—or resume his efforts to teach me what he called "the real game." Before today, except for our game of one-on-one, I never cared much for gambling, but Tee was determined to loosen me up, just like when he'd turned me onto weed. Now I was more receptive, since it looked like Dad was going to send me back to Chadwick no matter how much I protested. Out of sheer defiance and without telling Tee, I decided to give craps a try. Maybe if I learned the game well enough, I'd be able to teach it to some of my classmates. Tee would be proud.

"You still shooting dice?" I asked him.

"Got to, man. Nobody else going to give me the kind of money I need." He placed his hands inside his pocket and shook his pants leg so hard that I heard what sounded like several rolls of quarters clanking together. I envied the money he won, but he lost too often for me to want to be like him. On the days I witnessed his bad luck, it was easy for me to brag to him about why I didn't really indulge. It was a little harder to feel that way when he won, but those days weren't as frequent as the others.

His gambling was another reason my folks didn't really approve of my friendship with Tee. Like a lot of people in the neighborhood, they tolerated him but didn't think much of him as an exemplary young man. Dad always said, "He's a perfect example of why you need to get away from here, Isaiah. This kid is going nowhere, and if you keep hanging around him, you're going to end up going there, too."

Severing ties with a lifelong friend was easier said than done. Tee was someone you just couldn't turn off. He had come to my rescue when I fought, and I could count on him in a pinch. I just wished he were quieter and a little more discreet with his vices.

"You got time to teach me to play?" I asked him playfully as we neared my house. "If you do, I'll wear you out just like I'm gonna do you on the court when I get some rest."

"Yeah, yeah, yeah," he said, waving his hand. "You're all talk."

"No, really," I said. His skepticism affected me differently today. "If I decide to go back to Chadwick, I want to be able to teach them a new game." I felt inside my pocket for loose change and debated making a small wager to try my luck. I knew my folks wouldn't approve, but at this point I didn't care what they thought.

*   *   *

Tee lit up a joint just before we made it to my house, blowing the smoke at me. I'd already told him that smoking out wasn't a good idea, but he insisted on giving me a contact high. After the smoke hit my clothes, there was no way I could go through the front door. Mom would smell the weed, and I'd be in trouble all over again.

Luckily, her car was gone. I walked up the driveway to the creaking garage door, pulled it just a bit, and squeezed my way inside, with Tee right behind me. The refurbished garage wasn't big enough for a car, but it was just the right size to be our hangout, where we listened to music and relaxed after playing. I threw the basketball in the corner near the washer and dryer and cleared a laundry table of books, magazines with ripped covers, broken trophies, and an eight-track tape player with a John Coltrane tape stuck inside. I couldn't remember the last time I'd cleaned off this table. The stuff was still there from the summer.

"I want to make sure nothing gets in the way of our game," I said.

"You're serious, aren't you?" He regarded me with raised eyebrows, still unwilling to believe I'd finally decided to learn how to play dice.

"As a heart attack."

Tee pulled the red dice from his pocket and threw them on the table. "First, let me show you how to hold them." He grabbed them carefully, turned his palm up, and closed his hand. "This is how you lock 'em. If you lock 'em the right way, you'll get better results. You know. It's like shooting a free throw. You've got to have the right touch or you won't score." He moved his hand back and forth and threw the dice on the table. Seven. "I was trying to do that," he said. "Rule number one. You roll a seven or an eleven on the first time out, you win." He handed them to me. "You want to try?"

"Sure," I said grabbing them. It felt awkward to hold them, especially after my folks' warnings. It seemed like I was holding a newborn.

"Shake 'em up, man."

I raised them to my ear and began moving my hands back and forth like I'd been shown and then threw them across the table. I waited a moment, then counted the dots. Eleven. "I was trying to roll that," I said, mimicking Tee.

"Yeah, right," he said, cuffing me on the shoulder. "If you can throw that every time out, you're going to be a lucky man. Keep playing."

"So this is how they play in Vegas." I'd heard Mom and Dad talk so much about the evils of gambling in Las Vegas that I'd naturally assumed that Tee had learned the rules of the game from his father, whom he said went to Las Vegas all the time.

"Vegas? I don't know how they play there. This is how we play in the neighborhood. Rule number two: You throw a two, three, or a twelve the first time out and you lose."

The game, as he explained it, was simpler than I'd thought. I reached in my pocket to feel for change. "You want to play for quarters?"

"If you think you're ready." He rubbed his hands together eagerly, as if he were preparing for a delicious meal. "I should probably tell you rule number three first. If you roll a four, five, six, eight, nine, or a ten the first time, you establish what's called a point." He looked at me and waited for my nod. "To win, you've got to keep throwing the dice until you hit your point. If you roll a seven before you hit the point, then you lose and I win. You got it?"

"Yeah," I said, feeling a little shaky, wishing a little that I hadn't brought up money just yet. "I'll learn it as we go. Let's just play while I have the fever." I had shaken off the loss on the court, and now I was ready to gamble. *Strike while the iron is hot*, I told myself.

"You ready?" I asked.

"I'm game."

I held the dice with one hand and reached in my pocket with the other to grab several quarters. I threw a quarter on the table facedown and waited for Tee to do the same.

"You punk dog," I said after I'd won the first round. "You thought I wasn't going to be able to kick your ass, didn't you?" I picked up his quarter and waited for him to dig in his pocket for another.

"Shut up, man, and keep playing," he said, reluctantly reaching into his pocket for more money.

I threw the dice again and hit an eleven. So far, so good. "This'll teach you to fuck with me. When you saw me today, you thought I was gonna be a neighborhood boy, turned softy, huh? Man, I own you." I was beginning to see how the game could suck you in and make you talk shit, especially if you were winning.

"It's called beginner's luck. Roll the dice and stop talking."

My smile widened. I could tell the losing was getting to him. There was something about this game, this moment, that seemed to disturb him more than others. I'd beat him at hoops before, but something about his change of fortune this time was different. Gambling was his exclusive territory and academics were mine, yet I was making a shift right before his eyes.

The change felt good for me. Holding the dice, I felt in control of the outcome. That was certainly not the case when it came to Chadwick, where someone else was rolling the dice for me. At least that's how it felt.

Tee hadn't told me yet, but I also had to learn when to quit. Slowly the wheels were starting to turn. I sensed a change inside; I just couldn't put my finger on it. I was always under control but the dice game was showing me I could be more expressive. Free. That it was worth taking a chance, whatever that chance turned out to be.

"Do I sense a little hostility?" I tried to keep from smirking.

"Don't worry about it," he said. "Just throw the dice, man."

I threw the dice again and hit another seven. This was incredible. "You thought you were gonna teach me a lesson, didn't you? Well, I fooled your ass. You ready to quit?"

"Naw. Keep rolling."

The insults seemed to make him more determined. I could see it in his eyes as he put down another quarter. Sure, he'd been beaten before, but not by me. The jingle in his pants grew faint, and mine got stronger.

I put my hands in my pocket, shook my pants leg, and smiled. I started to roll the dice again, but in the distance I could hear footsteps pressing against the squeaky basement stairs. I grabbed the dice without looking at the results.

"Is something wrong?" Tee asked.

"Did you hear that?"

"Hear what?"

"Someone's coming."

"Ain't nobody coming, man. You're just paranoid. All the cars were gone when we got here. Come on, man, shoot. I'm trying to win my money back."

The noise grew more distinct. "Shut up. I think my mom's coming down here."

"Your what?"

I reached over to him and held his mouth so he couldn't make any more noise. "It's my mom."

"Oh shit." The warm air of his breath bounced hard against my palm.

I thought about what she'd say if she caught me gambling and, more importantly, what she'd do. Seeing Tee in the garage would make things worse. I wasn't prepared to endure another beating like the one in the bathroom at school, especially with my best boy around. I'd never be able to live that down. I still hadn't told him about that incident, but right now I didn't have time. I couldn't explain to him what I was about to do because he'd have too many questions, and we'd end up getting caught.

I took my hand from around his mouth and moved toward the window. In a matter of seconds, I removed the latch and pushed the pane slowly until there was an opening large enough for me to exit.

I grabbed the sill and pulled my body through. Outside, I glanced back at Tee's puzzled expression and then grabbed him.

"Where are you going?"

"I'm running away," I said, worried that I was running out of time. "I've just made up my mind. I'm not going back to that school."

"Man, you're crazy. You must have thought about that city championship, huh?" He was climbing through the window. "Where are you going? Where you gonna stay?"

"I don't care. I just know I want to get away. I heard Mom coming. If I leave now and don't come back, I won't have to answer her questions. It's the perfect setup. Plus, I'll miss the plane. They're not going to drive me all the way back now."

Tee landed on the grass next to me, brushed off his clothes, and followed me out of the backyard. We tried our best not to be seen.

"Come on, man, move quick, or you'll get us caught."

"I'm right behind you," he said.

*   *   *

The storage room next to the garage was dark. The cold air pushed through uncovered vents, and the dust clung to my exposed skin like static electricity. I was starting to smell. My armpits, once dripping with perspiration, were now dried must. A grainy film of salt still covered my forehead. I closed my eyes and prayed for water.

I'd found my way back to the house late that same night by sneaking back in the same window I'd left through. Melvin had locked it, but I knew how it worked. I'd fixed it so that on nights I wanted to sneak to the movies while my parents slept, I could adjust it without being detected.

I'd run away to the playground, the only place I knew no one would ask any questions. But as everyone left and it grew dark, I had no choice except to return home. Resting in the storage room gave me power, the power of nonconfrontation. Yeah. I was waging a war they couldn't understand and were powerless to change.

It was morning now, and I was hungry. As I crouched down, my stomach growled loud enough to give away my hiding place, but luckily, no one was around. Between nightmares of juicy steaks, fried chicken, and hamburgers, I thought about the reading assignment. I hadn't even started *The Old Man and the Sea*, and I was due back in a couple of days.

So many expectations had been placed on my shoulders that I felt overwhelmed. Not only was I carrying the hopes and the failures of my parents, but also they'd made me feel like I was the poster child for integration. The real truth was that I saw things differently—I wasn't obsessed with integration like my parents had been. I simply wanted to make sure white folks heard a black viewpoint once in a while and stopped treating me like an invisible man. My lone attempt to capture a wider audience in Hagman's class had failed, and now I was ready to take my ideas home to Oakland, where I thought they'd get a better response and where I felt more comfortable. At least I'd get to play on a pretty good basketball team.

I heard the footsteps and smelled the bacon cooking above me. Mom, Dad, and Melvin were awake and talking about my whereabouts.

"Have you seen him?" Dad's voice boomed above everyone else's. "I wonder where he could be …"

"I've asked Tee, but he said he hasn't seen him, either. Somehow, I don't trust that Tee," Mom said. "I know he knows where Isaiah is."

"He'll show up," Dad said. "And when he does …"

"Melvin?"

"Yeah, Mom?"

"Get me a clean dish towel. I need to dry these dishes. They're clogging up the sink."

"Where are they?" he asked.

"They're in the garage, on the dryer. Can you go down there and get me one?"

I smiled to myself when I heard the request. Melvin mumbled his answer, but I knew he'd comply. He usually did what he was told and didn't ask questions.

In a minute, I could hear his feet thudding down the steps to the garage. I moved from my hiding place in the storage room, pushing the door open slightly, positioning myself so I could see him through the crack. I wasn't sure how he'd react when he saw me, but I was too hungry to care. He was my meal ticket, pure and simple. He entered the garage and headed toward the folded clothes near the washing machine.

"Melvin?" I said. "Melvin?"

He jumped slightly at the sound of my voice, and then he turned toward the cellar's entrance. His round face and slender body were starting to look more and more like my father's. "Where the hell have you been? You been down here all this time? Whew. You're in a lot of trouble."

"I know, man, but I'm hungry," I said, trying to sound pitiful. "Can you get me something to eat?"

Melvin raised his eyebrows at me. "What do you want?"

"I don't know," I replied. "Just something to tide me over."

"Okay, but aren't you going back to school?"

"Stop asking so many questions, and get me some food."

He shook his head at me. "I wish I had your chance, bro. I wouldn't blow it like you're doing. You're really scared of becoming an Oreo, aren't you?"

"Shut up." I was taking a chance by talking back to him, but I didn't want to hear what he was saying. His reaction had let me know how much I'd been holding back from him, too. First it was Tee, now it was my brother who needed more than the smoke signals I was sending him. I wished there was more time to tell him everything, but I was growing impatient. My stomach was killing me.

"All right, man, I'll get you some food. Just remember—you owe me."

It was just like Melvin, always negotiating something for himself and making me beholden to him. As he walked up the stairs with the dishrag, I thought about our first trip to see my grandparents in Louisiana and the shotgun we'd found in Grandpa's bedroom closet. We'd been warned about playing with guns, especially real guns. But that time I had taken a chance. I had to see how things worked, and I did the unthinkable: I pointed the shotgun at him and pulled the trigger in fun.

Luckily, the chamber was empty. Melvin had a fit and threatened to tell my parents unless I agreed to shine his church shoes for a month. I did it to keep the peace, and now he was doing the same thing to me again.

*   *   *

"Where are you taking that?" The storage room's floorboards muffled Mom's loud voice. My mouth watered. I swallowed my spit, hoping to cut my appetite.

"I'm just going downstairs to eat."

"You know I don't allow you to eat down there. Eating all over the house brings rats. If you're going to eat, do it right at this table."

"But Mom …" I heard Melvin reply.

"Don't 'but Mom' me," she said. "What are you doing hungry anyway? Didn't you just eat?"

"Yeah, but I didn't get enough."

I was starting to get worried that Melvin would crack. I walked out of the storage area, moving closer to the garage's stairwell, where I could hear the conversation better.

"You know you don't eat oatmeal. You sure that's for you?"

"Yeah." I could hear Melvin's voice weakening. He wasn't a good liar. The weight of Mom's relentless questioning was wearing him down.

"Well, I want to see you eat every drop. You know about wasting food here. Sit down and let me watch you eat."

Damn. When I heard that line, I knew I was in trouble. I'd have to wait longer for my food.

"I'm full," he said after a few minutes.

"Boy, you haven't made a dent in that oatmeal."

"I know," Melvin whined.

"What's the matter, you sick now?" I could almost hear the suspicion and disbelief in her voice. "If not, you're going to sit there until you finish. I told you not to waste food."

He finally cracked. "It's for Isaiah."

"Isaiah?" Her voice shot up. "Where the hell is that boy?"

"He's downstairs," Melvin mumbled, "hiding in the storage room."

Shit, I knew he'd give me up, and why I'd trusted him, I didn't know. It was too late now. I thought about jumping out the garage window again, but I was too weak and hungry. I braced myself, like a prisoner awaiting sentencing, to deal with the fallout. The sound of shuffling feet meant Mom, Dad, and Melvin were all on their way down to see me.

I wasn't sure of the outcome, but I was ready to roll the dice. Living on my own, however briefly, had been instructive. After I had played more games of basketball and visited friends, and night had fallen, I had run out of things to do. Plus, I couldn't stop thinking about the hunger. My stomach was cramping, even now. How would I feed myself?

Breathe, I repeated, *breathe deeply.*

FIGHT

Dad entered the room first, and I let out the warm air filling my lungs, releasing the tension, too. Since he was usually more reserved than Mom when administering punishment, his initial entry before her was a good omen, I thought. His thick eyebrows were frozen in a V shape, his eyes clearly focused. His white cook's hat, normally worn straight, tilted to the side. The knowledge that I'd been in the storage room had clearly ignited his laid-back demeanor. His hands moved from his side and clasped together in front of his face. His fingers, gathered like a pyramid, rested against his lips.

"So this is where you've been hiding," he finally said. Mom and Melvin stood behind him.

"I guess you could say that." I scowled. "I told you I didn't want to go back to that school, but you weren't listening to me."

"Well, you might as well get ready, because tomorrow, that's exactly where you're going." His tone was determined, his look stoic.

I puffed out my chest, feeling belligerent. "I said I wasn't going back, and you aren't going to make me."

Before I knew it, Dad had moved closer and grabbed my T-shirt, the swift movement of his hands and fingers startling me. "I've been through this before with you," He tightened his grip. "Now I mean what I say. When I let go of you, I don't want to hear anymore of this bullshit. You hear me?" He kept his hands on my shirt and focused on my face as if he were trying to look through me.

I looked away so he couldn't see the emotions welling up inside me. I was beginning to feel wise, bold, and somewhat fearful, all at the same time. It was the fear of a cornered animal, forced by sheer instinct to respond. My arms moved back, my fists tightened, and my momentum carried them forward. The first blow I landed struck his temple. I didn't wait for his recovery; I immediately threw the next one that connected with his jaw.

His face darkened, his eyes narrowed, and he regained his composure well enough to hit me hard against the face.

I stumbled like a drunk, and the blow filled my mouth with blood. The room spun. He came at me again, but I struck out as best as I could, my fists landing hard against his flesh. I tried my best to make every swing count. The way I figured it, if I could take him out, I'd have nothing to worry about from then on.

I underestimated his power. Like a rookie catcher unaware of the intelligence and will of a veteran pitcher, I miscalculated and took for granted that youth would triumph over age. Wasn't that the way things were?

He struck me hard against the chest, like a boxer practicing his jab. I moved backward until I fell over my suitcase. My head bounced hard against the floor. I was tired, and he looked at me, confused and out of breath. His white shirt was clearly wrinkled; his face was starting to swell from the blows I'd landed.

"As long as you live, don't you ever hit me again," he said. "What's gotten into you?"

Mom moved closer, leaving Melvin near the door. She grabbed Dad's arms so he couldn't deliver another punch. "Take it easy, honey, I don't think he meant it," she said. This time, Mom was playing the role of a nonviolent peacemaker. How ironic.

"I'm not going to take this shit from this musty boy. I raised him," he said, moving toward me again. My defiance was making him angrier, perhaps creating the same tension that his own father had felt when Dad had made his decision to break the farming tradition and move to California. I'd stepped out of the box, and he'd done the same: his responses were generally tamed, intellectual, and preachy. History was repeating itself.

I stood up again and clenched my fists. He moved closer. My chest, now filled again with air, poked out, as if I'd successfully challenged a bully. Over his shoulder, I spotted Melvin mouthing the words, "I'm sorry, I didn't know." I knew he'd tell me later that he hadn't anticipated things getting this out of hand; but by then, it would be too late.

"Make sure you get your ass ready for that school," Dad said, punctuating his words with a finger jabbed at me. "You've got a day left here before you have to get back on that plane. If you aren't here when it's time to go, God help you. I set the rules in this house, and when you won't obey them, it's time for you to go."

The lecture was familiar, but somehow there was more meaning in it now. I didn't want to go back to Chadwick, but the alternative, I was sure, was that I'd be kicked out of my own house. If for some reason I wasn't kicked out, I knew that life here wouldn't be simple.

Tee had told me that I needed to be creative, and now my mind was racing. I didn't want to go back, but I had a solution. Since my folks wouldn't let me abandon my commitment, I'd deliberately sabotage my academic performance, making it even worse than it had already been. I vowed to barely study, defy authority, and bend the rules until the school officials asked me to leave. I'd end my career at Chadwick in shame, just like E. At least he was free of all the false expectations now. But he was wealthy, and his expectations had been different.

It was a weird pact I was making with myself, but I wasn't scared. When my parents had finally figured it out, they would swear I wasn't reaching my potential, and my teachers, without asking any more questions, would conclude that I never had any.

My return was ripe with possibilities.

THE RETURN

Thanksgiving vacation had lasted five days, but with all that had gone on, I had nearly lost track of the time. I tried my best to make my stay last longer. After saying good-bye to Tee, I had arrived late for the ride to the airport, but Dad, though angry, looked relieved that I'd finally made it. His threat had paid off.

Returning to Chadwick, the clang of the church bell and my hard dormitory bed were both waiting for me, the mattress feeling like endearing particleboard. To take my mind off things, I collapsed, thinking about the upcoming basketball game against Proctor. When I woke up, my vision was blurred, smoky, dark green.

I got out of bed and headed toward the sink to wash my face. My feet felt cold against the smooth concrete floor. Water. I turned on the cold, and then the hot. I couldn't wait for the warm water to feel comfortable against my skin. I cupped a small lukewarm puddle with my hands, leaned forward, and threw what remained on my eyes. I was fully awake now, but the images still lingered. I wanted to attach some significance to them, but I knew at that moment, it was best to wait. I had a feeling that if I didn't rush things, my answer would come soon.

After a few minutes of simply standing in front of the sink, I had it figured out. The basketball game against Proctor was making me uneasy and anxious. Big games got me pumped up, and I was freaking out.

I threw on my clothes and headed to the dining room to meet Richard, who'd pulled his lanky frame out of bed at the sound of the alarm and gotten dressed while I was having nightmares. He sat at the "black table," the place in the dining room where we discussed things we didn't want the white students to hear. Richard said he hated that designation, but he sat there nevertheless.

"Sitting at the black table this time?" I asked. "Something must really be bothering you, my friend." I set down my tray of pancakes and warm syrup and, like a nurse, felt his forehead. I hated the dinner food, but breakfast at Chadwick wasn't bad.

"So how was your vacation?" I asked between bites of my pancakes.

"It wasn't as fun as I wanted it to be," Richard said. "My grandfather got sick, and I had to spend a lot of time at the hospital. He's better now, but for a while, we were all worried. I hope your vacation was better than mine." He turned his head to avoid my gaze, and then touched the top of his 'fro to make sure it was still in place.

I'd heard about his grandfather; Richard had written about him in his admission essay. His biological father had been a chain-smoker who had died of cancer, and his grandfather had raised him.

I didn't want to continue on a low note, but I decided to say what was on my mind. "Well, I got in trouble for running away."

"Running away?" Richard looked confused. "Why would you do something like that?"

"I was trying to make a statement about this place." The way I said it made me sound as if I were proud of what I'd done, but I had mixed emotions. I could have told him that I'd learned to shoot dice for the first time, but I knew he wasn't going to be interested since he wasn't a gambler. I focused on what had happened after the crap game, saving the vague comments about having a really good time for a white boy.

"You know, you've been acting kind of strange for a while now. I know you're having a hard time adjusting to this place, but you ought to take my lead. Chadwick isn't as bad as you try to make it out to be." He shook his head, his upper lip curled up like he smelled something bad. "Isaiah, you're being too radical and confrontational, and the people here aren't ready for it. Didn't I tell you that you were wasting your time reading *Invisible Man*?"

"Yeah, I know." I said, trying to placate him a little.

Richard had been right about *Invisible Man,* but at other times, he just appeared as though he was scared of defending black people too strongly because he feared losing favor with some of the teachers, like Hagman. If that happened, he'd harm his chances of graduating from Chadwick in good standing. On the other hand, I thought I that if I kept pushing hard enough, I could change the school—and the way the students and the teachers thought about black people.

"But while I was at home, I got to thinking about Hagman, all these stupid white boys, and the fact that Chadwick has a lousy basketball team,"

I said. "You know, my buddy told me that if I came back home and joined the hoops team, Mack might win the championship. He also said I could help him raise money for the Panthers. It kind of got me to thinking along those lines. That's why I know this isn't the place for me." I sighed. "Look, Richard, from now on, I'm not going to be working too hard academically. If my parents are going to force me to come back here, it doesn't mean I have to work hard." To his confused expression, I said, "Yeah, I'm going on strike." I folded my arms tightly against my chest and then unfolded them to deliver a power salute to show my resolve.

"I don't know what to tell you," said Richard, pointing at me with his long fingers. "I think you're making another mistake. The white people here want you to fail. Can't you see that?" I could see the muscles in his face and neck become tense as he tried to drive home his point. Sometimes, it didn't take much to get him all riled up.

"Not really. They don't control everything I do. If I do fail, so what? Either way it goes, they're not going to know what to do about it." I finished my pancakes, scraping up the extra syrup with my fork. "Anyway, I just wanted to let you know what I was thinking about, just in case you notice something different about me or you get some strange questions from the faculty. You know how they try to get all into your business. "I can hear them now—'Do you have any idea what's wrong with Isaiah? He's been acting a little strange lately.' Yeah, when you hear that, I want you to think about what I just told you. I'm looking for a way out of here, and as Malcolm X would say, I'll get out 'by any means necessary.'"

* * *

Coach Wilkerson called the play for me. "Give it to Isaiah," were his last words before we left the huddle. Taking the inbounds pass from Frank, I dribbled calmly past half court between a slew of defenders toward the rim. Ten seconds left. Nine, eight, seven, six …

Picking up my dribble, I soared toward the basket. My slim body, drenched with sweat, inched higher and higher above the shiny gym floor until my fingertips, cupping the ball, were near the rim. I could have dunked it, but I dropped it through the opening without rifling the net, just before the buzzer sounded.

The roar of the home crowd and my teammates liberated me from my gloom. No one had expected us to win, but I'd been quietly confident. My bad dream had ended. Playing basketball was the only thing I liked about Chadwick, and I gave it everything I had.

"Isaiah?" I could hear the hoarse, high-pitched tone of Proctor's head coach calling my name as I headed toward the locker room. I turned at the sound of his voice and watched him walk quickly toward me, his cuffed golf pants bouncing with each swift step. Why was a basketball coach wearing golf pants? "Isaiah, I just wanted to congratulate you on playing such an excellent game."

"Thank you," I said nonchalantly. He was generous with his adulation, but I was leery of excessive praise.

He reached for my hand, and I could feel electricity as he shook it hard, and then he glanced at my coach, who was standing next to me now. I pulled away quickly.

The coach from Proctor nodded at Coach Wilkerson, saying, "Bill, where'd you get this guy?"

I watched him point at me, and I felt a little embarrassed for having played such a good game. I hated being the center of attention. I wanted my talent to speak for itself, and then I preferred to recede into the background.

Coach Wilkerson started laughing, a fake sound that let people know he didn't want to surrender any information. It was like he was protecting me. "He came from Oakland."

"What year is he?" The other coach was persistent. "Freshman? Sophomore?"

"Sophomore," replied Coach Wilkerson.

"Wow," he said. "Is he gonna be a player, or what? I mean, he already is, but he's gonna be fantastic next year and the year after that."

I couldn't tell whether the opposing coach was giving Coach Wilkerson a line or what. I paid more attention to him. His thin nose and crooked teeth made a lasting impression.

"You're right; he's going to be good," Coach Wilkerson said, "but he's got to improve his academics."

Coach Wilkerson had managed to slip in a remark about my classroom work. I wondered why—what was he trying to accomplish?

"He'll get it together," said the opposing coach. "I can tell just by looking at him." He winked at me.

How he could look at me and tell I was anything other than a good basketball player was a mystery to me. If he thought I was going to "get it together," he knew more than I did. I was ready to head back to the locker room, celebrate our victory, and end this madness, but his attentiveness and perceptiveness was distracting. I had played plenty of basketball games up to that point, but no one like this guy had ever sought me out. I wasn't sure how to take him.

"It was nice meeting you, Coach—what's your name?"

"Goodham—Ernest Goodham to you, Isaiah. You keep up the good work. Next game, we're going to have an answer for you."

"Okay, Coach," I said on my way to the locker room. I still didn't know what to make of this guy; he'd caught me by surprise, and I wasn't sure what to make of his questioning.

Frank, our center, greeted me as I entered the locker room. "We did it, didn't we?" He grabbed my shoulders and pulled me close. Our bodies and our uniforms were still wet.

"Yeah," I said, preoccupied, still thinking about Coach Goodham.

Sounding like he'd noticed the coldness of my response, he said, "Where've you been?"

"I was being introduced to Coach Goodham from the other team."

"Why were you meeting him?" Frank frowned. "What'd he have to say?"

I shrugged. "He just wanted to congratulate us on the win. He told me I played a good game."

"Was he surprised?"

"A little," I said, wondering why Frank seemed to know more than I did.

He laughed. "Well, we kicked their asses, and he probably wants you on his team now."

"I hadn't thought about that." The coach's odd behavior was starting to make a little more sense.

"Well, I did," said Frank. "Goodham is slick. He recruits good athletes, so you better watch out. He may try to snag you, and we need you here."

"Man, I'm not going anywhere," I joked. "I was just being polite."

"Good. I didn't want you getting any ideas. I've been here three years, and Mr. Hunter, the equipment manager, told me Goodham once recruited a junior high school basketball player from Hawaii to go to Proctor. The boy moved all the way from Hawaii to the Monterey Peninsula. Can you believe it? Goodham wants to win badly, and he'll do anything. He's definitely not your typical prep-school coach. How does someone from Hawaii end up at the Proctor School, anyway?"

"I don't know," I said. "This is the first time I've heard of something like this. I've always thought private schools like Chadwick care only about academics." I thought back to the boot camp. Davidson, the program director, had told us that academics were most important, but the reality of my interaction with Coach Goodham had changed things.

I thought a little more about Proctor and Coach Goodham. What he did to get that ball player may have been a little over the top, but just like the fight I had with my father, you do what you have to do sometimes, no matter how it looks.

"It's recruiting, plain and simple, Isaiah," Frank said. "And it's not fair. I don't want you to end up at Proctor."

The thought of bolting there crossed my mind. It was far-fetched, but not impossible. I thought of what it would feel like to announce that I was leaving Chadwick to go to Proctor and thanking Goodham for showing some faith in me. Goodham was looking more and more like a pretty smart man in my book, but I didn't want to get into any more debates with Frank about it. We'd won a game that we weren't supposed to win, and for now it made more sense to enjoy the victory.

"You're right," I said. "That man's somebody you can't totally trust. But let's just forget about that now. Who do we play next?"

THE ANNOUNCEMENT

"Don't touch that!" I hollered.

Chucky's meaty fingers neared the last piece of fried chicken. I could see the hunger and desire in his sky blue eyes the moment I'd carried the serving tray full of steaming hot chicken, mashed potatoes, and buttered sweet peas from the kitchen's swinging doors. His eyes had followed the platter until it rested safely on the table. Chucky, his jaws full and round, seemed to eat more than everyone.

My mouth watered for that last piece. The shout seemed to embarrass Chucky, no small feat, and his hand inched more slowly toward his target. It was the sophomore class's turn to serve the food, and I'd been looking forward to eating that last piece of chicken as payment for services rendered. If there was a school job that I hated, it was waiting tables. I couldn't wait for the day when I'd become an upperclassman. Their lives seemed hassle free.

Howard Twybell, the faculty member assigned to our table, never said a word. Chucky's parents were big contributors. They'd given a few hundred thousand to build the science center, and whenever they arrived on the campus, Rolls Royce and all, the faculty catered to them as if they were royalty.

Twybell's reaction wasn't all that surprising. His kids were faculty brats who ran around campus, making bold comments and tearing up things. He never corrected them. "You've got an overbite," little Ronnie Twybell had told me one day before dinner, after closely observing my skin and then my smile. He had stared at me the way kids looked at animals in a zoo. Where I came from, little white kids were seen and not heard. Of course I told his dad, but nothing ever became of the incident. After that, I never wasted another breath on them.

Correcting a fellow classmate for bad table manners was something I expected from a faculty member. Twybell's slow reaction only reinforced my opinion that the school catered to the rich, and that my feelings mattered only when it was of no consequence to anyone white or wealthy. It was a small incident, yet everything that happened was an example of what was occurring on a much larger scale. I was there physically, but like the book I'd read about the invisible man, I sometimes felt like a figment of everyone's imagination.

Chucky grabbed the chicken, and now everyone was watching him move the golden brown drumstick from the tray and place it on his plate. He didn't look up or around the table at any of us, probably because he knew he was out of line. As he ate, the crumbs fell onto his plate like ripe fruit from a tree. Mashing his fork against its smooth surface, he picked up the tiny morsels and stuffed everything inside his mouth. With Chucky, food was never wasted.

"Asshole," I said under my breath so only Chucky could hear me, and then I thought about ways of paying him back. I could short-sheet his bed, pop him with a wet towel in the shower, or pull his chair right out from under him. I was so mad I couldn't think straight. His soda glass sat near my elbow, and I pushed it so that the contents emptied onto Chucky's carefully creased slacks.

His gray pants, filled with ice cubes near the crotch, looked as though he'd peed in them.

He stopped eating and sucked in air with his mouth wide open. The chewed food inside his mouth looked gross. I knew how he felt because I'd knocked a water glass in my own lap once. He'd started to point his finger at me, but was interrupted by Twybell.

"Chucky, you can excuse yourself." Twybell grabbed at the lapels of his tweed jacket and waited for him to move.

With a mild protest, Chucky pushed back his chair, put his palms against the end of the table, and stood, shooting dirty looks at me.

I was glad, but surprised, that Twybell had given him what he deserved.

"Gentlemen," said Twybell, dabbing at the corners of his lips with a white cloth napkin. He waited until Chucky had left the dining hall. "Now that that's over, I've been told to make an announcement." The dining hall grew silent

Ignoring him, I grabbed my knife and fork and began awkwardly cutting through the chicken on my plate. I pushed my elbows out wide and moved the knife back and forth in a sawing motion until a bite-size piece fell from the bones. I quickly stabbed it with my fork and shoved it inside my mouth, savoring the taste, waiting for Twybell to continue.

"I know you've been hearing rumors, but I'd like to formally announce that in a few weeks, we're going to have a student exchange program with Yarborough, an all-girls school in San Diego. Mr. Breedlove will tell everyone in a more formal announcement at tomorrow's morning assembly, but I just thought I'd give you a sneak preview tonight.

I'd been so out of it that I hadn't heard the rumors. I looked around the table at the others, wondering how much they knew, and then remembered the color-coded charts I'd spotted in Breedlove's office before the break. I wondered if that had anything to do with this sudden announcement.

Still, I couldn't believe my ears. Yarborough! Yarborough! He couldn't be serious. I let the news sink in and then asked him the school's name again to make sure I'd heard him correctly. I thought I might be hearing things— having an exchange program with Jenaye's school was almost too good to be true.

"Could you repeat the name of the school?" I said.

"Yarborough Academy," he repeated, saying the words slowly, pronouncing every syllable.

I tried to contain my excitement, but as soon as he confirmed the name of the school, I threw up my hands toward the ceiling, joining in with the other boys in a shout of joy.

"Okay. Okay," said Twybell. He put up his hand to prevent the excitement from getting out of control. "Like I said, the faculty has been talking about a program like this for a few years, and now we've agreed to go ahead with the plan. Chadwick has had a long history of all-male education, but now we're going to experiment with coeducation. If all goes well, we may be adding girls to our school permanently." Twybell measured his words carefully, like the fifteen-year Chadwick veteran he was. His voice contained sadness for the way things were changing. His tone made me wonder if my presence at the school or the admitting of black students to the campus had in any way been announced like this. "We've decided on admitting at least twenty-five girls. Of course, they'll be living on campus."

I thought of what it would mean if the exchange program included Jenaye. The announcement had caught me off guard, especially coming on the heels of my fight with Dad and my decision to perform at less than my best academically. Twybell's announcement made leaving Chadwick less urgent. Maybe, with the girls attending, Chadwick wasn't going to be such a bad place after all.

"While the girls are here, we'll be sending a group of Chadwick boys to Yarborough. They'll get to see what it's like to go to school with mostly girls.

We think this'll be a good experience for everyone." He waited again before talking. "You boys are excited about this?"

"Yeah," I said, not waiting for the others at the table to respond. "Who's been selected to go?"

"Selected members of the sophomore and junior classes. These students will get a chance to see how things run from the opposite direction." He paused. "If the program works, we'll be sending more students next year."

I wanted to be a part of that initial exchange group, and if I wasn't, I wanted to make sure that Jenaye would be headed to Ojai. For the rest of the dinner, I thought about her. Hearing the news gave me the incentive to write to her again.

When I got back to my room, I penned a quick note telling her how I couldn't wait to see her and dropped it in the mail. Her response was swift.

December 12, 1973

Dear Isaiah:

I've missed you. Where have you been? We started off so well at the orientation program and during your first few days at Chadwick. You were really beginning to tell me about that school. I've been waiting for more. As for me, let's just say it's been really tough here, like I know it's been tough there. Don't ask me how I know. I've been thinking about what Davidson told us at RSP, and it's been all that and more.

When they announced the exchange program here in the morning assembly a few days ago, everyone got so excited that the headmistress couldn't finish her speech. Some of these girls have lived such sheltered lives that the prospect of going to school with boys was simply too much to take. Of course my excitement was for a totally different reason.

I've been selected to come up there next semester for the exchange program. I can't wait to see you. I'm still thinking about that dance and the way you moved with me on the floor. Everything ended so quickly and without a real kiss. Do you think we could change that?

This time I'd like to take things a step further, get to know you better, and see what you're really like. That would be fun.

After hearing about your displeasure in reading "Huck Finn" and after having to read some of the same things here, I'm beginning to see your point. Chadwick and Yarborough need to find more material we can relate to.

We didn't talk much about my family situation when we first met, but I just found out that my older sister, Rhonda, who's a senior in high school, just had her baby. I never got along with the father, and I don't see how she does it either. I'm glad I wasn't there, because my mom said that the baby was delivered in the car on the way to the hospital. She said blood squirted everywhere and that Rhonda yelled and screamed the whole way. You know how I feel about the sight of blood.

You think basketball is a release for you, but for me this school is the perfect place to escape that crazy stuff in my Camden neighborhood and in my family. I never want to go back there to live if I can help it. That's why I work so hard. There's nothing these folks at Yarborough can say or do to me right now that could possibly discourage or make me scared of them.

Although we're only a few hundred miles away, I hear it's warmer up there in Ojai. Is that true? I've never been there. All I know is what you've told me. I'm sure the weather and everything else will be fine once I get there. I've been counting the days ever since I heard the news. It's only a few weeks away.

Peace,
Jenaye

New Tradition

The first dinner bell cut through the early evening's warm air like a cool, slow-moving breeze. There would be two more chimes, both spaced five minutes apart, signaling that it was time for dinner. The first ring on this particular day sounded like any other, yet for me, the chimes really signaled the end of the school's all-male tradition and the beginning of a new one.

The girls from Yarborough had finally arrived. I'd heard the first sounds as I sat at my dorm room desk and thumbed through the letter Jenaye had sent right after the exchange was announced. I folded it and placed it neatly inside the pale green, lightly scented envelope. It was time for me to get ready for dinner. Richard was already dressed.

He wore a tweed blazer with patches at the elbows, a wide tie, white shirt, and penny loafers. He'd clearly abandoned the platform shoes he'd worn at the beginning of the school year and was ready to blend in with all the other kids. The only difference between Richard and some of our classmates now seemed to be his dark skin.

I couldn't figure out what to wear, even though I knew it had to be at least a tie and jacket. I got up from the desk and started pacing back and forth, nearly wearing a hole in the small rug that covered the linoleum floor between our beds.

"What's wrong with you, man?" Richard monitored my every move from in front of the mirror. "You act like you've never seen her before."

"I know. But it's been awhile. I need a Brooks Brothers jacket like the rest of these white boys. I want to make an even better impression this time."

"You'll be all right, man." He pulled at the bottom of his blazer to remove the wrinkles. "I guarantee you she's not half as concerned as you are about this," he said. He buttoned his jacket and headed out the door.

"How do you know?" I yelled back. I wondered how he knew she liked me, and where he'd gotten his information. She'd ignored me the first few days at boot camp. I didn't want that to happen again.

I had to hurry. I stopped pacing and headed to the closet. The second bell rang as I put on my blue jacket and the same clip-on tie I'd worn in the meeting with my parents and Breedlove. The outfit was good luck and had given me good fortune for the extra credit work. I wasn't superstitious, but I wasn't about to leave anything to chance, either. I straightened the tie one last time and headed toward the dining room.

I took long strides, rubbing my hands together, as if they were cold, to release the tension. I inhaled deeply, taking in the mountain air that sometimes left me panting. I wondered how much she'd changed and stepped up the pace. The wood planks next to the school's dining hall creaked as I stepped across them. I counted the spaces in between them. The letter she had written about us getting together was fresh on my mind, along with the tingling sensation she'd left me with after our first dance. By the third bell, I had zipped past the flagpole near the mailroom and was in front of the dining hall, looking right into her eyes.

There had been changes. The long black hair that had initially caught my eye was woven neatly into braids and pulled back in a ponytail, accenting her copper-colored forehead. A starched, white, long-sleeved blouse hung loosely over her breasts. I noticed they had become larger since our first encounter.

Some things about her were the same. She still wore those same silver bracelets around her wrists, and the sight of them made me recall the clinking sound they made the first time I'd grabbed her hand to dance. Dangling earrings gave her an added flair, a halo that set her apart from the white girls nearby who dressed as if wearing jewelry and bold colors was a sin. Like my mom and sister, she seemed to pay a lot of attention to what she wore.

"Isaiah?" Her smile met mine. Her new braces did nothing to diminish her charm. She interrupted her conversation with a classmate and focused on me. "It's been awhile. It's good to see you." Her high-pitched voice made me forget about looking at the round-faced woman she spoke to. I inched closer to embrace her. I held her, savoring the touch of her firm back and fragrant body. She released herself from my arms and stepped back. "You got taller. I think you stretched out more since the last time we saw each other. And look at that peach fuzz under your chin!"

"I guess so," I said, touching my chin and grabbing at the curly hairs that had started to sprout. I stroked them and then moved my hands away quickly, hoping my movements hadn't attracted the attention of any of the nearby faculty members. Chadwick males were supposed to be clean-shaven, and I'd clearly defied the rules to make myself look cool. I knew it was only a matter of time before a faculty member noticed and made me shave it off, but I'd wait until that time came.

"Let me introduce you to Becca," Jenaye said.

"Hi, Becca," I said. I recalled Jenaye's first letter telling me about her roommate. She wore a long white dress with spaghetti straps that accentuated her broad shoulders and a thin, gold necklace with a small pendant. "It's nice to meet you."

Becca flashed a smile without showing her teeth and barely grabbed my hand. "Are you an RSP student, too?"

Before answering, I looked at the part in her hair that started above her forehead and at the hairpin holding her long hair in place. She sounded as if she were determining my place in the school's pecking order. I wanted to say that my family was extremely wealthy, but I knew that answer would elicit even more questions.

"We met last summer," I finally answered, unwilling to offer any additional information, and returned my attention to Jenaye, whose face now held a playful pout.

"We're pen pals," Jenaye said to Becca. "But I'm not going to talk about the fact that he hasn't written me nearly enough." She looked at me. "You got all my letters, didn't you?"

"I got the ones that mattered," I said, trying not to say much while Becca was still close. I looked at Becca's puffy cheeks and then at the ground, noticing the cracks in the concrete, the small pebbles, and the broken leaves underneath my dress shoes. Deep inside, I was hoping that after the introduction, Becca would walk away to talk to the other students on the platform.

"Can we talk after dinner?" I said, pointing at my ears to let her know that I didn't want to shout over the conversations surrounding us.

"Yeah," she answered, smiling.

The crowd of students and faculty began moving toward the dining room doors that had been opened by the kitchen help. "Did you look to see what table you're sitting at?" I asked, hoping she was sitting near me.

"Come on, you two," Frank was yelling at us. "I don't know about you, but I'm hungry. Move along!"

"Where are the table assignments?" asked Jenaye.

"They're usually posted on the window near the entrance." I walked ahead of her and pointed to the list of names and table numbers on the dining room window, and then I grabbed her arm and pulled her so she could get a better look. "There it is." It wasn't necessary that I do this, but I just wanted to touch her again. "You're sitting at Mr. McDougall's table." I gazed at the red lipstick painted on her shapely lips and imagined kissing them.

"Is that good or bad?"

"You'll like him. He keeps the table conversations lively because he's not always serious like most of the teachers around here."

"And where are you sitting?"

"I'm at table three, with Mr. Saluto. He's taught Spanish here for years. All he talks about is chess. The last time I sat at this table, I thought my Spanish was going to improve, but I ended up learning more about good chess moves. But you took French, didn't you?"

"You remembered!"

"Of course I did," I replied. "Don't go anywhere when you finish eating. Just wait for me near the kiosk."

"Okay." She squeezed my hand and went into the dining hall.

At dinner, everyone talked about the Yarborough girls. I could barely eat as I thought of catching up. Visiting Jenaye's room and studying sounded good, but it was against school policy to be inside the girls' dorm. I tried to come up with something else, but I drew a blank.

If only we could have sat together, but that was nearly impossible, too. School officials tried hard, through strict seating assignments, to keep black students separated from one another, making sure the room looked integrated, I guess. After being at Chadwick for six months, I had never sat with Richard once at dinnertime. We were there, faculty members said, to make sure the white students got a taste of black America. Sitting together would have been tantamount to segregation and would have cheated the white people out of a chance to get to know us.

Knowing all that, I skipped dessert, hoping the time would pass more quickly.

*   *   *

"That's where we put all the important stuff."

After dinner, Jenaye was standing on the platform outside the dining hall, scanning all the announcements stapled to the kiosk. She pretended not to notice me, placing her palm against a memo.

"Don't interrupt me. I'm reading the schedule. It's time for homework now, right? We had study hall after dinner at Yarborough, too." She held her hands behind her back and turned to give me a big smile. Her cheeks were round and her dimples smooth and deep, like tiny measuring spoons.

Turning away again, she traced the printout on the bulletin board with her fingers while I admired her skin.

"Are you going back to the dorm?" I asked. I didn't wait for a response, but moved closer. "I'll walk back with you, all right?" The tie that I'd worn to dinner was starting to feel uncomfortable around my neck. I pulled it off and opened my collar.

"Sure." When she finally turned around and looked at me, her brown eyes were focused on my jacket and my open collar. "You've got the right idea," she said looking at the tie that I held in my hand. "I've got to change out of these clothes."

"You wanna study together?" I asked.

"We'll see," she said leading the way to the upper school dorm. "Let's go."

"Did you know that you're staying where the boys who left for Yarborough stayed? I know the place backward and forward. It's a nice dorm." We walked slowly up a narrow path leading to the edge of the campus. The walk was the perfect distance for talking and catching up. "So, has it been what you've expected so far?"

"Chadwick?"

"Yeah."

"Well, I didn't expect so many of these things," she said, waving off a fruit fly. "I was hoping I'd see some movie stars or famous people, but that hasn't happened. I didn't get to see much of anything on my way up here except the freeway."

I smiled. "Don't worry, you'll eventually run into someone famous." By coincidence, we were passing the entrance to the empty amphitheater, and I thought about the student actors who were part of the school's drama team, about their hopes of one day attaining fame and fortune. Jenaye, with her good looks, could have been an actress, but she seemed too starstruck to put in the necessary work.

"Like who? You're not talking about those people in the pictures on the dining room wall, are you?" She motioned toward the building behind us.

"That's a start. Did you see the one of Howard Hughes?"

"No." She had a cute way of furrowing her brow when she didn't know something.

"Well, he was a student here awhile back, and now Hugh Webb goes here," I said.

"Who's that?" Her brow furrowed again.

"You know Jack Webb from Dragnet?" At her nod, I continued. "Hugh Webb is his son—he's a weird dude, too. His roommate says he sleeps in the nude."

She made a face. "That's nasty."

"I'm just telling you what he said," I said, shrugging. "Anyway, his dad drives a Rolls Royce. You should have seen it on parents' weekend. He parked it over there." I pointed to the parking space near the alumni office, signaling that we were getting close to our destination. "I couldn't take my eyes off that car. It was better than the one my history teacher has."

"I can't wait to see it," she said. "On my way up here, I prayed that I'd run into the Jackson 5. The bus bringing us here passed right through Encino. That's where they live, all of them."

"How'd you know that?" She sure knew a lot about famous people.

"*Ebony* did a story on their mansion. Wanna see?" She reached inside her purse and pulled out a torn magazine page with a picture of the Jackson 5 posing in front of a huge house. I glanced at the picture and rolled my eyes. I was practically in love with Jenaye, but her obsession with the Jacksons— and any type of celebrity—was getting annoying. She wasn't likely to see too many famous people in Ojai, but I didn't have the heart to tell her just yet.

"I didn't know you were still into them," I said, handing the picture back to her.

"Into them? That's an understatement! I *love* the Jackson 5." She held the picture to her chest, affecting a dreamy look.

"Maybe you'll get lucky again," I said, recalling the story she'd told in the RSP orientation meeting about winning a contest through *Right On!* magazine to see the Jackson 5. *Maybe I'll get lucky, too,* I thought, hoping her dream of seeing the Jacksons again would fade and be replaced by a desire to kiss me. I changed the subject. "Speaking of getting lucky, how did your campaign for student government go? Did you win?"

"I postponed my candidacy for now. I've got enough think about with this exchange program. Representing the student body is a big thing. I don't know much about Chadwick, but at Yarborough, the girls are always trying to outdo each other."

"So, you're going to run next year?" I raised my eyebrows at her.

"Definitely! I'm trying to be the first one in my family to go to college, and the best way to make sure that happens is to pile up as many extracurricular activities as I can so the schools I'm applying to will think they're getting a model citizen. You know what I mean, a person standing for the right things."

"Oh," I said. This was all news to me.

"What about you?" she asked.

"I'm trying to go to college, too," I said, trying to sound like I knew what I was talking about. "I'm not thinking about running for school office, though. It's a waste of time. I'm too militant, and Chadwick isn't going to change. I'm going to be a great basketball player instead. I'll make it there on my basketball ability. Once the college scouts see me …" I jumped in the air and pretended to take a jump shot.

She laughed. "That's one thing that hasn't changed about you, Isaiah. You've still got your basketball dream."

It was good to finally have a black girl to talk to. With Jenaye, there was a little less explaining to do. We could speak or not speak and sometimes know exactly what the other was thinking about music, slang, careers, or whatever.

"What's wrong with that? You've got your dreams, and I've got mine." I watched her roll her eyes. "Look, let's not talk about the future, okay? Let's talk about something more interesting." I stopped in front of her, bringing her up short. The dorm was in clear view now. "Did you miss me?"

She blushed.

"After that dance … ," I looked into her eyes, "I know I thought about you." We'd been brought together as black students at predominantly white schools to correct the ills of the past, and in spite of our differences, the exchange program was a chance to solidify our bond—at least that was the way I was looking at the situation. Seeing another black person who was going through the same things helped me to make it through the long days. For a moment I even forgot about my vow to perform at less than my best.

"Wouldn't you like to know?" She stepped around me and walked a little faster, still blushing.

"Stop playing," I said, moving faster to catch up with her. "So how do you feel now that you're able to see me again?" I put my hand on her arm.

"It feels good." She shrugged off my hand, staring straight ahead.

"Good enough to kiss me?" I stuttered.

I'd crossed an invisible boundary. "Isaiah," she said, looking down, "I don't think we should be talking like this. We could get in trouble."

"I'm not worried about getting into any trouble," I said quickly, hoping I hadn't messed things up too quickly.

"Well, let's just continue walking and talking." She glanced over her shoulder. "Besides, someone's coming. Can we change the subject?"

I looked behind me and spotted Frank about a hundred feet back. Was he following us?

"Sure," I said. "Let's talk about the Hello Dance that's coming up. I hope you haven't forgotten how to slow dance."

"Oh, I haven't forgotten anything," she said, her voice light and flirtatious. "I've been working on some new moves, though. I know the music won't be the same as it was in boot camp, but we'll manage."

"Probably." I looked behind us, checking for Frank, and saw that he'd been heading for the library, after all. I wanted to shift back to the kissing conversation, but that discussion was long gone. I guess I'd bring it up again later on.

*   *   *

The Hello Dance took place the first weekend of the exchange and was run just like the others, except that there were fewer girls arriving from off campus. At the last dance, I'd spent much of my time holding up the wall until I'd seen Dofi, but those days were over. Jenaye's presence meant I wouldn't have to look hard for a dance partner.

While the band played, *Do a little dance, make a little love / Get down tonight, get down tonight,* Jenaye, who watched *Soul Train* religiously, showed me the pop lock and the robot in a secluded corner of the room. When they played a slow record, we danced real close, like I'd done at boot camp, moving with her without thinking about what I was doing. Oblivious to all the other girls there, I danced with her until I saw Dofi's face clear across the room. She was looking in our direction, and she wasn't smiling.

Clad in a kente cloth gown, dangling earrings, and a wooden necklace, Dofi stood there in disbelief. Not knowing what to do, I held onto Jenaye for dear life. "Aren't you going to put some space in between that dance?" She put her hands on her hips and waited.

Stunned by her appearance, I was speechless. How had she found me? Did she know I'd be getting dancing lessons from another girl? I had some explaining to do. How would I explain Jenaye to Dofi and vice versa? I'd had my chance to tell Dofi about Jenaye the moment I'd heard about the exchange program, and I could have written Jenaye to tell her about meeting Dofi at the school's first dance, but I'd kept the news to myself, thinking this situation would never happen.

Jenaye stopped dancing with me and disappeared into the crowd without looking back.

"She was just showing me some dance moves," I said, giving Dofi what I hoped was an endearing look.

"It looked like more than that," Dofi said, rolling her eyes. "Why weren't you on the dance floor with everyone else, and not in this corner?" She pointed down at the floor and waited for a different explanation from me, but never having been in that situation before, I was still speechless. "That's the last time I'll lend my input to you for any sort of extra credit project you're engaged in. I hope she's a good student like me. You can resume your dancing lessons, too, I'll find someone else." She stormed away, flicking the end of her kente cloth gown over her shoulder at me.

As the music continued to play, I stood alone in a corner of the dance hall, sulking at the outcome of an event that had started with so much promise. Jenaye had been the first to walk away, and now I was about to lose Dofi. I wanted them both as friends, but I knew I'd have to choose only one, especially after the way I'd handled things during the dance. I'd learned a little about both of them, but still there was a big difference in how I felt about Jenaye. I knew I'd have to do something to make it up to her. We had a common history as participants in the Rising Stars Program and a relationship that had grown through constant correspondence. I wasn't about to let all of that go so easily. It wasn't that I didn't like Dofi. It was just harder finding common ground, harder getting used to her accent, and harder understanding who and what her African background meant to her. That relationship would take a lot more time to repair.

When the lights came back on, signaling that it was time to go back to our rooms, I replayed a spirited rendition of the slow song the band played in my head, over and over, and waited for Richard. He'd know—or at least have an opinion on—what my next step should be.

Richard was wearing a white turtleneck and the tweed blazer he wore frequently to dinner. He wasn't smiling, which meant he hadn't met a new girl. His response to happiness was a serious face that hid his jumping-around emotions.

"What'd you think of the dance?" I said, straightening my high-boy collar and tugging at the waist of my bell-bottoms.

"It was all right. I mean, the band played K. C. & the Sunshine Band music all night. I wish they knew more songs, but they were pretty good." He laughed, doing a quick bit of footwork. "I can't wait for the next dance."

"Why?" I was puzzled by his sudden transformation from stoic to happy.

"At the next dance, maybe I'll get a chance to dance with Jenaye a little more." He winked, placing the palm of his hand against the lapel of his jacket, near his heart. "I saw you two in the corner, and so did everyone else. You guys looked pretty into each other … and then I saw her again right before the lights came on. She looked upset. What happened?"

I shoved my hands in my pockets and started walking next to him back to the dormitory. "We were trying to catch up." I cleared my throat, feeling embarrassed. "But Dofi was there, too."

"Oh, no!" He put his palm flat against his forehead to acknowledge his disbelief. "Was there a fight?"

"Nah." I let him know all the details, hoping to garner some sympathy, but he still didn't believe me. He wanted to believe there was a fight.

"I could have told you that would happen. You and Jenaye were spending a lot of time together. It hasn't been a month, and I hardly ever see you. Now it looks like you've blown it with both of them. So what's your plan now?" He kept a smirk on his face, looking certain I'd never revive either relationship.

"The first thing I'm going to do tonight is to see if I can make it up to Jenaye. I've got to apologize for what happened. Anything wrong with that?" Determined to remove that skeptical expression from his face, I considered visiting Jenaye's room before bed check to set the record straight.

"I hate to burst your bubble, but these girls will get you into trouble. I mean, look at it like this: we've already got a whole new set of rules. Did you see the list on the kiosk?"

"Look who's talking! Since you were looking, what time do they turn off the lights on weekends now? Did that change?"

"It's one of the first things I checked," answered Richard. "And it's still midnight."

"What time is it now?"

Richard looked at his watch. "It's past midnight," he said.

"Let's go by the girls' dorm," I suggested. "I've got to talk to Jenaye again before we have to go to bed."

"What about Dofi?"

"I'll talk to her later," I said. "So, are you going?"

Richard veered off the smooth gravel path and onto the grass like I'd pushed him. He shook his head back and forth. "Not me. I heard that if you get caught inside their dorm, you'll get expelled, and I'm not gonna take that chance. Suit yourself. The faculty will be watching that dorm like hawks, especially now. These girls haven't even been here a month." He let me walk slightly ahead of him.

"You're right, but I bet I could get in there with no problem," I mused.

"Didn't you already get caught for smoking weed?" He folded his arms and waited for my answer.

"Yeah, but that was different."

He put his palms against his forehead and moved his head back and forth like he couldn't believe we were having this discussion. When he was finished, he kept walking toward the dormitory ahead of me, except now I didn't feel like going inside. My adrenaline was still pumping from the dance, and I had something in mind. I turned and ran back in the direction of the auditorium.

"Where are you going?" Richard called after me. "Bed check is coming up!"

"I forgot something," I called over my shoulder. "I think I left it in the auditorium. If the prefect comes looking for me, tell him I'll be right back."

RENDEZVOUS

I jogged along the winding, moonlit path to the girls' dorm. It was quiet except for the occasional hoo-hooing of owls perched in the pine trees. I thought about Jenaye as my feet hit the densely packed gravel behind the art studio and observatory. I was determined to get back in her good graces, no matter what it cost me.

I gave a wide berth to a cat-faced raccoon stirring in the garbage can, jogging along the path that rose to give me a view of the rolling mountains and then descended past the academic building to give a clear view of the upper school dorm. The arched doorway of the adobe-style building was clearly illuminated by the lanterns placed on either side to ward off intruders like me.

Jenaye had mentioned she lived on the first floor, and as I scanned the windows on the bottom row, I could see that all the lights were out. The dance hadn't been over an hour, and she was already in bed. I wasn't about to let that stop me. She couldn't possibly be asleep.

I looked around for a female prefect or Mr. Warrel, the other prefect on duty, and when I didn't see anyone, I walked around the building to her window, rapped my knuckles against the pane, and waited. I considered Richard's warning and what he would do and say if he knew where I was. I didn't care anymore. When she didn't answer, I tried again.

"Jenaye. Jenaye." I whispered, keeping my tone low. "Open the window. It's me, Isaiah."

After a few minutes, I heard the sound of her house slippers, like sandpaper rubbing against the tile floor. My stomach fluttered as I watched the dingy white curtains move and Jenaye stick her head through the small opening.

"Isaiah? What are you doing out there?" She snapped the latch and pushed the window open. You know you're not supposed to be hanging around our dorm."

"I came to talk about what happened tonight." I said, moving closer to the building. She wore flannel pajamas embroidered with seashells. The front buttons came apart enough for me to see her small cleavage. "Plus, I want you to braid my hair. I didn't tell you how much I liked the way yours looked tonight. And since it looked so good, I want you to do the same to mine." I patted my small, knotty Afro and tried to appear sincere. If Mom or Dad knew what I'd just asked for, they would have killed me. I'd had a hard time convincing them that Afros were in style. Now I was asking for braids. They'd never understand.

"Yeah, right," she said, straightening her night clothes. "Tell the truth."

"Stand back," I said. "It's getting cold out here. If you let me in, I'll let you run your fingers through my hair." I slid my hands across the top of my head and down the back until my hands reached the nape of my neck. My skin felt like cold metal. If I hadn't been in such a hurry, I would have gone inside my room to get something warmer.

"All right," she said, "but don't think I'm going for that lie you just told. You know I can't braid that rough stuff on top of your head. I'm just letting you in because I want you to explain what happened at the dance." She pulled the curtain back so that I could climb through the window and then headed toward the door to turn on the light. I landed feet first on her desk. The brightness hurt my eyes.

"Turn off that light," I said, knocking over an alarm clock and the books and papers on the desk. "And try that one." I pointed to the small lamp that hung over her unmade bed.

She moved from the window to the light switch, grabbed her white terry cloth robe from atop the pink bedspread, and sat down Indian-style on the bed. "Come sit next to me," she said, smoothing out the covers.

I pulled my legs onto the bed and folded them in front of hers. Her perfume smelled like lavender and honeysuckle. I peered over her shoulder to refrain from looking too hard into the brown eyes that had made me forget about everything, and I noticed that her head was framed by a giant collage of Michael Jackson stapled to the mahogany-paneled walls behind her.

"So now that you're here, do you want to finish telling me about that girl who cut in on us?" she said, moving closer. "I was too upset to talk earlier, but I'm all ears now," Her legs were crossed on her lap so that her kneecaps rubbed against my thighs.

"I met her at our first dance, but it's nothing serious." I was talking fast, trying to get it all out, as if my entire future hinged on this conversation. "It's not like us. She didn't have anyone to dance with." I tried putting on my most sincere face, hoping that she'd accept my explanation and cut the inquiry short.

"Well, she didn't sound that way," said Jenaye, leaning back. "It sounded more like you two had talked a lot and had made plans."

"We were gonna talk about an extra credit assignment, but that's all, honest." I turned away to look at her alarm clock, noticing the time. It was way past bed check, and I'd have to hurry my explanation if I wanted to make it back to my room before getting in trouble. "I wish I had more time to really explain what happened."

"I do, too," she said. "You've certainly got a lot of making up to do." She winked.

I tried to relax, racking my brain, thinking of all the things I could do to make up for what had happened at the dance. I was waiting for some type of signal from Jenaye.

"So what are you going to do?" Jenaye moved her head to the side and behaved as if nothing less than a kiss would help ease the tension. Was I off the hook?

"I'm thinking." I reached out my hand and touched her calf. She was trying hard to stay wrapped up, but as she rocked back and forth, her robe came loose, and I felt a sudden sense of fear. I hadn't felt this way since Linda Bowler, a girl from home, had told me she had a crush on me. That was months ago. The feeling wasn't mutual, but the whole incident left me wondering what kissing felt like if you did it with someone you really liked.

"Are you through thinking?" She sounded impatient.

"Not really."

"The boys in Camden are different." She folded her arms in frustration.

"What does that mean?"

"Some of them have tried stuff," she said, shrugging.

"Like what?"

"You know … stuff." She turned her head away and looked down.

"Kissing?" I finally took the hint.

"Maybe," she said. "But, that's a personal question, and my mom said I don't have to answer personal questions." She pulled back again, but her eyes were begging me to at least hold her. "Do you really want to know?"

"Not really," I said, trying to remain calm. I slid my hand down her calf, grabbed her ankles and pulled her legs across my lap.

"Look at you. You really want an answer, don't you?" She took her hands and put them in mine. Like me, she was loosening up.

Our palms were touching, and I couldn't resist the urge to get the kiss that I'd been wanting since we'd met last summer. I began to understand why I liked her so much. She was the first girl who had really listened to me, the first girl I really wanted to get to know. First the Hello Dance, and now our reunion, had stoked a fire that refused to go out. It didn't hurt that we were both black kids tucked away at a practically all-white boarding school, but that was beside the point.

Jenaye must have known we were playing a dangerous game—meaning that I needed to get back to my room before one of the prefects caught us—but I was much too close to my goal to turn back now. I had to seize the moment.

My fingers found the spaces between hers, and I clasped her hands tighter, gently tugging at her arms, moving her forward, until her chest was touching mine. Her face and that smooth brown skin were close, and I closed my eyes and rested my lips against hers. A strong current, like a river, moved through my body.

Her lips felt moist, but not slippery. I pushed my tongue inside her mouth. A breath of surrender escaped her nostrils and landed where my mustache was starting to grow. My tongue explored her mouth, slipped from side to side, carefully avoiding the metal braces.

She was right where I wanted her, and as I used my weight to push her back toward the cover, she pulled me closer. I felt the warmth of her body against mine. The feeling was better than a dream.

Sliding her hands down my body, she loosened my shirt and moved her hands along my bare chest. My heart raced. If things went far enough, making love to Jenaye was going to be my first time.

Her legs, moving as if on hinges, caressed my butt. She moaned softly as if she, too, had been waiting for this moment, when we would finally be together, holding each other with no interruptions.

I was so mesmerized that I barely heard the keys rattle and the door open. At the sound of another woman's voice, I was immediately transported back to reality. We were caught.

"What in God's name is going on? Isaiah? Jenaye?"

I rolled off her and turned to look in the direction of the noise. Jenaye moved as far away from me as she could, closing her robe. Goddamn. It was Mrs. Buellton, the dorm prefect, and Negley again! I tried to close my shirt. I was speechless, embarrassed, and afraid. I felt terrible for Jenaye. She hadn't been here a month, and I'd already gotten her in trouble. Had a few moments in paradise been worth getting caught?

"Did you two know that this visit is against school policy?" Mrs. Buellton folded her thick arms, her jaws set.

"I'm sorry, ma'am," I said, trying to sound as freaked out as I felt. "I was just leaving."

"No, you certainly were not," she responded. "And you, Jenaye? What's your explanation for this situation?"

"I don't have one," she said, her eyes fixed to the floor. "I told him that he wasn't supposed to be here."

"It didn't look like that to me," Negley said, moving from behind Mrs. Buellton. He'd replaced Warrel as the prefect and had busted me again.

"Honest, Mrs. Buellton, I did tell him he wasn't supposed to be in here. He just ignored me."

I was disappointed that she was blaming everything on me, but I understood why. She had to do it. She was intent on making a favorable impression, and I had put her in a bad spot.

"Well, let me tell you that this is not acceptable behavior, especially for you, Mr. Issacson," she said. "You know the rules. This is immediate grounds for expulsion. I suggest you get yourself together and leave right now. Mr. Negley and I will wait here until you do."

I straightened my clothes. I wondered what would happen to us, to me. Negley glared in my direction.

"Are you going to tell the headmaster and my parents about this?" I asked him.

"We'll see," he said ominously.

I didn't know Mrs. Buellton, but I could tell that by his response, Negley was considering something drastic. This wasn't good. I'd already been in trouble, and now I'd gotten someone I cared about in trouble, too. I hoped we weren't both expelled.

CONSEQUENCES

I was hoping I wouldn't end up in the headmaster's office, but I didn't have any such luck. At breakfast the next day, Negley told me to report to Breedlove's office before the morning assembly. I gathered my books and the unfinished homework I had taken with me to the dining hall and headed to the headmaster's office. I greeted Breedlove's aging secretary and was pointed through the lacquered door to his carpeted office.

He was waiting for me this time, intently scribbling notes on yellow lined paper. His mahogany desk revealed a cryptic filing system, with piles of books and stacks of stapled papers sitting strategically nearby. When I entered, he threw down the sleek, silver Cross pen, leaned back in his chair, and grabbed the steaming blue and gold coffee cup sitting on his desk blotter, moving it slowly toward his chapped lips. The cup covered his mouth and nose, but left his piercing blue eyes unobstructed. His stare made me uncomfortable. He seemed to be looking through me, searching for the clues to my actions. He finally took a sip, and the slurp was the only thing I could hear besides the hum of the air conditioner. The steaming java made the cup sweat.

"I thought I'd never see you in here again, Isaacson," Breedlove's voice boomed as he sat upright in the squeaking chair, placed the cup on a square green coaster, and then extended his wrinkled hand in the direction of the smooth, tan leather chair in front of his desk. "Sit down, young man. We've got a lot to talk about. Obviously, you're hard of hearing."

"No," I said, placing my stack of books on his desk and taking my seat. "My hearing works fine." I tugged at my earlobe.

"We've got a real dilemma," he said. "I'm sure you're aware of the school policy about visiting the girls' dorm. Just in case you aren't familiar with this policy, it states that you're never supposed to go inside the girls' dorm. Period."

As he talked, I followed the deep folds imbedded in his forehead, timelines that helped me mark the seconds until it was my turn to respond. "I couldn't help myself, sir. I just thought—"

"That's precisely your problem, Isaiah," Breedlove said, cutting me off. "You don't think."

"I made a mistake," I said, trying to defend myself.

"You've made enough mistakes here already with your erroneous thinking." He folded his arms and rested them against his stomach. His breathing was slow, measured. "We've got to do something about that. The future of this school is riding on this exchange." He unfolded his arms and grabbed the cup again. Fingers firmly around the cup's exterior, he raised it for another taste. "The faculty members and a whole lot of alumni want this experiment to go forward. But I'm not about to let you ruin it or sully Miss Jenaye's reputation, either."

He was on a roll, his words darting out of his mouth and bouncing off my partially ironed gray sweatshirt like a rubber ball against the asphalt. I wondered if what he was telling me was really meant for my ears, or whether he had just gotten caught up in the moment and said too much. I had no need to know about the heartfelt desires of the alumni or the faculty, but at least now I understood why my actions had triggered such an immediate response.

"I've been thinking about this situation since I first heard about it from Negley," Breedlove said. "It took me by surprise because when you came into my office for smoking marijuana last semester and I put you on work crew, I thought you'd begin exercising better judgment." He scratched his head. "You've put me in a bad spot. You understand?"

I nodded. "Yes, sir."

"Things will be a little bit different this time." He cleared his throat and swallowed, his face growing solemn. "I think you're a good kid—or at least have the potential to be one—but ..." He filled his cheeks with air, blowing it out slowly. "As your punishment, I've decided to dismiss you from the basketball team for the rest of the season."

The news hit me in the pit of my stomach, traveling quickly upward to create a painful knot in middle of my throat. We'd made the league playoffs for the first time in school history, and college scouts had become interested, but Breedlove's ruling meant I'd be unable to play. I thought about the damage to my dream of leading Chadwick to a league championship, how the dismissal would affect my chances of one day making it to the NBA. Every game leading up to that glorious day was important. Each time I entered the gym,

I had visualized the winning banner being raised as I received congratulatory remarks from my classmates.

Now I was being kicked off the team. Yes, I could certainly change my behavior enough to stay away from the girls' dorm and keep my nose clean, but I pushed those goals out of my mind, preferring to dwell on how I'd survive on the sidelines.

How would Mom and Dad take the news? This situation was clearly different from the weed-smoking incident. In that case, I'd blamed everything on peer pressure. I could see them getting upset, but in my mind they shared the blame for selecting a boarding school that couldn't contain my sexual urges.

And what about the reaction of my best friend at home? Tee's voice sounded clear in my head as my mind drifted. *See, man, I told you that your parents shouldn't have accepted that scholarship. You're getting screwed. We've got plenty of girls here, plus we could have won the championship with you here at McClymonds. Now, you've gone down to that school and got in trouble. What kinda sense does that make?*

"You have anything you'd like to add to this conversation?" Breedlove saw me struggling, and his voice snapped me out of my reverie.

"Yeah," I said. The more I thought about Breedlove's words, the angrier I became. "Don't you realize what this is going to do to our team?"

"Of course I do. I'm an ex-baseball player, but I never got kicked off the team like you. Your teammates will adjust. You'll see." He turned his chair around and pointed to the awards on the wall behind his head, but I wasn't impressed. I'd noticed them on my last visit. He quickly turned back so he wouldn't lose his place. "You need to learn that you can't keep breaking school rules willy-nilly and not expect to pay the consequences."

"Can we talk about this again?" I towered over the desk and his short frame, trying to intimidate him.

Breedlove pulled the chair closer to his back and braced himself. "Isaiah, your season officially ended today."

NO LONGER NEEDED

The playoff game was almost over. The first half had been a blur. Our green and gold uniforms had merged in my mind with the opposition's red and white, erasing all semblance of order. I sat on the hard bleachers near the rear of the gym between classmates and watched a bald-headed man take notes on a clipboard. Anxiously tugging at the sweatbands I wore in solidarity with my teammates, I cursed Breedlove for making me sit on the sidelines.

"You got busted in the girls' dorm?" "What happened?" "Are you on probation now?" "What about Jenaye?" The questions had come from all angles until I wanted to disappear. I didn't intend to sit through the entire game, but I was curious to see if Breedlove's prediction about the team adjusting to my absence proved true.

A day after Breedlove's decision, I had searched the stands looking for Jenaye, finally noticing the back of her head behind the Chadwick bench. I'd left my classmates and headed down the aisle to take a seat next to her. As I approached, she narrowed her eyes, reluctantly cleared a space for me to sit, and then focused her gaze on the sleeve of her jacket, pulling at the loose strings as if they were more important than speaking to me. Her reaction let me know that I'd screwed up big-time by visiting her room, and there were no kind words waiting for me, only indifference.

"You're freaking out, aren't you?" she finally said, looking first at me, and then at the scoreboard. I didn't know if she was asking me whether I was freaking out about the silent treatment she'd been giving me or about my inability to play the game. I glanced at the score again, tied 48–48 with only five minutes left.

"A little," I said, moving closer to her. I stared at her a moment, smiled, and then looked at the bench of the opposition, a scrappy public school from the city of Moorpark. They'd called a time-out to set up a play, and I watched as their coach drew a diagram on a faded green chalkboard. "If we hold on, we can do it," I said, crossing my fingers and looking back at her.

The tight score drove home the fact that being at a boarding school was only an advantage academically. When it came to sports, the public schools almost always had better players because coaches could choose them from a larger talent pool. Chadwick's talent pool was limited by the small size of the school, the high cost of tuition, and the predominant focus on academic achievement rather than athletics.

"They need you," she said, looking at me and the sweatbands I wore. I pulled at one, letting it snap back against my skin. "And you're obviously ready to play."

I shook my head. It was the first time that I'd sat on the sidelines watching my own team since Dad had taken me out of a Little League game in the middle of an inning for not hustling after a routine fly ball. I'd learned a lesson from that episode, and my inaction right now was killing me.

"I knew that Negley was gonna fink," I replied. "That's all he does—tell on people. He told Breedlove that E was smoking a joint in the forest, and he's been monitoring my every move since I failed that first quiz. Maybe he wanted to expel me along with E after my first mistake, but I wish he'd focus his attention on someone else. I think he just wishes he were the headmaster. He didn't have to get us in trouble. He could have just given us a warning."

The action still hadn't resumed, and a group of cheerleaders from the opposition took the court. Performing a quick routine, they threw their pom-poms in the air. I watched them soar and then glanced back at Jenaye.

She threw her hands up as if she couldn't believe I'd made that statement. "How'd you know it was Negley who told?" she asked. "Mrs. Buellton was there, too, right?"

"It was him, all right. Look at the results. You got probation, and I got kicked off the team. He shouldn't have been patrolling the girls' dorm, anyway."

"You were late for bed check, remember?" She shook her head again, looking upset that her message wasn't getting through.

"Yeah," I said, still thinking about the reason for my visit—making up for what had happened at the dance.

"At least we didn't get kicked out, right?" She sounded relieved.

"You got probation, and I got kicked off the team," I said, lamenting the unequal results.

"Like I said, we're still here." She crossed her arms.

"That's true." I was beginning to see her point, especially since I could have been expelled.

"You ever gonna say you're sorry?" She cut to the chase as if she'd been waiting all game for the opportunity to elicit another apology from me, this time for getting caught in her dormitory room.

"I wasn't trying to get you in trouble." I put my arms around her shoulder.

"But you did."

"Sorry," I said. "I know I messed up, but you don't have to rub it in."

"Is that it?" Her nostrils flared a bit, and she took a deep breath.

"I should have left after I explained what happened at the dance, but once I got started on the other stuff, I couldn't help myself."

"I could tell," she said.

"Don't remind me," I replied.

The Moorpark supporters roared as their team took the court after the time-out. I clapped my hands to try to show my support for Chadwick, but my voice was faint and sad. Another player had replaced me at forward, and he played nervously.

"Look at them," I said, pointing to the ball sailing out of bounds. "They're scared to death. If I could play, this game wouldn't even be close." Watching them made me regret my decision even more. If I'd have straightened out everything with Dofi when I'd found out about the exchange program, I could have avoided my predicament.

"Well, you might as well forget about it, Isaiah. Your playing days are over."

"For the time being," I said, "unless I come up with something to get me back out there." The statement was meant as idle chatter, but deep down I was hoping to find a way to make Breedlove change his mind.

"You're dreaming."

I turned my head to look at her sideways. "There's nothing wrong with that." Jenaye was always trying to keep me grounded.

"Just save your energy, Isaiah. It's not going to happen."

"Then I'll kick Negley's butt." I was trying to evoke another response from Jenaye, making sure she hadn't tuned me out.

"Isaiah, you're talking crazy. How are you gonna do that?" The volume in her voice was rising, and she turned around to look behind her to see who was listening. I looked, too. Becca was there, but she pretended not to hear our conversation. Our team had taken the lead, and only seconds remained.

"Easy," I said, shrugging my shoulders. I hadn't formulated any concrete plans.

She grabbed me with both hands. "You need to stop talking like this," she said. "Aren't you in enough trouble, Isaiah?"

"I know," I said, trying to catch myself. "It's just a wild thought. But you've got to admit that this man has been out to get me. He said so on the first day." I pounded my fist into my palm as hard as I could.

"Okay, Isaiah. That's enough. Let's just watch this game."

I looked at the scoreboard. We were now comfortably ahead, and the prospects for advancing to the championship looked favorable. When the buzzer sounded, the game ended with a 62–58 Chadwick victory.

The win was surprising, and Breedlove had been right. The team had been successful, even without me. I maintained a faint hope of getting back on the team, even though Jenaye thought it was far-fetched. There had to be a way.

I was eager to share in the victory with my teammates and stood up next to Jenaye, who was still shaking her head about my comment. She had forgotten all about the game, but I hadn't. I was beginning to feel like she was really rubbing the dormitory incident back in my face. I knew I'd made a poor decision, but I didn't want to hear it, and I really didn't want to accept that I'd never play again. Celebrating with my teammates would at least provide me with the illusion of being connected to them. It was a cliché, but Mom and Dad always said that you never missed your water until your well ran dry. I was sorely missing the camaraderie of my teammates after they'd won an important victory without me. I never thought I'd miss being with them like this.

"I'm going inside the locker room," I said.

"Why?"

"To help them celebrate."

She twisted her face, looking as if she wanted me to stay with her and talk a little while longer. Although her sincere expression made me wish I could take everything back, the game wasn't the best place for apologizing. I blew her a kiss, but she turned her head to let me know that I wouldn't get back into her good graces that easily.

I walked toward the locker room, hoping my former teammates could put me in a better mood. They had pulled the game out without me, and Jenaye was giving me a cold shoulder. I shoved my hands deep inside my pockets and headed for the exit, hoping that once I got together with my former teammates, everything would be all right.

RESCUE WAGON

I walked from the gym to the locker room, keeping my hands inside my pockets and my eyes riveted on the door ahead. The smell of fresh paint sprayed on the hard metal surface made the hairs inside my nose tingle. As I moved closer to the celebration, loud yells and hand claps escaped through the door's narrow cracks, like the aroma from a good meal. I listened from afar, taking in the excitement, and then pulled the door open to watch them celebrate their good fortune.

Mark Young stripped down to his jockstrap, stood near the door and threw his socks in the air, shouting, "We did it! We did it!"

Frank stood on one of the skinny gray benches mounted in front of a row of orange lockers, stretching his arms toward the ceiling. His fingers were curled hard against his palm in a tight fist. "Yeah, boy! Yeah, boy!" Frank said to no one in particular. "We kicked some ass." His words echoed throughout the locker room as the thick wad of Bazooka Joe gum nearly spilled out of his mouth. Losing his balance, he stuck his hand against the locker, righted himself, and then stepped down.

Coach Wilkerson hopped on top of the bench like it was a podium, extended his arms, and quieted the room. His youthful face was beet red, and his gray wool jacket with matching suede elbow patches was soaking wet around the shoulders. The oval-shaped glasses he wore rested against his face crookedly. He straightened them, and then ran his hands through his closely cropped hair. "Calm down. Calm down, everybody. We've got another game to play," he said, trying to maintain his balance.

The noise of the water from the shower competed with Coach Wilkerson's hoarse-sounding voice, and the dense cloud of steam settled against the ceiling and fogged up the mirrors. The heat made it difficult for me to keep my letterman's jacket buttoned; I unsnapped it and listened.

"I don't know who we're playing next, but I'm sure they'll be tougher." He surveyed the room, moving his head back and forth at the team that had gathered underneath his outstretched arms. "We'll need everyone to be prepared. This is just the start." He moved his hands together as if he were shaking something, and then narrowed his eyes, catlike, to gaze around the room until he was looking at me.

Surprised, I removed my coat, threw it over my shoulder, and then made eye contact with Frank, who was clear across the room. If I'd heard the coach correctly, he'd said that he needed everyone to be prepared. Maybe he'd support any reasonable effort toward getting me back on the team for that final game. Coach Wilkerson wanted to win.

"That's all I want to say," the coach said, rubbing his hands together and rocking back and forth, trying to contain his excitement. "Go ahead and celebrate. Just remember we have practice tomorrow." He stepped down from the bench, sidestepping wet towels and discarded Ace bandages.

Frank was beaming. "So, how'd I look today?" We'd made it part of our postgame routine to evaluate each other's performance. His head bobbed when he talked, as if he were listening to a perpetual rock beat. He extended his palm, face up, and waited for me to slap it. A white boy from the suburbs of LA, Frank had finally learned to be cool. The other students had called him "nigger lover" for befriending and sometimes imitating me, but that didn't bother him—or so he said.

"You did okay," I said, slapping his palm. "But I would have tried to post up more against that dude that was checking you. When you've got a shorter man on you, you've got to take advantage of it. You've got to ask for the ball like this." I pushed my butt against his midsection. "You did all right. Just think about that move for the next game."

"Do you think those scouts saw me?" Frank put his hand on my shoulder, looking excited.

"Scouts?" My stomach felt queasy. "I didn't see any." My eyes grew big, and I could feel the wrinkles above my forehead. My jaw dropped as the news hit me like a thunderstorm on a sunny day. The presence of scouts at a game had been something I'd been waiting for. All the practice and hard work I'd done had been intended for this moment, and I was missing out on it completely. Frank was going to get my opportunity, and there was nothing I could do about it, never mind my big talk to Jenaye.

Frank continued, "I know there was a scout out there from Santa Clara University. I'm sure that was him. I met him at a basketball camp last summer. I spotted his bald head and those thick-rimmed glasses a mile away. He sat on the last row of the bleachers and made notes on a clipboard." Frank started taking off his wet jersey. His chest was small for a big man; he could have used some extra weight lifting. "I think my letters are starting to pay off."

At my suggestion, Frank had started a massive letter-writing campaign to a number of colleges, letting them know about his interest in playing college basketball. He wasn't asking for a scholarship, just a shot at the big time. His enthusiasm for the game had led to our friendship, and his approach highlighted a brutal fact of life about sports in a boarding school. No one cared about you or thought you could compete on the next level unless you generated your own noise.

"Naw, I didn't see him," my voice cracked as I lied. I tried to hold back my sadness. If college scouts were in attendance, I had just missed a great opportunity to showcase my talent. With my lips pressed firmly together, I closed my eyes.

"That's why we've got to get you back out here," he said. Holding his jersey, he pointed his index finger at me and pushed it gently against my shoulder. "We can make this a package deal."

My eyes were still glazed over.

"If you want me to," Frank said, "I could talk to Breedlove for you. Maybe if he heard from one of your teammates about how sorely you're missed, he'd change his mind." He nodded his head and winked at me. He knew just what to say.

I liked the suggestion, especially since it was a scenario I hadn't thought about. The offer gave me a little more hope. "That's a start," I said. "You two seem to have a good relationship. I'd considered asking him again, but your idea is even better. Maybe he'll be more objective if it's not coming directly from me."

"Consider it done." Frank tossed his uniform into the big pile, holding his arm straight and flattening his wrist as if he were shooting a jump shot. "Next time I see you, you'll be back in uniform."

*   *   *

Happy that Frank had volunteered to talk to Breedlove about reinstating me for the championship, I left the locker room and headed off to the snack bar. On my way, out I swung my jacket above my head like a victory flag. I'd been injected with the energy and strength of a superhero.

When I tired of swinging my coat, I put it back on and immediately felt my shirt sticking to my damp body. I was still burning up from the stuffy locker room, and as I made my way back up the hill from the gym, I thought about kicking Negley's butt again but quickly removed the thought from my mind. If I were reinstated, I could forgive his actions.

The COLD DRINKS & ICE CREAM sign I spotted as I neared the school's snack bar cooled my thoughts. The building, a one-story rectangle in the middle of campus, was open after every game. A butter-pecan ice cream cone topped with hot fudge sounded good.

As I entered, I could see that Richard was already sitting there, his fat tongue pressed against a creamy mound of rocky road. The melted portion dripped onto his soiled napkin, down his fingers, and onto the books sitting in front of him. He was oblivious to his surroundings, which was nothing new.

"I should have known you weren't going to the game," I said, looking in his direction and then around the snack bar at the chairs pushed underneath the round tables. Several students besides Richard were assembled near the large picture windows decorated with stenciled pictures of popcorn kernels, cookies, and soft drinks. The room smelled like hot fudge, and the stereo system played symphony music.

"Loren already told me who won," he said. A pigeon-toed, wannabe, former point guard who had been cut from the team, Loren used every opportunity to poke fun at the team's misfortune.

"That's good," I said, turning my back and looking up at the chalkboard menu hanging from the wall. I already knew what I wanted, but I stared blankly because I just didn't want to hear any of Richard's smart remarks yet.

"I'm surprised they won without you," he said. "What was the score?"

"I don't remember it exactly, but we won by four points," I said.

"So, they didn't need you, huh?" Richard smirked at me.

"I wouldn't be too quick to say anything like that," I said after ordering my ice cream. "They struggled against a team that we should have blown out. If I'd been out there, the game wouldn't even have been close. Now that we've made it to the next round, my services will really be needed."

"You hope they will," he said.

"I *know* they will," I said, handing my money to the pale, old white woman behind the counter. "I could tell by the way the coach was talking to the team after the game. Looking at me, he said we're gonna need everybody against our next opponent."

"Where are the rest of your teammates?"

"Still celebrating," I said. "You shoulda heard 'em."

"It's probably a good thing you got kicked off the squad." Richard looked up at me. "Now you can focus on your studies. You won't have to worry about practices or anything like that anymore."

"Yeah, how does it feel?" Loren chimed in nastily, sitting across the table from Richard.

I'd laughed a bit when he'd been cut from the team, and now he took pleasure in my misfortune.

"Everyone's heard about you being caught in the girls' dorm," Loren sneered. "That'll teach you to walk around here like you're God's gift to basketball. You've messed it up for everybody. Now the faculty checks and double-checks our beds every night at eleven. You should feel proud."

"Fuck you," I said. I moved close to him and stuck my finger near one of his nostrils.

He jerked his head back.

"I haven't given up yet." I turned my attention back to Richard. "Frank's going to talk to Breedlove and try to persuade him to let me play in the next game."

"That's nice," Richard said. "But, if you want my real opinion, I wouldn't waste my time. You know Breedlove. Once he makes up his mind about something—remember what he did to E? He's never looked back."

"I hear you, but you've got to admit that sending Frank in to do the dirty work couldn't hurt anything." I turned my attention back to Loren. "You have any thoughts, asshole?" He wasn't my favorite person, but maybe, since he was a white boy in the school's good graces, he could shed some light on the situation.

"What if Frank goes in to plead your case and Breedlove still doesn't change his mind?" Loren asked.

"I'm not even thinking like that." I said. "Everything's positive."

I finished my ice cream and placed the empty cup on the table in front of Richard and Loren. "Frank's cool. He'll get it done. You'll see."

*   *   *

After practice, Frank inhaled huge gulps of air as he walked toward me. Coach Wilkerson always made him run extra wind sprints to improve his conditioning. With all the running, it was amazing that he never dropped basketball and just ran track.

I waited underneath the basket after Frank's last lap, eyeing each step, searching his face for clues to the results of his meeting with Breedlove. When he was close enough, I popped the question.

"So, did you talk to him?"

"Yeah," said Frank, leaning over to grab his shorts. He closed his eyes between gasps.

"Well, what did he say?" I moved in as close as I could without touching his long, sweaty body.

Frank wiped the sweat from his forehead. "He said no."

My body slumped forward and my shoulders dropped as I listened to the news. I felt as though someone had driven a knife through my chest.

"It's just not fair," Frank continued. "I tried to tell him you'd just made a mistake, that we really needed you in the final game, but he just ignored me."

I looked toward the court and spotted a thick-seamed leather basketball rolling my way. I kicked it as hard as I could toward center court. My foot stung. "Well, even if I'm not playing, I'll be in the stands rooting you guys on. It's my fault. I should have used better judgment." I threw my hands in the air.

"I didn't mean to get your hopes up." He stood up straight and put his arm around my shoulder. "I know how you must feel."

"I kinda knew that was going to happen." I laughed, tightening my cheek muscles into a fake smile, but nothing was funny. "I appreciate you standing up for me."

The tears were starting to well up in my eyes as the reality of not being able to play for Chadwick again began to sink in. Unwittingly and against all logic, I had gotten up my hopes about playing in the championship. The gym's air, once welcoming, was now stale and musty, making me feel claustrophobic. I had been able to hold back the tears up until this point, but suddenly they came pouring out of me like water through a broken levee.

It was no use holding back. I needed air.

STAND

One week after Frank's failed efforts to get me reinstated, Chadwick's team was defeated in the league championship game. Now, sitting in Frank's room a day after the loss, the pained expression of Coach Wilkerson and the words of the pep talk I'd given during halftime, urging the team to keep fighting, were still fresh in my mind. Coach Wilkerson had blamed the championship loss on poor execution of the game plan and the fact that some players didn't know how to conduct themselves off the court. Everyone knew he was talking about me, and I felt bad that I'd let him and the team down.

"That speech you made at halftime really got me fired up," Frank said, sitting on his bed, wearing a purple, blue, and yellow tie-dyed shirt, running his hand across the comforter.

I sat on the other side of the small dormitory room, thinking about how I could have made a big difference in the team's one-point loss.

"I didn't think Coach Wilkerson was gonna let you talk, but after you came in there yelling at everybody, he just let you go. That was real cool. I thought for sure we were going to win after that." The comforter didn't need straightening or smoothing out, but Frank never seemed to want things out of kilter, and he kept his hand moving. Maybe it was just a nervous habit.

Frank's walls were carefully covered with pictures of his favorite musicians: Jimi Hendrix, the Beatles, and Sly and the Family Stone. I sat at his desk, staring up at the picture of Hendrix, an embroidered headband squeezing his big 'fro, his knees bent and eyes closed, sweat pouring down his chest between the lapels of his unbuttoned silk shirt. Hendrix was intense. Frank got the idea for wearing colorful headbands from staring at the picture.

151

During games, he wore a green one around his fire-engine red hair to keep his curly locks in place.

Next to the poster, in the spaces above his desk where he was supposed to keep his textbooks, Frank stored albums from his massive record collection. The overflow was kept in the gold spray-painted milk crates he'd pushed flush against the walls. I'd started my own collection since I'd come to Chadwick, since there was nothing to do on weekends, but mine was only just starting to grow.

"I thought I could fire you guys up and help you win." I looked around the room for the leather basketball he sometimes kept lying around. I needed to feel it in my hands to make sure I hadn't lost my touch. Sometimes just rubbing the surface lifted my spirits. When I couldn't locate it, I scanned the thin edges of the album covers, looking for some soothing music. "Play some Sly," I said, finally spotting something that seemed appropriate.

"Sounds good," said Frank. He got up off the bed and pulled out the album. Everything was alphabetized. "Yeah, I thought we were gonna win," he said, trying to pick up where he'd left off. He dumped the album out of the cover and slid the edge against his palm. He was careful not to touch the record's surface because his brother had told him that putting your fingerprints on the shiny, black plastic was the quickest way to scratch an album. He talked about his brother a lot, reverently, almost as if he were a god.

"We could have won the championship if it weren't for Breedlove dismissing me," I said. "It wouldn't have even been close."

Frank turned on the stereo and lifted the cover to the turntable. He flipped the lever controlling the cartridge, and the needle descended slowly and safely onto the track. We listened for a minute, bobbing our heads to the beat of "Stand." His blue eyes were distant, seemingly focused on the voices coming through the speakers. The noise temporarily drowned out my memory of the loss.

"I still can't believe he didn't let you play," Frank said. "We came a long way this year. I've been here four years, and this is the closest we've ever come to winning anything. I was sure he'd drop the punishment. Wasn't he an athlete?"

"Sure he was, but his decision didn't have anything to do with that," I said. "I think he felt like I'd already blown it too many times before."

Frank sat down on the bed and leaned back. His elbows made a dent in the bedspread. "I thought I had some kind of inside track after he gave me that award for most improved student, but he told me not to get involved and that you needed to learn a lesson."

"He told me that, too."

"At least he's consistent," he said. He checked the record. "Sometimes I hate this place."

The music grew louder. Sly Stone's raspy voice was ringing inside my ears, with Frank singing along: "*Stand for things you know are right / there's a midget standing tall, and the giant beside him about to fall / Stand / la, la, la, la, la, la, la, la, la, laaaa.*"

"You really like this music, huh?" I asked.

"Love it, man," Frank answered. "It's got a message."

"Like standing up for the right thing," I added. I followed his movements as he walked toward the overflow crates to hunt for the next album, but I wasn't about to let this moment pass without following up. The words traveled from the pit of my stomach, up through my chest like a burst of energy. "Talk about standing up, I told Jenaye that I was gonna pay Negley back for keeping such close tabs on me. He caused this."

Frank looked surprised. "You shouldn't have gone to Jenaye's room. It wasn't his fault he caught you."

"Well, I had to," I said, thinking about what happened at the dance. "I know it was wrong, but I had to do it. What about you? You ever want to kick somebody's ass?"

He paused before reaching down and flipping through his collection. "Not like that."

"I've even considered other stuff." I threw jabs at an imaginary punching bag, pretending I was sparring with Negley.

"Like what?" he asked, amused.

"Messing with that Lamborghini he's so proud of ..."

"Shit, Isaiah, that's crazy."

"I know it, but I gotta do something. Messing up his car is safer than a punch. Wanna help?" I stopped throwing punches to look at him.

Frank moved his head back and forth like I'd lost my mind and walked away. He propped himself against the door. "You got any other bright ideas?"

"Not yet." I patted my foot to the beat. "What's the deal, you getting scared? You were on my side. Talking to Breedlove didn't get us anywhere, and now you've lost the championship. It's all Negley's fault for ratting me out."

"I've got limits. Negley was just doing his job. Plus, I'm a senior. I don't need any screwups this close to the finish line. If I'm caught, I'd ruin my chances of getting in college, and you know what that means. No more hoops."

"You haven't heard the real plan yet." I got up from the chair and walked toward him. "It's gonna be foolproof. Don't laugh. Hear me out. If I screw up, I'll take the heat. I don't need you to do anything, really, just help me with the little details."

"Details? I don't want my name in it." He held his hands, his palms facing forward.

"Your name won't be on anything. If we get caught, I'll say it was my idea. Got it? Besides, you owe me for helping you become a better player. Without my coaching, you'd never have gotten any scouts interested. Remember our postgame chats? And what about the letters I helped you with? Just think about how much satisfaction you'll get for getting back at Negley for everything. You'll thank me later."

I looked at him and shook my head back and forth, attempting to shame him into participation.

He wasn't budging.

But neither was I.

Too High

D–day. That night, I slept with my eyes open. It was 3:00 AM, and the room wasn't completely dark. Rays of moonlight snuck through cracks in the curtains, while chirping crickets sounded off as if they were singing in a church choir. I tried closing my eyes, but the thoughts rushing to my brain kept me from dozing off. I saw myself running, sweating, and breathing hard. Moving my hands, I tugged at the ragged T-shirt I was sleeping in. It was damp and smelled like Tide, which I'd poured too much of into the last wash.

My breathing intensified, so I removed the brown and white blanket from my heaving chest and sat up. The *Ojai Times* lay neatly on the desk in front of an unopened set of textbooks. The paper was two days old, the headlines stale. I jumped up and headed toward the desk. I clicked on the light and pulled the fully intact sections toward my body, trying my best not to rustle the pages. Richard was still asleep. He snored loudly, like something was wrong with him.

I adjusted the lamp and stared at the print. Nothing made sense. Richard's snore momentarily ceased. He smacked his lips against the room's silence and cleared his throat hard. I looked back at his bed and at his body, face up. Most times he slept on his back, with hands folded neatly on his stomach. He shifted his weight and opened his eyes.

"Isaiah?" He squinted. "What are you doing still awake? Don't you know what time it is?"

"Yeah, I know. I couldn't sleep. So I decided to sit up here. I'm just staring at the newspaper." I turned back to the pages in front of me. "Go back to sleep."

"That light is bothering me," he said, taking the edge of his hand and placing it over his eyebrows like a visor.

"Just try," I said. "I'll be finished in a minute. I'm getting a little tired."

I waited until I heard him snoring again and then got up from my desk and walked over to the dresser. I opened the drawer just enough to get my clothes, got dressed, and walked outside into the night air. The joint was lodged deep inside my pocket, a remainder from the stash E forgot to take with him when he left months ago. I hadn't smoked since Mom's beating, but this time I was more careful. After the first few hits, I thought about calling the whole thing off, but the weed was messing with my head. I kept moving.

The shed sat near the soccer field on the other side of the campus. I'd spotted it during a game but never thought I'd feel the need to go inside, until now.

The door was open, and I turned on the light. Beneath its dim glow, I spotted several lawnmowers and a brown bag filled with dirty rags. Rows of farm tools were hung neatly on mounted wall racks, and the smells of freshly cut grass and gasoline filled the air. The petroleum odor knotted my stomach, and I held my belly button, hoping the pain would quickly subside.

I walked around, moving empty boxes and plastic trash bags, looking for the spray can. When I found it, I picked it up and shook it, hopeful that it would contain just enough paint to get the job done. It was full.

I walked the rest of the way toward Negley's house, trying my best to move quietly, but the liquid inside the can swished like ocean waves hitting the shoreline. I slowed the pace to preserve the quiet. Finally, Negley's one-story house came into view. Dry leaves crunched underneath the weight of my sneakers.

Just as I'd planned, I sprayed the garage's exterior, covering it with graffiti. Paint covered my fingertips. I stopped to wipe my hands against my pants, hoping that would give me better control over the spout, but a flash of light from inside the house and a loud noise nearby kept me from continuing. I'd have to come back for the Lamborghini. Scared, I dropped the can and sprinted from the scene.

Out of breath, I arrived at my room, eased my way inside the door, removed my clothes, and threw them on the floor. I could still smell paint on my hands and clothes. I jumped in bed wearing only my underwear and pulled the covers over my head, nearly suffocating myself. Underneath the covers, the stuffy air let me know I needed a shower or at least a chance to get rid of the smell. I jumped out of bed, threw on my robe, and headed down the hall to the bathroom. I quietly turned on the faucet, trying not to wake up the entire dormitory as I washed the paint from my hands. Rushing back to the room, I thought of hiding my clothes, but decided against any further movement. It was best to pretend that nothing had happened, that I'd been here asleep all this time.

The knock on the door came as my chest heaved in and out rapidly. It was hard to tell in the darkness if Negley or someone else had spotted me running.

"Isaiah? Richard? Are you two in there?" I recognized Loren's high-pitched voice. I threw the covers back and answered.

"Yeah. We're in here," I said, looking over at Richard, who was slowly waking up.

"What's going on?" Richard asked. He wiped the matter from his eyes and turned his head toward me. "And what's that I smell?"

"Shut up, man," I said, waiting for Loren to finish. He was still outside the door, and I could hear other voices in the dormitory piercing the quiet.

"You guys better get up. The prefect wants to see everyone. Now."

*   *   *

During the headcount, I stayed calm. I rubbed my palms in a circular motion, observing the faces of my shocked and angry classmates, upset they'd had their sleep disrupted by a prankster.

Negley had managed to discover the damage right away. No one suspected me of doing anything, but the high was starting to wear off and all the fanfare was giving me a dose of reality. I began to wonder what I'd need to do to protect myself from the eventual fallout and investigation. How would I keep this deed under wraps? How could I maintain a straight face? What if Breedlove and Negley found out it was me?

My hands were clean, but I put them behind my back, rocked back and forth on my heels, waiting for a signal that we could go back to our rooms. I could hear Sly and the Family Stone singing in my head. The beat, sounding like a broken record, never stopped.

AFTERMATH

I didn't want to bring any unnecessary attention to myself, so I started arriving twenty minutes early for morning assembly. I was usually one of the stragglers, a latecomer, but after a few days, the investigation intensified. Richard had started to study later and later, becoming more withdrawn whenever I entered our dormitory room, and I was getting paranoid that something bad was about to happen. I checked my name off the seating chart as I entered and found my assigned spot in the small auditorium. It was a foamy, padded chair, covered with worn fabric, near the front of the elevated stage. I'd begun to unravel the loose ends without even realizing it.

My new arrival time took some getting used to. The Chadwick nerds, the boys—and now girls—who were members of the Chess Club, Drama Society, Bible study group, and Astronomy Club, arrived first, followed by members in the Horse Program, who had to get up early to feed their animals. Like good kids, they got the standard eight hours' sleep, while the all-nighters and procrastinators like me slept late, grabbed a quick breakfast, and usually strolled in seconds before the headmaster took his place in front of us.

I twisted and turned each morning, waiting for Breedlove, quickly deflecting questions from the nerds about my early arrival by saying I was turning a new leaf. Some of those white kids believed anything I said, but not Jenaye. As one of the early birds, she knew what was happening.

"Why have you been arriving here so early?" she whispered from where she sat behind me on the second day.

"What are you talking about?" I kept my face focused ahead, trying not to hear her. It was difficult because she didn't take no for an answer.

"You know," she insisted. "We talked about this but you didn't listen." She patted me on the shoulder as if to signal that I was on my own, and then sat back in her chair, waiting for the start of the assembly.

Breedlove stepped up to the podium wearing his standard baby blue seersucker suit, a starched white shirt—without his usual necktie—and a scowl, that same one he displayed when he'd had me in his office after the weed incident.

"I'm sure you all know what happened the other night at Professor Negley's house." He talked slowly, ignoring the formal announcements that were part of his morning routine. His voice trailed off into a whisper, not the fiery diatribe I expected, at least not yet. He spoke like a man on a mission. Measured. Precise. Unflappable. He shifted his weight and grabbed the podium even tighter. "Since then, I've talked to a few of you." He looked down and back up again. "Ladies and gentlemen, someone in here really crossed the line." He let the podium go and tugged at his sport coat as if a wrinkle would have distorted his message. "That means I'll be escalating this investigation and interviewing everyone until I find the culprit."

He placed his hands in his pockets, walked away from the podium, toward the edge of the elevated surface to get a closer look at us. He was a short man, but now he appeared ten feet tall. No one talked, laughed, or coughed. "Since I've been here, we've never had an incident like this. It hurts me to have to point the finger at one of you. We've always prided ourselves on honesty here, and if you know something about this situation, I suggest you come forward now. I'm not going to tell you right now what the consequences will be if you wait." He removed his hands from his pocket, stroked his thick eyebrows, and moved back behind the podium. "But the punishment will be swift and thorough."

I was scared. Trying to release the tension, I started drumming my fingers against my thigh. I thought about the punishment, Breedlove's scare tactics, whether I'd be able to keep my actions secret when my name was called. I wanted out of there, but not by being expelled for spray-painting Negley's garage. I had imagined a more graceful exit, involving long, drawn-out farewells and lots of gloating over my newfound freedom. After Breedlove's speech, I knew that I'd gone a little too far. I tried to remain calm and comforted myself by believing all I needed was more time for things to die down and blow over.

"I don't want to talk about anything else this morning," Breedlove said. "If there are any other announcements, make sure you post them on the kiosk today. Now let's get to class."

He motioned for Coach Winstrom, the eighty-one-year-old chaplain, to deliver his morning prayer. He started in his usual manner, "God grant us the serenity …" and then added a line about the garage. "Dear Lord, we hope one of our great students has not carried out this evil deed. And if they have, we ask that you grant them the power to repent and muster the courage to come forward …"

As he rambled on, I closed my eyes and whispered my own words of wisdom. I prayed for God's grace without realizing that the chaplain had finished his prayer already, and my classmates had left me there all alone, my head bowed.

* * *

As soon as the assembly was over, I made it a priority to find Frank. We needed to talk about the speech and some damage control. He was making long strides toward the academic building, a chemistry book tucked underneath his arm, his biceps straining under the odd weight. I grabbed his loosely fitting shirt as he reached for the door handle to Twybell's class.

"Did you hear that speech?" I asked.

"Yeah, I heard it," he replied, turning back and looking over his shoulder. He let the door handle go, moved away from it, and took a deep breath. "I told you this was a bad idea."

"I know," I said. My fear of being discovered grew.

"You sound a little concerned."

I put my arm around Frank's neck and pulled him out of earshot of his classmates. "I am."

"About what?" Frank asked.

"Richard smelled the paint on my clothes," I said.

"And what did he say?"

"He mentioned that something smelled funny that night, and he left the assembly this morning before we could talk."

"Do you think he's gonna fink?"

"I don't know," I said.

"Then you've got to talk to him." Twybell began calling out Frank's name, and I knew it was time for him to go inside. He turned toward the classroom. "Shit, you're his roommate. You know him, so you've got to do everything in your power to keep him from talking. If he pins that incident on you … you're going to be in a world of trouble.

"I don't care what you do." He moved closer. "Just don't mention my name."

* * *

I spotted Richard during the morning break, camped out near the silver bowl of graham crackers and the container of milk the kitchen crew placed outside for us daily before third period. His expression bore a seriousness I'd only seen before an exam. He took one bite of his morning snack and met me halfway across the platform.

"So it was you that messed up that garage, huh? Did anything get on that fancy car?" He got in my face, and I pushed him back. The sudden jolt made him drop one of the thin, rectangular crackers. He looked down and hesitated before picking it up.

"Can you keep it down?" I asked. Picking up the cracker, I moved in close to him.

"Why?" He knew I wasn't going to try anything, particularly under these circumstances, with everyone standing around, but he egged me on. "You know that wasn't right. You just did it because Negley got you kicked off the team."

"I didn't do anything," I said, trying to defend myself.

"Well, Breedlove hasn't asked me anything, but if he does, I'm going to tell him how you were acting that night. You're not going to get me mixed up in this mess." He moved away from me like what I'd done was contagious.

"What if I hook you up at the snack bar every night for the rest of the year? Would that help?" I asked.

"I don't want your money," said Richard, smiling and shaking his head. "Like I said, if Breedlove asks me, I'm going to tell him what I know and what I saw that night."

"Come on, man," I said, pleading with him.

"I'm not making any promises," Richard said. "You should have thought about this before you did what you did." He finished another cracker and picked up his books. "You better say your prayers."

*   *   *

That same night, in study hall, I got a note from Breedlove's secretary.

I was flipping the pages of my history textbook, the murmur of the air-conditioner and the tapping of pencils against desktops interrupting my thinking. The paper was neatly folded in small squares, the pink edges frayed with pieces of plastic. As soon as I started to unfurl it, my hands shook. I looked around, wondering if anyone was glancing over my shoulder and could tell that I was next in line to be interrogated. No one was paying attention. Folding it open, I read the words that said he wanted to see me right away in his office. Things were moving fast now.

Realizing that I'd made a bad decision, I wanted to take it all back, but I knew I couldn't. I'd acted out of spite, and now I wished I'd taken my time to really sort things out.

I refocused on the pages of my textbook and made an attempt to study. As I turned the pages, I planned a brief explanation and denial and hoped Breedlove was oblivious to what had really gone on. Maybe he was calling me to ask questions, like he'd done with the other boarders. I got up from my desk, showed Breedlove's note to the study hall monitor, and excused myself to walk back to the headmaster's office.

I entered confidently, but he didn't look up. He stared down at a piece of paper inside a manila folder, which contained a long, typed message, and waited until I'd gotten comfortable. I inhaled something that resembled fresh paint. I scanned the room, overcome by the odor, imagining that night. Breedlove continued reading and looked up.

"Well, Isaiah, I hope you can explain a few things." He looked tired. His eyes were bloodshot and his hair was slightly uncombed. "It's come down to me and you again."

"Yeah, I guess so." I pretended not to know what he was talking about, but clearly he was expressing his frustration at seeing me in his office for another misdeed.

"Richard told me you were awake that night and that before we called everyone together, he smelled a strong odor in your room." He leaned back in his chair and took his time.

"Sometimes, it's hard for me to sleep." I said. "And that odor ... I smelled the same one, too. So what's all this got to do with me?"

"A lot," he said. "Did you talk to him about retaliating against Mr. Negley when I kicked you off the team?"

"No. Did he tell you that?" I said, trying to turn things around. "We talked about me getting kicked off the team, but nothing else."

He took a sip of the water that sat in the crystal drinking glass. I followed the design and stared through the damp prisms at his moving body while he leaned back and looked underneath his desk. When he had found what he was looking for inside a paper bag, he grabbed it and threw it on top of the desk. I recognized it as the pants that I'd worn that night and wanted to kick myself for not getting rid of them.

"What are you doing with those?" I asked.

"They're yours, aren't they?"

At first I wanted to deny it but then realized it was no use trying to stonewall Breedlove or myself anymore. If he knew about the pants, there was no telling what else he held underneath his desk. Maybe it was best to come clean. Perhaps I could escape a harsh punishment.

"Yeah. They're mine."

"Well, that's all I need to know." He rubbed his hands together and swallowed hard. "Now I want you to start packing your clothes and getting your things together. We no longer want you here."

I was stunned. I thought about E and how he must have felt getting the same news. I wanted to tell him that Negley had been out to get me from the first day, and now he'd gotten his wish. I didn't want to be at this school, anyway. Getting the boot now meant I didn't have to think of any other way to make an exit. I was dazed, but largely relieved, glad to be free of the expectations that had been placed upon me. There were only a few things troubling me at this juncture. How would I tell my parents, and how would I say good-bye to Jenaye?

"You have anything else you want to say?" he asked.

I recalled my conversation with Frank after the assembly. *Just don't mention my name.* Now that Breedlove had dropped the bomb, I was all alone.

"I'm sorry about what happened," I said, not really meaning it. "I didn't know what I was doing. I just got carried away." My eyes were starting to water, but I wasn't going to cry.

"That's unfortunate, Isaiah. This is what happens when you lose control."

THE VIBE

I left Breedlove's office and headed back to the dorm. I opened the door, hoping to find Richard, but he was still at study hall. I stood in the middle of the floor, staring at my music collection and the posters tacked to the wall. The record collection reminded me of my dispute with E, and the poster of Tommie Smith and John Carlos, the 1968 Olympic protestors, made me remember my first days as the reluctant newcomer.

Months after arriving, I'd made a vow to get myself kicked out, without realizing I'd be reunited with Jenaye as part of a coed exchange. I'd finally gotten my wish. Even the exchange program wasn't enough to alter my attitude, because deep down, I never saw myself as a full-fledged member of the Chadwick community. What would she think of me? What would she say now that I'd been expelled? Would she still care about me?

I sat on the bed and told myself to start emptying the clothes from the dresser drawers, to worry about the small things later. I leaned back and wondered what home would be like. How would my parents react to me coming home? What would my teachers think? And what would my new school be like? I tried to put a positive spin on things and immediately thought about the opportunity I'd have to play on the McClymonds basketball team. The season was over, but I still looked forward to competing with Tee and all the others at the right time.

I ran my fingers across the ribbed bedspread and sucked in a breath of fresh air. I held it for a moment, and then blew it out slowly, feeling momentary relief that the pressure of excelling at a practically all-white institution was being removed from my life. There were other things to think about now.

At my new school, I knew I'd have to convince my friends that Chadwick's square environment hadn't rubbed off on me.

There was no knock; the sound of rattling keys and a creaking door hinge signaled an intruder. I got up from the bed when I saw the door swing inward, hoping it was Richard. For what seemed like the longest time, no one entered. Richard must have felt my vibe.

His skinny arms finally pushed the door closed behind him, but before he could turn completely around I jumped out of bed and was in his face. He held his books tight, the spines grazing my thighs. I lifted my right arm and grabbed his neck, squeezing it like a rubber ball.

"Why'd you tell?" I snapped. I kept my eyes focused on his.

He looked down. His droopy eyes made him look like he was barely awake. "What are you talking about, Isaiah?" Richard strained to get the words through his compressed windpipe, past those crowded teeth.

"I just got kicked out of here. Breedlove pulled me out of study hall a few minutes ago and told me that he knew what I had done and that I was no longer welcome here. He said you tipped him off. On top of that, he had a pair of my pants. Did you give 'em up?"

"I have no idea how he got those pants," he said, looking away.

"Yeah, right," I said. I held onto his neck and jerked him away from my body. When his books hit the floor, I let him go so he could pick them up. As he bent down, I took my fist and tagged him on the chin with an uppercut.

He looked at me like he was going to puke. "Man, that shit hurt." He was gasping for air.

"It's supposed to." I waited until he had grabbed his books and stood up straight. He rubbed his chin in a circular motion with his free hand in the spot that I'd tagged. "And you're gonna tell me the truth. I ain't got much time. If you hold anything back, I'll pummel you some more."

He turned slightly so I wouldn't have another clear shot at him. "I told you I was gonna tell him exactly what I saw that night."

I eased in closer to keep the pressure on. "But why did you give up the pants? What did he promise you? Glowing letters of recommendation? An extra day of vacation? Membership in some Chadwick secret society? It had to be something."

"It wasn't really a promise," said Richard, loosening up a bit. "He kept questioning me over and over about the same thing, trying to get more information."

"And you gave them up, didn't you?"

"He wouldn't take no for an answer," Richard whined. "He started talking about how the perpetrator was putting everyone in the school at risk, and that the sky was the limit for someone who would engage in something like that. Breedlove suspected you anyway, and he said that if he found out that you did it, and I didn't tell what I knew, I'd be kicked out, too. He had my file out while I was talking to him … and then I broke down."

"What do you mean?" I rubbed my throbbing knuckles while he talked.

"I sorta panicked. I gave him the pants and told him some of the things you did that night. He's the headmaster, you know. He's got keys to everything." He stretched his arms out now as if there was nothing he could do.

It was hard for me to feel sorry for him. Listening to his rationale infuriated me. I felt a rage that had been building inside since he'd made me look bad in Hagman's English class while we were reading *Huckleberry Finn,* and now it came pouring out of me. Richard's choice to take sides with the authorities was bad then, but his decision to rat me out now was the last straw. In the past, I had been more restrained, but now there was no school code to stop me from lashing out at Richard—no matter the cost.

"Come on, man," he said.

I watched his body move toward mine in an effort at reconciliation, but instead of embracing him, I let my fist go until it connected with his forehead and followed it with another punch until I could hear him yelling for me to stop. The more he yelled, the more I continued, until I felt strong hands grabbing at my arms and trying to hold them down.

"What's going on?" It was Loren's voice. He held me in a bear hug, his arms locked in front of my chest as if he were a trainer and I was his prize boxing pupil, unmercifully taking advantage of a cowardly fighter.

"You see what I'm doing," I said, trying to wrestle my arms loose to finish the job. "I'm kicking this boy's ass. Let me go."

"Did he do something to you?" Loren asked.

"I'll let him answer that." I wasn't ready to tell him of Breedlove's decision to dismiss me yet because I knew that with time, he'd know more and tell more about the situation than I'd ever reveal.

"Well, I just came to tell you that your father is on the phone outside." He let go of my arms, and I turned my head around to look at his messed-up hair, sweating face, and big arms. For a small guy, he was stronger than I thought. "Are you gonna answer it?"

This was one time when I was glad that students weren't allowed telephones in their rooms. I turned away from Loren, ignoring the question, to look back at Richard before heading to the phone. I thought of skipping Dad's call, but how smart would that be?

Richard was sobbing, his head nearly touching the floor, both hands spread across his face. I wanted to finish the job, but with my dad waiting on the phone, I didn't want to make him any angrier than I knew he'd be already.

"Yeah, I'll get it," I said, still looking down at Richard's body. "Don't bring your ass back to Oakland," I spoke to the back of his skull. "I know where you live."

ON THE ROAD

My folks wired me money for a one-way bus ticket to Oakland. Dad said he wasn't about to pay for an expensive plane ride or wait another day to see what else I could get myself into. After hearing about the fight and seeing what I'd done to Richard's face, Breedlove quickly sided with him. With the little time I had left, I penned farewell messages to Jenaye and Frank, but I knew they deserved more. Those notes only told a part of the story. With Jenaye, it had started with a dance and letters. It was only fitting, now that I was dangerously close to never seeing her again, that it would end that way, too.

I rode the yellow school bus alone through Chadwick's gates for the last time, toward Ojai's Greyhound station, where the driver of Chadwick's creaky contraption dropped off me and my oversize footlocker at the curb and sadly shook my hand like we were former business partners.

It was really too early in the morning for a long bus ride, but that's all I had to look forward to. Entering the depot at 7:30 AM, the smell of hot chocolate, coffee, bacon, eggs, cheap perfume, and cigarette smoke all combined to make me sick to my stomach. Unshaven passengers, hippies, crying infants, and the voice of a male clerk bellowing out destination points through a static-filled PA system let me know that I was about to face the sharp-edged world that Chadwick had temporarily shielded me from.

I stood in line to purchase my ticket and then sat down next to an old black man with coarse hands. He wore a light brown suit jacket, and his khaki-colored duffel bags were slung over a sturdy shoulder. As I looked at him, he mumbled something to himself. His beard was thicker than Dad's, but the self-talk, the staring into thin air, and the movement of his lips reminded me of the way my father prepared himself to deal with tough situations. Dad was probably talking to himself now, getting himself prepared for our inevitable, face-to-face meeting.

Before he'd hung up the previous night, he mentioned that Breedlove was expecting payment for the thousands of dollars in damages I'd caused by spray-painting Negley's garage. *Oh my God.* If I promised to pay, Breedlove would erase all evidence of the incident from my academic record. Dad said that upon my return, I would have to find a job or something, nothing specific. He was leaving things open, which in itself was a little scary. It was the first time he'd talked to me about making money during schooltime. I suspected that he stayed away from the subject thus far because it brought back bitter memories of his own childhood and his stern father, Henry, who'd stressed hard work in the form of manual labor, and, when time permitted, school. For the most part, Dad lectured me on the need to get a good education, but now he was more interested in having me make enough money to pay for a mistake I'd made. I could tell that was eating him up.

The sound of the PA system snapped me out of my thoughts. It was the first—and only—boarding call for Oakland. I gathered up my small record collection and a few books and walked toward the ticket-taker. I climbed up the narrow metal stairway, walking down the aisle of the bus until I found a window seat. I sat down and stretched out my legs.

Staring out the dirty window at the brown, hilly terrain surrounding the station, I mentally said my good-byes. This time, I grew nervous as I thought about going home and the reception that awaited me. I'd seen a book titled *You Can't Go Home Again*—one of those catchy phrases that stuck with you. I couldn't get it out of my head because it seemed so appropriate for my journey back. It was just one of those things people repeated without paying much attention.

The desk clerk had said the bus was an express, but my experience on Greyhound told me "express" could mean anything. Soon enough, I'd be home.

For better or for worse, I'd finally gotten my wish.

THE WORLD TOMORROW

The Greyhound bus traveled west from Ojai toward the California coast, and then north to Oakland on Highway 101. I stared out my window at the vacant farmland and the distant mountain ranges, enjoying a moment of serenity.

The ride was smooth and quiet until the old white woman sitting next to me diverted my attention. I'd been avoiding her periodic glances, preferring to remain anonymous among the passengers crammed in this tiny space, but the incessant tapping of her left foot was hard to ignore.

"You got a problem?" Her long silver hair was combed back in a bun, and her bottom teeth were covered with tartar. What I could smell of her breath reminded me of dishwater.

"That noise is bothering me." I motioned toward the heavy soles of her black shoes. "You mind?"

She looked up from the book she'd started to read, over the top of her glasses, which were connected, near the ears, by a small chain. "You're a little young to be telling somebody my age what to do."

I'd always been taught never to guess a woman's age, but based on the crowded lines at the edges of her eyes, I figured she was much older than my parents.

"No disrespect, ma'am." I ran my hand along the side of my face and then placed it squarely on my lap. "It's just that this is supposed to be a long ride."

"So what? I have the right to tap my feet. You should be in school, anyway. What's your story?" She ceased making the annoying noise and angled her torso so that her knees pointed in my direction. Underneath the baggy black sweater, her waistline was nonexistent.

"I'm headed back to Oakland." I filled my chest proudly with air after answering and stuck it out so she would notice. When given the opportunity, I enjoyed letting people know where I was from. "And you?"

"San Francisco."

"So, we're almost going to the same place," I said, trying not to sound disappointed that we'd have to ride the entire trip sitting together.

"Almost. Why are you going back to Oakland on a weekday? Aren't you supposed to be in school? It's not a holiday."

I looked at my watch. It was still early, and at Chadwick, it would have been time for graham crackers and the morning break.

"Well?" She closed her book so I'd have her undivided attention.

Leery about telling this total stranger, a white woman, the reason I was on the bus, I regretted that I'd even said anything about the noise. I gave it more thought. Why did she want to know? She was weird-looking and curious. But then … what did I have to lose? I was on my way back for a lot of reasons. I recalled Richard's bloody face, and the threat I'd delivered to him before departing made me cringe. Maybe I'd been too tough in warning him not to come home. I had mixed emotions about discussing Negley's garage and my subsequent dismissal, but I knew talking things out with this stranger would help me explain myself better once I was face-to-face with my parents. I'd have to give them a recap of events, too.

"You first," I shifted the conversation and focus back in the other direction. "Why are you going to San Francisco?"

"It's my home, but I was here celebrating my birthday. I own a small gift shop and haven't taken a break in years. I don't like to fly, and now that I'm getting older, I refuse to turn into a hermit. Ojai's the perfect place just to relax. And you?"

I chuckled to myself. I'd never looked at Ojai like that. It was amazing how two people could be in the same place and see it differently.

"I got dismissed."

"You what?"

"They kicked me out of school." I changed the wording a bit, hoping it would sound better.

"You look like such a nice kid."

"It was my parents' idea for me to go to prep school, not mine. They said I'd get a good education. I was homesick the whole time."

She nodded her head like she understood. "So what are you going to do now?"

"Go to a public school," I said.

She took in air and leaned back a little in her chair. Her hands gripped the armrest. "Nothing wrong with that, I guess."

"You ever been in that type of situation, where you didn't want to leave home?"

"Believe it or not, I'm a long way from home now. I grew up in Russia, and my family left after the Communists took over. I was a kid like you, and I didn't want to leave my native land, but my father said we had to. My mother died during childbirth. I seldom traveled, but I had to make adjustments." She reached down near the foot she'd been tapping, grabbed her purse, and pulled out an old photo. Within the worn edges was a picture of a beautiful young woman wearing a crown, white gloves, and a robe. Behind her was a small stone fortress that resembled a castle.

"Who is that?" I asked.

"It's me," she said, sitting erect. "Someone took this a long time ago. I come from royalty. My father was an officer in the Russian Imperial Army. He was a prince. Our roots extend all the way back to the czars and noblemen of the ninth century, which makes me a princess. My name is Victoria. And yours?"

"Isaiah," I said, feeling humble.

I looked at her in disbelief, and then back at the picture. In the photo, her teeth were straight, her smile brighter, and her hair, now in a bun, touched her shoulders.

"A princess?" I still couldn't believe it.

"That's right," she said. "I was much prettier then." She loosened the pins holding her hair and grabbed a silvery strand so that it hung down a bit over her eyes. "My hair was jet black, too."

"So what happened to you?" I leaned my elbow against the armrest between us, leaning forward so I wouldn't miss anything.

"It was the Communists," she said, sounding angry. "After the revolution, the Bolsheviks took over, and it was difficult for my family to live in peace because my father had fought in the Imperial Army against them. It wasn't safe in Russia for anyone who had fought them or anyone with any affiliation with royalty. Once they took power, the Bolsheviks tried to get rid of anyone who'd participated in the old regime." She removed the hair from her face so I could see her eyes again.

I wanted to know more about the Bolsheviks and how they had become so powerful. "And that's why your family left?" I was riveted.

"Yes, that's what my father told me. I was very young at the time, so I don't remember all the details. He said we moved to Paris in the 1920s, right after the revolution started, and I remember having to get used to it. Paris is a pretty city, but I didn't like it there at all. When I got old enough to work, I had a hard time finding a job. I borrowed some money, moved to San Francisco with some relatives, and that's how I ended up here. I like it much better now." She paused to take a deep breath and look outside the window at a train heading in the opposite direction.

"So, it feels like I've been in an alien environment all my life," she said. "In spite of all the changes, I've just learned to adapt. As you can see, I'm no longer on a pedestal." She made a quick motion with her hands so that I'd look at her closely. "You're pretty young now, but one day, you'll learn what it means to fall from grace. And what you'll have to do to get back up."

I shook my head, feeling a little confused.

"Look around you." She pointed out the window and the train passing on the opposite track. "The only constant we can depend upon is change."

When I looked again, the train had passed us. I stared at the rolling hills and crumbling rock formations, whose shapes were altered with each bend in the road. Victoria's age and her wisdom had made me remember my own grandfather, who had passed away. What would he have said about what I'd done? For the first time, I began to ponder how I could have dealt differently with my situation at Chadwick. Hearing how Victoria had handled and survived the changes in her life made me think seriously about how I'd adapt to the looming changes ahead of me, growing closer as the bus edged closer to home. I wasn't on a pedestal anymore, either.

"So what's the name of the book you've been reading?" I asked. The cover bore half of the face of a white man with a single eye staring at me.

"*Toward a Psychology of Being.*" She held it up.

"Is it any good?" The picture on the cover was striking and unforgettable. What kind of book would have such a cover?

"If you ever want to learn how to make good decisions, it's excellent."

"Maybe I'll pick it up." She'd answered my question, but I still wondered if the book would say anything else about dealing with change.

"You should—it just might change your life."

Before long, she had resumed the annoying tapping, but the sound no longer bothered me as much. There were other distracting noises. I glossed over the images outside my window. Closing my eyes, I tried falling asleep, but a boom box behind me kept me awake. Before I knew it, the bus was weaving its way between trucks down the Nimitz Freeway, past the Oakland Tribune Tower, Jack London Square, past blocks of old Victorian homes, and finally came to rest inside the Oakland bus terminal.

I looked out the window in the direction of the passenger terminal, searching for my parents, but only managed to catch my reflection and a silhouette of the old woman riding next to me. I knew they were close; on matters concerning education, they were always on time. Feeling nervous, I waited until everyone, including the woman who'd sat next to me, had left the bus and then made my way inside the building.

Dad was inside the waiting area, standing out among the sea of faces in his brown and white gaucho sweater with the high collars and big brown buttons. Without smiling, he elbowed his way to the front of the crowd. He offered no embrace and gave no indication that he was glad to see me. He shook his head back and forth in front of me, as though he couldn't believe what he was seeing. He'd had a similar expression the first time I'd gotten into trouble at Chadwick, but this time, he closed his eyes and buried his face inside his palms for a long time. Looking up, he regained his composure and grabbed the small duffel bag I was carrying.

"I see you made it back." He squeezed the comment through tight lips.

"Yeah, I did." I didn't really know what to say. "Did you come by yourself? Where's Mom?" I wanted to delay talking about my dismissal and the inevitable punishment.

"She's in the car," he said.

"That's different. She was out of the car the last time, waiting with you."

"Well," he said, squeezing his lips together, "there's a reason for that."

"I know," I said, angry at myself for not choosing my words more carefully. "Can we go get the rest of my stuff?"

We walked to an area on the far side of the terminal. The baggage claim area was different from the one at the airport. Here, the drivers unloaded their own cargo onto carts and wheeled it inside to a small room. There were no conveyor belts. Everything here was done manually. I liked riding airplanes better, but riding the bus was a sign that my life was changing again. I was no longer on the verge of privilege. Those days of riding in assigned seating, or being served soft drinks at the drop of a hat, had come to a close, to be replaced with having to fend for myself. But all wasn't lost. In spite of the change, there were some definite plusses. I didn't have to worry about being the only black person in class anymore or making sure I carefully measured my words. At home, I could relax a little, put away my suit and tie, play James Brown music without a confrontation, and slip back into the neighborhood, where getting an Ivy League education was rarely the most pressing goal.

The driver opened the door to a roomful of suitcases. "There's my stuff," I said.

"Is that it?" Dad pointed to the lone blue footlocker that sat upright on the pavement.

"Yeah, that's it." I stepped past the driver, grabbed my footlocker, and then followed Dad to the parking lot behind the terminal.

Dad finally broke the ice. "So what happened? I told Breedlove that something like this was totally out of character for you. I know it must have been a setup."

He was trying to give me a way out.

I told him that Negley was out to get me and that I'd made up my mind on the spur of the moment to get him instead. I left out the part about smoking weed.

He listened, walking with his eyes focused carefully on the lines in the asphalt. "I'm speechless, Isaiah. Disappointed." He stopped. He was taking deep breaths, sounding like a teakettle. "You spray-painted someone's garage, Isaiah? What were you thinking? You know I taught you better than that. One day, you'll wish you had that chance again. I could strangle you right here. Just wait 'til I get through with you." I wasn't looking forward to a beating, but I could handle the tongue-lashing.

I swallowed. "I tried to tell you I didn't want to go back."

"Your reasons weren't good enough."

"Well, now I can go to a public school," I said, hearing the defiance in my voice.

"Can you hear yourself?" Dad threw up a hand. "What a waste."

We walked through the parking lot until we got to the car, and Mom, seeing us through the sideview mirror, jumped out. The car radio was tuned to *The World Tomorrow,* a familiar religious program, and Garner Ted Armstrong, the radio evangelist, shouted through the small speakers on top of the dashboard. His messages predicted terrible natural disasters, plagues, and the imminent end of world. An apocalyptic program seemed fitting, considering what was probably in store for me.

"Isaiah … I honestly don't believe what you did. What the hell is wrong with you?" Mom was in my face before I could put down the footlocker. Her fingertips poked at my chest, and her lips were pushed up and out. She shook my shoulders. She'd removed her glasses and held them by her side. Her face had more lines since the last time I'd been home. "Who do you think is going to take care of you, little boy? I should whip your ass right outside here, but—"

"But what?" I said, putting my belongings down and rubbing the place in my chest where she'd had her fingers. I met her focused stare with one of my own.

Standing next to me, Dad grabbed at my arm and squeezed it hard, a clear indication that I needed to watch my next move. The gesture made me remember our big fight at Thanksgiving. I knew that if I went there again, I'd eventually lose.

"But," she continued, "you're getting too old for that." She backed away.

I was confused and relieved at the same time. It sounded too good to be true—no more spankings. What had changed?

"I whipped your ass before, and it seems like none of that worked. So, from here on out, it'll be nothing like before." She cleared her throat. "Naw, you're not gonna get your ass beat anymore, but don't think for a minute that you're totally off the hook. Tell him, babe." She backed away from me and headed for the passenger side. Flipping her hand in my face, she signaled for Dad to finish.

"You know what we talked about." He looked at me. "Breedlove said the damage to Negley's garage was extensive. Your mom and I have decided that you'll have to take an after-school job to pay for the repairs. He's gonna send me an estimate this week. If you pay, he'll forgive everything. You got anything else you want to say? You thought about a part-time job?"

"That bus ride wasn't long enough for me to decide anything," I said, thinking about the conversation I'd had with the old woman. "There wasn't enough time to think about a job. I got distracted."

"Well, you don't have a lot of time. I suggest you start getting your act together right now." He was still holding my duffel bag. Reaching inside his pocket for his extra set of keys, he opened the trunk of the car. "I've told him that you'll be making some payments to him within the next thirty days. I don't want you to stop looking until you find some kind of part-time job around here. You hear me?"

"Yeah," I said, opening the car door to the backseat and sitting down.

He put my baggage in the trunk, and I hopped in the seat behind Mom. She was still fuming. "Boy, when are you gonna learn? I keep trying to tell you that a hard head makes a soft behind."

* * *

Dear Isaiah:

I received your farewell letter. I couldn't wait to write you. Hope you are better. I tried to warn you, but I see you had to learn things the hard way. Getting Negley was something you needed to do. I hope you got it out of your system. Now you can really move on. A new school should be the perfect opportunity for you. At least that's what I hope you decide to do. You've got the opportunity for a new start. Don't blow it this time. We just came back from a camping trip. You should have seen yours truly out there. For a city girl, I think I did pretty well for myself. The camping trip helped me clear my head. Out there I had plenty of time to think.

Jenaye

P.S. I've forgiven you for getting me in trouble. Given our feelings for each other, what we did was bound to happen. I just wish things hadn't ended so quickly.

*   *   *

I couldn't sleep. I woke up before daybreak and grabbed the round, palm-size alarm clock from the nightstand. At 5:25 AM, the sun's rays squeezed through the window shades, and I sat up, ran my fingers through my hair, and stared at the black-and-white poster on the wall. ALL POWER TO THE PEOPLE. Huey Newton was holding a rifle in front of his ammo-filled belt. Like me, he was gazing into the future, preparing himself to face the unknown.

With his image still in my mind, I pushed the covers from my legs, rolled out of bed, and took a long shower. My chest pounded like a bass drum. It was only 5:31 AM. Time was moving slowly.

Getting dressed, I pulled on my blue jeans and held up the preppy, short-sleeved shirt I'd often worn at Chadwick. Looking in the mirror, I wondered if I'd be overdressed for my new school and decided to put on a T-shirt that I'd worn only once. There was still time to mess around, so I listened to "Midnight Train to Georgia," trying to memorize the words.

In a while, Mom and Dad were awake, too. I could hear one of them close the door and flush the toilet in the bathroom that served as the divider between our two bedrooms. I didn't know if they were aware of it, but I could often hear them talking while they were in there:

"He's going to get a lot of questions from those kids up there about why he isn't at that private school anymore," Mom said. "I don't think he should say anything. You know, he should just briefly mention that things didn't work out. Don't you agree?"

"Yeah. You don't want to invite too many questions—and those that they do ask, you don't want him to answer if it can be avoided," Dad said. "We'll talk about it on the way to the school. You almost ready?"

"Just about," she said.

"What about Tee? Are you going to tell Isaiah what happened?"

"We'll see," Mom said. "I don't want him hanging out with that boy now that he's back. It might be best if we just keep quiet."

I turned down my music and moved closer to the bathroom door, hoping to hear more of the conversation, but things quickly quieted down. I wasn't sure if Dad heard me listening, but he opened the door to look inside my room.

"You ready to go, son?"

"Almost." I walked toward the kitchen and played like I hadn't been listening. Dad was already dressed in a short-sleeved shirt and loafers, and Mom was wearing a khaki-colored blouse and a pair of black shoes that she usually wore to go shopping. They'd never have worn those outfits to Chadwick. The change in clothes was the least of their worries. Now they'd have to pay closer attention to the people I hung around, the classes I took, and make sure I was on the right track. Attending a public school meant no hand-holding by school officials, no influential alumni to tip the scales of a college admissions committee. Public school meant no guarantees—period.

"When you finish in the kitchen, Isaiah, wait for your mother and me in the car. We'll be there shortly." He gave me a long, measured look. "We'll give you a ride on your first day back, but after this, you're on your own."

I grabbed a quick bite to eat and climbed into the backseat, wondering what it would be like at my new school. I'd gone to public school before, but it seemed like a long time ago now. I wondered if the boys would be meaner—or tougher—and if the dances would be anything like the ones we used to have back in junior high. Given the new surroundings, how would I perform academically? I shifted in the seat and toyed with the window switch until my parents came out. I thought about the old woman on the bus, about all we'd talked about. I didn't know why it took getting kicked out to realize it, but I was suddenly beginning to feel more power over my situation than I'd ever had.

Dad started the car and, while it idled, told me about the meeting he'd set up with my new guidance counselor. Mom played with the buttons on the radio, keeping silent. He drove several blocks until I could see the building with the school's name carved into the concrete blocks above the large white pillars that framed the school's entrance.

I looked at the kids sitting on metal benches and milling about the campus, waiting for the bell. It was like a fashion show. My new classmates wore apple hats, puka shell chokers, platform shoes, and big Afros, like the kind I'd marveled at in *Superfly*. I looked down at my shabby T-shirt and felt like going back home to change, but it was too late now.

I said good-bye to my parents and jumped out of the car. A warm spring breeze pushed against my face as I ran up the stairway to see if I could spot Tee before meeting my new counselor. Not recognizing anyone, I pushed toward the entrance, pulled open the heavy, metal doors and walked inside. The halls were a maze of gray lockers and closed doors with shaded windows. The sound of my footsteps bounced off the closed classroom doors and the smooth concrete walls. I walked slowly, looking for a sign or something that told me I was headed in the right direction. An arrow pointing to the business office was tacked on the wall next to the library. I spotted a tall white man with a stack of folded paper. His eyeglasses were tucked inside the front pocket of his monogrammed golf shirt, and his sideburns joined his salt-and-pepper beard.

"Isaiah?" He slowed his pace and moved the papers he was carrying to his other hand. I nodded, and he extended his right hand. As we shook, he gripped my hand firmly and looked at me as if he were trying to match the description given by my parents with person in front of him.

"That's me," I said, squeezing his hand. "Glad to meet you."

"I'm Mr. Lever, your new counselor."

I looked him up and down to get a better feel for what I was dealing with. His stomach hung slightly over his waist, but his pants were creased professionally. His shoes were lace-ups.

"I see you found your way. I was looking for you. Come on into my office. We need to talk." He turned toward the business office and walked us past his secretary, into a spacious, paper-filled room. He grabbed a chair across from me and then motioned for me to sit.

"You'll need to fill out some paperwork before we get started, but don't worry, it won't take long. You'll get a list of your classes before you leave." He handed me a pen and one of the papers he was carrying and waited while I filled everything out. "So, you're the one from boarding school." He looked down at the information sheet that contained my emergency phone numbers, birth date, and home address. Filling out these forms, he'd emphasized, was standard procedure. "You must not have liked it there?"

I weighed his statement for a second, my mind jumping back to the conversation I'd overheard between my parents. They had promised to talk to me about these types of questions, but somehow, it had slipped their minds. They had even forgotten to tell me about Tee. What was up with him? What had changed? I tried my best to stay focused on Lever's question.

"That's true," I said carefully. "But I'm here to make a new start."

"Starting over is not so bad," he said. "Sometimes it's for the best."

"I hope so. My parents aren't too thrilled about me going here, but that's another story. I want to do better here."

"If you keep that attitude, you'll do quite well." He paused. "Believe it or not, I didn't like the first high school I went to, either. I got expelled. I think that's why I became a counselor. I knew I could tell my story to all the students if they got in trouble. I used to cut class to go to the movies. I loved James Bond movies more than I loved studying—he was always calm under pressure."

"You really got kicked out?" I felt an immediate connection. Here was someone who hadn't lived a perfect life.

"Yes, I've been where you're sitting. I figured it out later, though—at some point, you realize that if you want to be successful, you have to go to class."

"That's good to know." I was beginning to feel like I wasn't too far gone. In spite of getting kicked out of Chadwick, I was seeing living proof that miracles happened.

"It's the truth," he said.

I felt myself relaxing a little. How much did he know about my situation? Did he care? Hearing about his life put me at ease. I immediately wanted to stay on his good side because he'd been so honest and show him that I had what it took to make it at McClymonds.

"By the way," he continued, "your parents told me that I'd have *carte blanche* to keep you in line. They said to see to it that you do what you're told. I wanted to make sure that you knew I had the green light to keep you in check." He rested his elbows on the desk, propped his face on his palms and smiled, his lips held tight.

It was difficult for my parents to give up their disciplinary hold. Were they starting all over again? They'd gotten close to Breedlove at Chadwick at the start of things, bringing their Bibles and quoting scripture about discipline at our first meeting. It sounded as if they were trying to set up a similar relationship with Lever.

"Your father asked me about student jobs and career placement. He said Chadwick didn't have much of that. He is determined to keep you busy." I watched him move his bald head back and forth, following the shaded hairline as it met his beard. "I told him that a lot of our kids deliver newspapers and hold after-school jobs to help them keep some spare change in their pockets. In fact, we've got a work-study program here. It's unfortunate that you're starting so late; I could have gotten you in. Mr. Boller, our career options instructor, only works with about twelve students during the year, and his class is full. I can make sure you get in next year. I'll keep my eyes open for you." He grabbed the stack of papers on his desk, straightened them between his fingers, and leaned his body forward against them. The weight of his torso bent the edges of the papers. "So, tell me, Isaiah, what do you want to know? Any questions?"

"None," I said. "I'll probably have more as time goes on, but none right now." I sat on the edge of my seat, waiting for the interview to end so that I could get to my new classes.

"Well, if there are any problems here on your first day, I would hope that you'll seek my input. Like I said, this is a totally different environment from Chadwick. As a matter of fact, I've thrown in a class on your schedule that will show you that this will be a more supportive place."

He handed me an index card with a list of classes, and I looked them over before leaving.

"Mr. Sykes will be your U.S. history teacher," he said. "He's always included black history in his lesson plans, and I've heard nothing but great reports from some of his former students. He recently showed a documentary about the Civil Rights Movement." He looked at me and smiled.

I wasn't sure what to make of this gesture, but it showed me that Lever paid attention to politics. What was he trying to tell me? Did he know about the *Huck Finn* incident from my English class at Chadwick? I'd never expected Dad to say anything about that, considering how disappointed he was at my dismissal and how concerned about appearances he'd seemed on the way here. This was a good start. I folded the list and kept it handy for future reference.

After leaving the office, I moved slowly down the hallway, reading the student work displayed on the bulletin boards and glancing at the school newspaper tacked inside the glass display case. The headlines were about a new campus lunch program allowing students the freedom to eat off campus. Reading the story made me think about how wonderful it felt to be home and eating good meals. Thank God there'd be no more formal dinners or table-waiting.

The campus was large and impersonal. All of Chadwick's students could have fit in several of the large classrooms. Still awaiting the first bell and curious about class sizes, I peered through the portals inside the sunlit classrooms and mindlessly counted empty desks. The classes I selected for viewing was spacious enough for at least thirty students. My classrooms at Chadwick had been small and intimate. I imagined my first class being full and fretted over being introduced as the new kid.

The cover of a book propped up against the lip of a chalkboard resembled the old woman's book on the bus. She'd said it was about change. I had to find a way to get it and satisfy my curiosity. I wandered the hallways a few minutes more until I found the library. Heading toward the checkout counter, I spotted a freckle-faced librarian wearing wire-framed glasses. She'd been eating her breakfast and was wiping her small hands and the edges of her mouth with a paper towel.

"I'm looking for a book called *Toward a Psychology of Being*," I said.

"Is this for one of your classes?" she asked. She looked surprised, almost as if she'd never gotten this request before.

"No, a friend recommended it to me."

She tossed the paper towel into the trash and walked around the counter to a nearby file cabinet and began looking inside.

"I've heard of it, but I'm not sure we have it," she said. Her fingers flipped through the index cards quickly. "By Maslow, right?" She had stopped going through the cards, sticking her finger between them to maintain her place.

I shrugged. I wasn't sure of the author, but I made sure she wrote down the call letters on a piece of paper and then headed to the section where I thought the text was located. I'd know the book when I saw it. I walked across the carpeted floor, past shelves of books, staring at the letters and numbers on the spines, until I had found what I was looking for. I pulled it from the metal shelf and caressed its surface. This was the book, all right. The black-and-white cover bore half of the face of a white man, a single eye staring mysteriously back at the reader. I opened the book to find water-stained pages, key passages underlined with a yellow marker:

Each person's inner nature is in part unique to himself. ... Destructiveness ... seems so far to be not intrinsic but rather they seem to be violent reactions against frustration of our intrinsic needs, emotions and capacities.

I skimmed this statement, mulling over its meaning, and then read further: *Anger is in itself not evil ... of course it can lead to evil behavior ... Human nature is not nearly as bad as it has been thought to be.*

I closed the book a moment and tried to figure out what was being said. The author seemed to be on my side. In so many words, and in just a short time, he had begun to reassure me that putting graffiti all over Negley's garage, though awful, had not made me a bad person. Wanting to read more, I carried the book back to the front desk, and I smiled as I carefully handed it to the librarian.

"Looks like you found the book," she said.

"Yeah, I just need time to read it." I looked at the clock that hung behind her and began to rush. I was already late for my first class. "Can I check it out?"

"Of course," she replied. "I just need to see some proof that you're a student here and after that, you'll have two weeks to return it."

"What if I lose it?" I wasn't sure I'd be able to read it in the time allotted and considered keeping it beyond the two weeks.

"You'll just have to pay the fines and replace it."

I showed her a list of my classes, which was enough to check the book out. I couldn't wait to get started.

*   *   *

Lunchtime came after geometry, Western civilization, and U.S. history. Hearing the noise made by the students assembled inside the airy cafeteria was intimidating compared to the usually quiet and formal atmosphere of the Chadwick dining room. The eating surfaces inside the McClymonds cafeteria were without tablecloths and reminded me of the sterile, rectangular mess hall tables at an old summer camp. The food choices were limited to prepackaged fast food and one hot entrée. Some students carried bag lunches. As I soon found out, the food at McClymonds, like the food at Chadwick, was terrible. No wonder the students wanted an open campus for lunch.

The lines were long. I stood behind an overweight black kid, whose wrinkled T-shirt read: I AM SOMEBODY. Becoming momentarily distracted by a table full of girls with open notebooks, I landed on his heels. He turned his broad shoulders around and looked up at me.

"Who are you?" He tilted his head to the side, crossed his arms, and looked at me without smiling. His 'fro was neatly combed, and his almond-shaped eyes were squinting.

"I'm new," I said.

"That's obvious. You stepped on my heel and didn't apologize. Some people say, 'Excuse me.'" You could have put your finger through the gap in his front teeth.

"And what are you gonna do if I don't?" I lifted my chin, sucked in my stomach, and threw my shoulders back.

"Teach you a lesson, new boy," he said, moving closer to me. "You understand?"

As he moved closer, I made a fist but didn't swing. I waited on his next move and thought about Lever's comments about good conduct. I didn't want to get into a fight on my first day. I needed to defuse the situation, and I pushed him back gently so I'd have more space.

"You aren't gonna teach anybody a lesson." The voice behind me was unmistakable.

Tee's gruff voice was a welcome sound. I took my eye off the fat kid and turned in his direction. Tee's frame had filled out, and the scar that had been evident underneath his right eye during Thanksgiving break had healed.

"Hey, fuck you, Tee. You need to stay outta this," said the fat boy. "You might be king of the school, but this is between new boy and me."

"Russell, you need to settle down—this here is my boy." Tee stepped around me and closer to Russell, who had dropped his backpack and was poised to retaliate. "He just got back from prep school. He's cool. Why you giving him such a hard time?"

"He needs to learn some manners," said Russell.

"Like you, huh?" Tee said. "I think you two just need to let it ride this time. It ain't that big of a deal." He took his eye off Russell and noticed the gap in the food line growing. "Now grab your stuff and move up."

Russell turned around slowly and refocused his attention on making up the space in the line. Some of the other student bystanders, who had moved in closer to hear the confrontation, began moving away.

"That's how you handle that," said Tee, rubbing his hands together and loud-talking him in a way that let Russell know that he wasn't scared. "That boy might be bigger than me, but I'll give him a run for his money."

"I'm sure you will," I said, surprised to see him, but happy he'd found me. "So, it's true. You run this place now?" While I was at Chadwick, he'd bragged a lot over the phone that he'd become the most feared man on campus. I'd been skeptical of his telephone boasts until I witnessed Russell's retreat with my own eyes. He'd solidified his reputation while I was away at Chadwick by beating up Freight Train in one of the school year's biggest fights.

"Nobody messes with me or my friends, if that's what you're trying to say." He looked me up and down in the usual way. "Did you get your classes?"

"Yeah. I met with Lever this morning."

"What time you got gym?"

"Sixth period."

"Damn. I thought we'd at least have one class together." Tee knew that it didn't matter whether you were a sophomore, junior, or senior when it came to gym class. This was the only time all the students were mixed together, regardless of age.

"My parents don't want us hanging out." I said jokingly. "I heard them talking about you this morning. What'd you do this time?"

"I didn't do what *you* did. The word's already out. What happened? Did you paint the entire campus?"

I thought again of Mom and Dad's conversation about my dismissal. If the word was out, it was no use holding anything back. That strategy was history.

"Almost," I volunteered. "But I ran out of time, and then my roommate finked."

"Your roommate?"

"Richard Bonar."

"His folks live next door to the New St. Paul Baptist Church, right?" He was shaking his head as if he were trying to pop a clear picture of Richard into his mind. "He's a real square dude, right?"

"Yeah, that's him. He was always trying to please the teachers and the headmaster, and so he told on me."

"You took a big chance with that paint, man. That school was too small." He smiled. "Well, I knew it was only a matter of time before you found a way to get back here. During your last break, you tried to pretend like you weren't receptive to my suggestions, but when you left, there was something in your voice. And then I reread a few of your letters before I started counting down the time."

"Did I sound confused?"

"Not at all," said Tee. "Just different."

The lunch line moved quickly now, and I stepped inside the kitchen, grabbed a tray, and moved it along the smooth surface in front of the prepackaged food. "So, are you gonna tell me what happened to you, or what?" I picked up the charbroiled hamburger and French fries and slid the tray toward the cash register.

"We didn't win the city championship and the OAL, if that's what you want to know."

"You know what I'm talking about. What's the rest of it?" I asked. "I ain't talking about basketball."

"You mean Saretta?" he said.

"I don't know. You tell me."

"She got pregnant," he said.

"Pregnant?" I said it louder than I wanted to. "You got Saretta pregnant?"

I was surprised, but then again, I wasn't. Saretta was the girl he'd been closest to since we were kids. From our conversations, I knew they'd had sex and that Tee never cared for birth control or condoms. He was using something he called the "rhythm method," which meant he just pulled out when he felt himself getting too excited. It had worked—up until now.

Saretta was one of the only people who really listened to his crazy, moneymaking schemes and radical ideas and laughed at his jokes. The rest of us took many of the things he said with a grain of salt. He'd always said he'd wanted to marry someone who supported him, and now he was making progress toward marriage and fatherhood right before my eyes. Outside of Saretta's support, I didn't see what got him so excited, especially since she wasn't the prettiest girl I'd ever seen. The zits near her forehead were so large sometimes that I wanted to pop them. But then again, that was Tee. He had a style and tastes all his own. Hearing him talk about Saretta made me think back to Jenaye, how what I'd done after sneaking in her room could have easily resulted in the same thing.

"You sure it's yours?" I asked.

"Who else could be the father?" He filled his chest with air. "She was only seeing me."

"You never know," I said.

"Man, that baby's mine. Now I gotta start thinking about making some money."

I waited until Tee had grabbed a cheeseburger, and we walked to the other side of the cafeteria.

"You happy about that?" We found a seat in the far corner, away from the crowd. I looked over my shoulder before he responded, to see who was listening. The next closest table was a few feet away, but none of the kids paid any attention. Everyone was talking about the upcoming senior prom.

He gave me a bland shrug. "Yeah, I guess." He took a big bite of his hamburger, but I'd lost my appetite.

"So you didn't think about adoption?"

"Naw, man. She ruled that out a long time ago. Her parents, once they found out, wouldn't go for that. Mine were pissed when they found out, but there was nothing they could do. So we've decided to move forward. The baby'll get taken care of some kind of way."

"But how?" I folded my arms, leaned back, and waited for his reply. Even with his knack for coming up with moneymaking schemes, I didn't see how Tee would ever make enough money to take care of a newborn baby.

"I'm thinking about quitting school and getting me a hustle. I've got to support a family now—or at least start thinking about it. This school stuff is nice, but I'm not going to be able to depend on anyone else to support my kid."

"What's your mom say about that? She got strong feelings about you dropping out of school?" I unfolded my arms and rearranged the fries on my plate, tossing one in my mouth. I thought about my visits to the beauty shop and how much she'd bragged about Tee in the past. I wondered what she'd brag about now.

"I haven't told her."

"And so you're going to drop out, just like that? What about the hoop team next year? And our plans? You've got to come back so that we'll have a chance at the city championship. I'm back now." I grabbed the ketchup bottle and smacked it hard near the bottom. "You trying to tell me you changed your mind about everything?"

"I've got other priorities." He tried to sound confident without looking me in the eye, but that reaction and his tone were dead giveaways that he was scared about the future.

"Chump." I didn't want to hear it. Things had changed. Basketball had slipped in importance. The reality was that we needed to make money to pay for our mistakes. "I've got to figure out a way to earn some extra money, too. The headmaster at Chadwick sent my father a letter telling him I'd have to pay for what I did to that garage. Since I've been back, all Dad's talked about has been finding a part-time job. He said it would teach me a lesson. But I still ain't giving up basketball. And you shouldn't, either."

"How much do you owe?"

"A few thousand," I said, shrugging. "It's enough for my father to worry about."

"So, how are you gonna get outta the hole?"

"I could work at a theater, a car wash, or even get a paper route."

"But that's not going to bring you enough money, is it? A paper route?"

"Maybe not," I replied. "It'll be enough to keep my dad off my back for a while."

"You need something a little more lucrative." He took a bite of his food and reached underneath the table to shake the loose change in his pocket.

"Like what?"

"We don't have much time to talk right now, but if you want to go into this a little more, come and find me."

"You aren't talking about anything illegal, are you? I've already been in enough trouble."

"It's nothing you can't handle, nothing you've never been exposed to." He took a deep breath. "Relax, man. Being at that school seems to have gotten you all uptight." Tee stuffed the last of his food in his mouth. "What you doing Saturday?"

"Nothing that I can think of."

"Good. We'll take a little walk and talk about this some more. And like I said, man, just relax. You'll thank me later."

COTTONFOOT

"You ready to go?" Tee's voice came through the receiver clearly as my head rested on the pillow, and my eyes, barely open, searched for light.

"It's too early to be going anywhere on a Saturday morning," I said, mumbling a bit while half-asleep. "Plus, I haven't eaten any breakfast."

"Hey, man, the early worm catches the bird," Tee said, laughing. He was always getting sayings wrong. "We've got an important stop to make today, and if you want your father to stop pressuring you about getting a job, you need to stop thinking about your stomach for a second, get out of the house, and hang with me. Your cash problems are about to be a thing of the past. So hurry up."

"At least let me wash up," I said, pushing my fingers into the soft corners of my eyes to dig out the sleep. "Meet me in front of the house."

"I'll be there in no time."

I jumped up and, thinking we were headed for a job interview, threw on a dressy blue shirt, some boots, and a light jacket to shake off the morning fog. My parents were still asleep, but they would have been happy if they'd seen me looking as if I was headed to a job interview. I waited for Tee outside the house on the porch so he wouldn't have to ring the doorbell.

"That was quick." We slapped palms.

"You mentioned money, so I hurried. Am I dressed okay?" Tee had on a collarless shirt and some cords.

He looked at my carefully ironed shirt, the crease in my pants, and the new shoes, and then nodded in approval. "You're all right. Let's go."

We walked down West Street, past a small grocery store, an auto repair shop, and the church. I'd traveled this way before, but only on my way to the grocery store or to church. As we walked, I tried to guess where we'd end up, but the further we walked, the harder it got to imagine.

"Where are we going?" I asked.

"You'll know when you get there."

We continued a few more blocks, until we arrived at a concrete, two-story building with a metallic blue Rolls Royce parked nearby. I hadn't seen a Rolls or a car this fancy since Negley's sports car, and it looked out of place next to a secondhand store and a car repair shop holding Chryslers and Fords.

"We aren't going in there, are we?" I examined the building through the holes in the tall fence. Its windows were protected by security bars, and the metal door held a small peephole.

"Yeah, this is our stop," he said, pulling out a piece of paper and looking at his scribbled handwriting, matching what he'd written with the address on the building. He leaned against the ringer for a long time and waited for someone inside to open the door. As it moved inward, I noticed the shiny wingtips before I saw the face and the smile of a small, fair-skinned black man flashing his gold teeth.

"Hey, Tee, you're early." The man's complexion was red, almost the color of Louisiana's red clay, and his wavy, jet black hair made me think of Nat King Cole.

"I see you brought someone with you." His voice was deep, like it belonged to a man much taller. He walked with a slight limp toward the gate. "He looks kinda familiar."

"You know Isaiah," Tee said, pointing in my direction. "He's the kid everyone was talking about that went to that private school, but he's back here now. He just started this week at Mack …"

"Say no more. I know who he is." The man, who was older, looked up at me as he held the door open. "Come on in, Isaiah. And in case you didn't know it, I'm Lonnie, but everybody calls me Cottonfoot." His awkward gait explained his nickname.

I couldn't help wondering how Tee knew this guy. As we entered the building, Cottonfoot motioned for us to take a seat next to each other on a sunken couch. The fabric was covered with hairs from a mean-sounding dog that barked from behind a closed door. I quickly brushed them off my sleeve, but in a manner that would not offend our host. I didn't know what he had in mind or what the place was really used for, but I had my suspicions after eyeing the brand-new tape decks and racks of new clothes with tags on them. If this were a department store, he would have made a healthy profit.

"Have you thought about what we discussed?" Cottonfoot sat across from us in a wicker rocking chair, posing the question to Tee as if I weren't even there.

"That's why I brought Isaiah here with me," Tee said, nodding at me. "I want him to hear it, too."

"I guess that means it's safe to talk?" Cottonfoot pushed his feet out in front of his body so that his heels rested against the floor.

"Put it like this, Isaiah needs some extra money right now, just like me," said Tee.

"Well, are you going to do it or not?"

"I thought about it," said Tee. "And it sounds like something we can do."

"'We'?" I said, looking at him in amazement.

"Yeah, Isaiah. I haven't told you yet, but Cottonfoot's gonna help us set up our own business. Right, Cotton?" Tee looked toward Cotton, who nodded his head slowly.

"What kind of business?" I asked.

"I'm going to front you some money to set up a little gambling operation," said Cotton. "Hand me the dice, Tee."

Tee reached into his pocket and handed over the dice he'd been carrying. Cottonfoot looked at them momentarily and then showed them to me. The edges of the dice had been filed down suspiciously.

"You see," Cotton said, "If you play with these, you're guaranteed not to lose. Tee's the expert. He's already told me that he's shown you how to hold them and how to throw 'em."

"Are you talking about playing with loaded dice?" I interrupted the presentation. "Man, you're crazy. I just got out of trouble. I'm not interested in something like that. I'll be in hot water all over again. If that's how you plan on making money, I'm outta this now." I stood up in front of the couch and signaled to Tee that it was time to leave. "I didn't mean to come in here and cause a ruckus, but you didn't tell me about this plan, and there's no way I'd get involved in what Cotton's proposing."

"What if we used the money to help the Party?" Tee asked. "He's willing to split the profit sixty–forty to do this. He'd get sixty, and we'd get forty. Sounds fair to me. And if we're successful, you could pay off your school debt, I could support my new baby, and we could use the rest to help the Panthers. It's time for you to make a contribution and join the Party, anyway."

"I'm not ready to join the Party," I replied. "I'm looking for a real job," I said, holding up my hands.

Cotton rocked back in his chair. "I think you need to talk to your boy a little more, Tee. He ain't ready yet."

"You're right," said Tee. "I don't know where he thinks he'll find a job around here. I'll talk to him on the way home. After I get through with him, he'll reconsider."

"And if he doesn't change his mind, you'll just have to do it alone. There'll be more money for your new family, and the Party will love you."

Paying off my school debt and helping the Party sounded good, but I knew I'd need to get moving quickly on finding a real job to prove them wrong. I began to feel empathy for Frank, my old Chadwick buddy. Now I knew what it must have felt like to be put on the spot, how much courage it took for him to listen, knowing my intentions were less than noble.

"Yeah, let's go," said Tee. "I didn't plan on this happening. I'll have to get back to you, Cotton."

*   *   *

"What's it gonna take, big fella?" Tee asked as we walked out of the building to the sidewalk.

"You know my situation, Tee," I said, trailing him slightly. "I'm looking for a *real* job. You know, maybe I can find something in the classifieds. I've seen my mom looking through them. She's gotten lucky, and maybe the same will happen to me. I'm not trying to make a big killing like you are. I'm just hoping for something that will keep me moving in the right direction."

"Cotton's willing to front us some money, which we can use to help ourselves and the Party. How can you pass that up? We'd kill two birds with one stone." Tee was talking and shaking his head like he couldn't believe what was happening.

I had talked a good game and supported him in the past, but when it came down to it, I was scared.

"You really got spooked when they kicked you out of that place," Tee continued. "You need to put that behind you. You're gonna miss out on a lot of things if you keep up this attitude."

"That's just the chance I'm going to take," I said, still insisting that this operation wasn't for me.

"Man, I thought I taught you better than that." He shook his head.

"I'm just learning to pick my spots," I shrugged and then walked ahead of him, trying my best to leave Cotton's proposal behind me as fast as I could. That wasn't my idea of a small business.

Tee caught up. "Well, since you're 'picking your spots,' you wanna hear about something else?" He waited until he had my attention again.

I wondered how Saretta put up with him. His sales pitches were nonstop. "Now what?"

"I've been riding the bus a lot lately and watching these dudes making gobs of money playing three-card monte. I think we could team up and do it. I'll teach you the game, just like I did with shooting dice. You could be my decoy."

"Decoy?"

"He's the guy that pretends to bet his money, like he's got nothing to do with the game, and the other folks on the bus don't know that he's really a partner."

"Oh, yeah, now I know what you're talking about." The description brought back memories of an Easter weekend when Melvin had gambled away the money Mom had given us for buying new church clothes. I'd sat next to him near the rear of the bus the day after Good Friday as we headed downtown and were distracted by a group of three-card monte players who made finding the red card in a sea of black look easy. In their hands, they carried rolls of money bound by thick rubber bands. If you bet on the right card, you won a fortune.

That day, Melvin got carried away and wagered everything in his pocket on the wrong card. We rode the bus all day and eventually got our money back, but he nearly got us killed by betting without any backup. I think they got tired and let us win just to get rid of us. Two young boys begging for their Easter money in front of a bunch of potential customers was bad for business. That crazy day was still vivid, and I wasn't about to go there or tangle with those fellas again.

"You game?" Tee asked, snapping me out of my reverie.

"Man, that's too risky."

"So?"

"We'll get into a fight, I know it."

"You're a pessimist," he said.

"I gotta think about this. I'm not good at gambling. You saw how I was with the dice." I could feel myself getting hungry. It had been an early morning, and now it hit me that I hadn't eaten breakfast. Maybe, after I'd put a little something in my stomach, I'd have a better response to things.

"Well, don't wait too long. The longer you wait, the less money we'll have." He took the back of his left hand and smacked it against his palm to make his point.

"I hear you," I said. "Do you have any other stops for us to make today?" I was in the mood to eat, get out of my clothes, and shoot some hoops.

"Not anymore. You're free to go. The next time you see me, if I've got a pocketful of money, I want you to think twice before asking me for a loan. Remember, you had your chance."

PRESSURE

I unlocked the front door, pushed it open, and headed toward the kitchen. I checked the refrigerator door; underneath a magnet, I found a serious-sounding note from Dad, telling me to stay up until he got home. Maybe he'd heard me leave earlier that day and wanted to talk about my job search.

I grabbed a bite to eat, pulled up a chair at the round mahogany table, and picked up the paper to read the sports page. Flipping to the want ads, I started looking for safer alternatives to the one Tee had presented. He was clearly headed in the wrong direction, and as I turned the pages, I thought of severing ties and somehow limiting my future contact with him. But how was I going to do that? We'd been through a lot together, and he'd been a major part of the reason why I wanted to come back. Now I had to make some hard choices.

The front door slammed shut, and the sound of Dad's footsteps made its way across the hardwood floor into the kitchen. Dad hummed a church tune, a sign there was a lot on his mind. Saturdays were usually taken up by shopping, and when he entered the kitchen, he stopped singing and placed some grocery bags on the table. He turned to look at me, and when I didn't move, he just stared. This gesture was part of the new way he was handling things between us now. He didn't tell me what to do anymore. He made funny faces.

"When you get through with that page," he said, "I want you to put these groceries away. You hear me?"

"Yes." I folded the paper and watched him as he arranged the partially filled grocery bags to make sure they didn't fall off the table's edge.

"I see you got my note." He didn't wait for an answer. "You've been out all day. Were you out looking for a job or just working on your basketball game?" He pointed to my shirt, still damp from playing.

"Both." I dropped the paper and got up to help him. I pulled a few soup cans from the closest bag.

"Any luck? I mean, with the job search?"

"No," I said, stacking the cans neatly on the table.

"Where'd you look?"

"Just around the neighborhood." I didn't want to go into any details about my trip with Tee and my meeting with Cottonfoot.

"I'm glad to see you haven't forgotten about what you're supposed to do. You got some mail today." From inside his coat pocket, he pulled out a thick letter with a Chadwick return address. It was hard to tell who it was from. It looked official and my name was printed neatly across the front. Thinking it was from Mr. Breedlove, I shoved it inside my pocket.

"Anyway," Dad said, "I got a call from your counselor."

"Oh yeah?" I said, recalling my initial meeting with Mr. Lever.

"Well, he told me that he had a contact out at the RC Cola plant and that they were hiring students on a part-time basis. It's work I think you can do, and it looks like it won't interfere with your schoolwork." He pulled out a piece of paper from his pants pocket that had been folded several times over. "Here's the name and number. I want you to call him."

"Okay," I said reading the name on it: Auggie Sutcliff. I stuffed it in my pocket, along with the letter. "I'll do my best."

"I hope so," he said. He stood there for a moment, watching me put away the groceries. "You need me to give you some job advice?"

"Go ahead." I tried to pretend like I had it all under control, but the letter distracted me. He talked for a long time, but I never heard a thing until the end. I appreciated his concern.

"If you really want the job, make sure you look the interviewer in the face. Don't mumble, and dress neat. I think that's all you need to know right now. If you remember all that, you'll go far. You understand?"

"Got it."

GOOD NEWS AND BAD

The next day, as I nervously waited to board the bus for my interview, I thought about meeting with Cottonfoot and Tee, wondering if I'd reacted too quickly in rejecting the offer to help. What if Tee became successful and earned the money he'd talked about? After he supported his family, would he use the leftover funds to help the Party? Would he laugh at my real job and rub it in if the salary was meager? Would he feel sorry for me and decide to share? Cotton's idea was too risky, and even if we got the operation under way, there'd be no guarantee that I'd become a proficient enough gambler to raise the money to pay off the damage to Negley's garage. I preferred to take my chances with a conventional job at the cola plant.

I bit my lip and peered down the street to see if I could see the bus coming, but it was still nowhere in sight. What was taking it so long? Reaching inside my pocket to make sure I had my fare, I found the letter Dad had handed me the day before. Realizing that I had delayed opening it out of fear that it was from Breedlove and a sure reminder about the damage bill, I finally mustered up some courage to face the inevitable, pulled it out, and tore it open.

May 1, 1974

Dear Isaiah:

It's been a little quiet closing out the year without you, and so I thought I'd write you a letter to find out how things were going. A lot of people are still talking about that paint job at Negley's house, but I hope your disappointment over getting booted from the team is over and you've moved on.

Since you left, I got accepted into Claremont College. It's a big difference from what I expected (I always imagined myself at an Ivy League school), but I hear it's a good school. And coming from here, it's just the right size. Because it's small, I have a feeling that I won't get lost in the shuffle like I would at some Ivy League school. I've already talked to the basketball coach and it looks like I'll be able to at least try out for the team next year.

Remember that coach at Proctor? The one I called a "big recruiter"? Remember the story about the kid he recruited in Hawaii? Guess what? He's been asking about you! I hope you don't mind it, but I took the liberty of writing him and telling him about what happened to you. He wrote me back, and believe it or not, he's interested in talking to you. I thought it was the least I could do for you since you've been real loyal to me. He's always been interested in building a good team. It's another prep school, but so what? I know you can do it.

Maybe if you have the time you can call him and see what he wants. There's no obligation. It couldn't hurt. I've put his number on the back of this letter. It would be another way to get a brand-new start.

Think about it. I hope I'll hear back from you soon. Let me know what you think. The end of school is only a couple of weeks away. I can't wait.

Frank

It was an understatement to say the letter surprised me. I read it over a few times, and then folded it and shoved it back in my pants when the bus arrived. Our games of one-on-one had improved Frank's game so much that now he was in a position to make a college team. He appeared to be returning the favor. How could I forget Proctor's coach and his comments to me after that game? Was it possible to go back to boarding school now? He made everything sound so easy, but I knew there would be more involved.

When the bus arrived at RC Cola, I tried to shift my thoughts from the letter to the upcoming job interview, but I was having a hard time. I buttoned my suit jacket and straightened my tie as I approached the building's entrance. With each step toward the door, I tried to put the letter behind me. I'd been on interviews before, but this time I'd have to banish an unexpected distraction and face a potential employer without the help of my parents.

I greeted the receptionist as I entered the building and then examined the pictures of soft drinks and the company's fancy logo in the spartan lobby while she paged Auggie Sutcliff. She pointed me down a long hallway through the facility to his office.

As I wandered through the plant, trying to remember Dad's advice, Auggie Sutcliff stepped out of his glass-enclosed office to greet me. Strands of Auggie's thin brown hair rested on his forehead and above his deep-set eyes. Extending his arm, he shook my hand firmly and showered me with stale breath that he tried to cover with a Lifesaver.

As I followed him into his office, I looked around in amazement: workers were lined up, adjacent to noisy bottling machines, making sure the bottles were filled, capped, and boxed for transport. I sat in a chair near the desk, like I'd done with Breedlove, Hagman, and Mr. Levers. Behind Sutcliff's head, I spotted safety manuals in white plastic binders and a poster of two white hands clasped together in brotherhood. On the desk there was a stack of papers that measured an inch thick.

"I see you found me," he said.

"It wasn't hard. I just followed the directions your receptionist gave me."

"That's a good sign. You listen well." He peered at my shoulders. "And you're certainly built for the job. You're the ideal candidate. There's just one small thing ..."

"Okay," I said, wondering what was next.

"Did you fill out an application?" He pointed to the stack of papers on his desk. "Before you came, I looked for one."

"No," I said looking back at him. "I didn't know I had to. Mr. Lever didn't mention any application."

"It's just a formality. You mind filling out one for me? It'll give me a better idea of your abilities." He reached inside his drawer and handed one to me. "Take your time and fill everything out. I've got to leave for a few minutes, but when I come back, we'll talk."

He allowed me time to complete the application, and when he returned, he took it from me.

"I see you have a little work experience." He placed it flat on the desk.

"I've had a paper route and a janitorial job. They didn't pay a lot, but I was there every day." I wanted to show Sutcliff that I was dependable and had the drive to do what was necessary.

"This job will be quite different. But you knew that, right?"

"How so?"

"We're looking for part-timers to help us out during the supermarket strike."

"A strike?" I asked, a little surprised. No one had told me about this, and I thought about getting up from my chair and looking for something safer, but I stayed there, hoping to hear that there was a catch or something.

"Yeah," Sutcliff said, "the store clerks at all the major supermarkets are on strike, and some of our regular drivers and delivery boys don't want to cross the picket line. We've got a lot of product to sell, and we need fellows like you to help us with the deliveries until things get back to normal. Is that something you can handle?" He folded his arms and waited. "It might get a little hairy, but you'll be all right. You'll be paired up with a veteran. He's been through these things before."

"I guess that means I have the job?"

"Sure," he said. "If you want it, it's yours."

"Of course I do." Thinking of Tee, I reached for another application. "Can I have another one? I have a friend who might be interested."

"Take as many as you'd like."

The offer not only meant I'd finally be able to get Dad off my back, but also it was living proof that I didn't need Cotton or Tee's wild moneymaking schemes. As I headed for the bus, I broke into a light jog. The soles of my feet grazed the pavement as if I were being pulled along by a conveyor belt. I could barely find my fare as I tried to imagine Dad's reaction after briefing him on the strike. I toyed with the idea of not telling him about it, afraid he'd be overly concerned for my safety. But knowing his current state of mind, he'd most likely downplay the danger and then tell me to find a way to make things work.

I poured the loose change in the fare box like it was a piggy bank and found a seat near the rear. I shook the rest of the change in my fist as I looked at a young passenger whose face resembled Tee's. Staring at that passenger made me wonder about Tee, what he would say about my new job. I hadn't gotten back to him about his wild plans, and the new job offer, if Dad approved, made it unlikely that I'd ever participate in his schemes. I couldn't wait to tell him about it. I'd grabbed an application in the hope of convincing him that working at RC Cola was a better alternative to hustling money on a bus. I'd make sure that he filled it out. Anything could happen.

Before leaving the bus, I practiced telling Dad about the new job, but not Frank's letter. I wasn't sure if he'd welcome it. Another boarding school suggestion would keep him glued to the past. It was much too early to talk about a second chance.

*   *   *

I rushed through the house to the kitchen and found Dad sitting in a chair peeling potatoes, getting them ready for a pot roast. I liked to sit with him when he prepared the family's meals because he usually lowered his guard and told me what he really thought about things. He'd placed a brown grocery bag between his legs to catch the skins, and his fingers were coated by a chalky white film. He glanced up at me with watery eyes, watching my chest heave from the long run. Something was clearly wrong. He didn't return my smile and kept swallowing his words, stopping just before making a sound.

"Why are you looking so down?" I finally said. "I've got some good news. I got the job at RC Cola."

He twisted his lips slightly, raised an eyebrow, and got up to wash his hands. It wasn't like him to just ignore me, and it certainly wasn't the reaction I was looking for. I expected him to jump up and hug me, but he was calm.

"That's good news, son," he said. "But have a seat. I've got something to tell you."

"What?" I didn't want to sit down.

"It's your friend, Tee," he said.

"What about him?" I asked.

"He was shot on the bus today. He's dead."

I took a breath. The news hit me hard, fast, and out of nowhere. I felt numb, like my whole body had been shot with Novocain. I dropped the job application on the floor. Without looking up, I stared at the blank spaces on the application.

"No. It can't be."

I sat with my face in my hands without moving. Images of my time together with Tee came to me one after another. I thought of our weed-smoking, the playground, our plans to play at McClymonds, and his latest moneymaking schemes. I wanted things to be different. I wished I'd been riding that bus with Tee, and that I'd been the victim. He had a kid on the way. Who was going to be the father?

"He's gone, and that's all I know," Dad said. He walked to the refrigerator and wiped his wet hands on the dish towel that hung on the door handle.

"Who told you?" I asked. I looked up and tried to keep a straight face, but the tears started to come.

"Diane." That was Tee's sister. "Mrs. Lassiter was too distraught. Diane said they took him to Highland Hospital, but he was dead by the time they got him there."

"Did they catch the shooter?"

"I don't know," he said. "I didn't get that far. Once she gave me the news, she just broke down. Maybe you should call her or go by the house."

"Okay," I said. "But I should have talked him out of it. I should have been there. Me. Me."

"Talked him out of what?"

"It's hard to explain," I stuttered. "I could have stopped him."

"What could you possibly have done?" Dad stood in the middle of the floor with his hands outstretched, waiting for me to continue. "I know he was your friend, but that boy didn't listen to anybody, including you. Do you see what we were trying to tell you? Does it make sense now?"

"Yeah." We had our disagreements about Tee, but this wasn't the time to get into a debate with Dad. Tears flowed freely now as I began to think about what life would be like without Tee. I couldn't stop thinking about him, and now he was gone. His desire to make money at any cost had resulted in his death. I could no longer sit. I started to walk back and forth to the sink, turning on the faucet, letting it run without placing my hands in the water.

"Don't you want to sit?" As I walked toward him, Dad reached up and tugged at my arm.

"Not really," I said. "I'm not sure what I want to do right now."

"We need to talk about this." Dad was still tugging, trying to get me to settle down.

I considered heading back to my room, where it was quiet and I could be alone in my grief, but I knew I'd feel better if I shared my loss with him. I sat back down.

"Tee was trying to set up a gambling operation on the bus to make money so he could help his pregnant girlfriend and help me pay off that damage bill. We were going to use the extra money to help the Panthers. He was a good dude; he just didn't think things through."

"Like you, huh?" Dad never hesitated to take advantage of an opportunity to get his point across.

"You know what I mean," I snapped back in defense of my friend.

"Sure do," he said. "Just let what happened be a lesson to you, son. You've got to stay away from the wrong people and get your education." He leaned forward in his chair and continued peeling the potatoes while I let the words sink in a little. "You said he was trying to help the Panthers with a gambling operation on the bus?" I could tell he was wrestling with the logic.

"Yeah," I said confidently, going into detail about our meeting with Cottonfoot. I even told him about Tee's three-card monte scam, carefully emphasizing how we'd use the money.

"That was stupid. You know how I feel about gambling."

How could I forget? He'd removed the dice in the Monopoly game.

"That's why I didn't want you getting involved with him in the first place," he continued. "I know it hurts right now, but you've got to look at this as a lesson. Now you see why I wanted you to go to Chadwick, and why I didn't want you to come back to this neighborhood. I knew what you'd be up against."

His comment made me think about Frank's letter. I hadn't mentioned it yet—maybe another change of scenery was something I needed. Maybe the letter was the thing that would get Dad off his soapbox. Maybe he'd consider Frank's suggestion a godsend and think about sending me to another boarding school, where I'd get a chance to finally make him proud.

"Do you remember that letter you gave me?" I said.

"It was from Chadwick, right?"

"My friend Frank sent it to me. He told the coach at Proctor, another boarding school, asked about me. He thinks that school will be a good fit for me and wants me to call the coach and see what happens."

Dad stopped peeling potatoes. "Let me see that letter," he said.

I pulled it from my pocket and handed it to him. He took a few minutes to read it over, and then handed it back without comment, a sign he wasn't as excited as I was.

"So, what did you think?" I asked.

"Your buddy is looking out for you, that's for sure," he said, nodding his head and giving me a weak smile. "But we've been through this before with the Rising Stars Program. Remember?"

"How could I forget?" I said, recalling my initial introduction to the program. I remembered not wanting to go, but this time my attitude was different. Tee was gone, and now that I knew what to expect, getting away from the heartbreak of the news seemed more appealing.

"I don't think you should get your hopes up about some vague proposal. You don't know enough about Proctor or this coach your friend is talking about." He finished peeling the last of the potatoes and wiped his hands on a nearby rag. "Besides ..."

"What?" I answered.

"No one in their right mind would ever let you back in a boarding school after what you've done."

DON'T SHOP HERE

Days before the funeral, I started working at RC Cola. When he got over hearing about Tee's death, I told Dad the details of my interview, and he was so pleased with the offer that I left off the part about the strike. The assignment sounded dangerous and morally reprehensible, considering the unfavorable impact on the full-time workers, but on the positive side, I'd earn extra money to pay off my debt—and as a practical matter, working as a scab was a safer alternative than getting involved in a gambling venture. Plus, it provided the perfect diversion from thoughts of Tee. I'd recovered from the initial shock, but I knew that once I witnessed his body going down into the grave, I'd want to scream and cry out for his return.

Inside the well-lit bottling plant, the activity was intense. Workers with earplugs stacked crates of finished soda bottles next to the noisy conveyor belt. Among the crowd, I looked for the man that Sutcliff had told me I'd be paired up, with but no one fit the description. Outside I spotted a charcoal-complexioned man with rough skin, almost like leather, and a wiry frame. He was leaning against a red, white, and blue delivery truck, smoking a cigarette. His biceps were smaller than I expected for a man who'd spent his life delivering beverage crates. Considering the job ahead of us, I wondered if he could lift more than his weight.

"You the new guy?" he asked as I walked closer. The cigarette smoke hovered near his face.

I nodded my head and shoved my hands deep inside my pants. "Yeah." The fingers of one hand found my house keys, and I shook them over and over until the guy took notice.

"Relax. I'm Jacob Gibson, but Mister to you. As soon as they load us up, we'll be moving out. Take this." He handed me a long-sleeved, heavily starched white shirt that was worn by members of the delivery crew. "You drink coffee?"

"No," I said, recalling the first time my stomach cramped after sampling a cup. "I'll just wait here until they finish." I put on the shirt as the forklift guy loaded our truck with soda cans and bottles.

"Suit yourself," he said, dropping his cigarette to the ground and mashing it underfoot. "I need a boost. They should be ready for us when I come out."

He went inside briefly and then stepped out of the break room, caressing a white Styrofoam cup, lines of steam drifting from the top. "You're in for a real treat, Isaiah." He took a sip and glanced at the RC Cola insignia inscribed on the side of the truck in bold letters. The forklift operator had finished his job. "Did Sutcliff tell you about the strike?" We moved toward the truck.

"He didn't say much," I said.

"Well, he should have."

"He just said you'd teach me the ropes."

"That's Auggie for you," he said matter-of-factly. "Right now he just wants to get some bodies in here. I've been in this business about thirty years, and let me tell you, every strike's different."

"How?" I asked, getting into the truck.

"You'll see. If it lasts a long time, things could get real nasty. Just keep your cool—and whatever you do, don't take your eyes off this vehicle." As he started the engine, he pounded the palm of his hand against the dashboard for emphasis.

"I won't."

We pulled out of the plant parking lot and headed toward the highway.

"Good. You'll need to learn how to operate a hand truck, but I'll teach you before the day is over. This first delivery should be a piece of cake."

As we cruised along the Alameda shoreline, I peered out the window at the mounds of sand, the distant San Francisco skyline and the bay, watching the small waves hitting the shore. I thought about working during the strike, keeping my cool and making sure I kept my eyes on the truck when we got to the grocery store. Remembering all these things seemed like a tall order on my first day, but I was determined to make sure everything went smoothly.

As we drew closer to our destination, focusing was difficult. At a stoplight, a young woman crossed in front of our truck holding an infant. Saretta, who was carrying Tee's unborn child, entered my mind. I wondered if she'd thought about what Tee would be like as a father, if he'd have measured up to her ideal. The slow, jerking motion of the truck shifting into gear after the change of the traffic light brought me back.

Mr. Gibson drove around the back of the grocery store to the delivery area and pulled alongside the loading dock of the grocery store, avoiding a crowd of strikers at the front who were carrying handwritten picket signs and fliers.

"Like I said, keep your eye on the truck at all times." Mr. Gibson looked through his rearview mirror and cut the engine. "You open the side bays, and I'll unload the sodas. While I'm working, watch my back. Now, let's get cracking!"

I pulled the door handle, headed to the rear of the truck, and began unloading the cargo onto Mr. Gibson's hand truck.

"Hey, scab!" A gray-haired picketer with day-old stubble and a red beanie came around the corner. His shirttail hung outside his dingy white pants. The sign he carried read: DON'T SHOP HERE.

"You're taking food outta my baby's mouth," said a younger white man, wearing shorts, a baseball cap, and dark shades. The comment made me anxious, and I wanted to see his face without cover. Was he telling the truth? I thought for a minute about Jacob's warning. If I kept my cool, we'd get through this. I'd earn some dollars, and I'd have a story of survival to tell, just like Mr. Gibson.

"I ain't taking nothin'," I said. I tucked in the shirt that Mr. Gibson had handed me and puffed my chest out to make my frame look like I was a weight lifter. Maybe I could scare them into leaving me alone.

"How old are you?" The beanie man put the picket sign down and rested it against his dark sweatshirt. He was sizing me up the way my fat classmate at McClymonds had done on my first day.

I looked at him hard, determined not to reply. The way he had asked, it sounded like a test of some sort, and I wondered what he was prepared to do with the information if I gave it to him. If he asked a follow-up question, I was prepared to tell him I was much older, just to keep him off balance. I remained silent, waiting for him to make the next move, but instead of beanie man saying something, Mr. Gibson did.

"Fuck you, man. Mind your goddamn business. You got something to say, you say it to me," said Gibson, rubbing his knuckles and staring at the striker with fire in his eyes before moving the stack of sodas toward the entrance. I was glad he'd come to my defense. His vocal support made me feel as if I was part of a team. I turned to watch him pushing the heavy load through the doorway, and when I turned back around, the strikers were gone. There was a long silence, time enough for me to think about Tee. I wished he were here to see the money that he could have made. Recalling Mr. Gibson's warning, I walked slowly along the side of the truck to see if I could locate them. I was too late.

The morning quiet was shattered by the sounds of breaking bottles crashing against the pavement. I got up from my knees and ran to the other side of the truck. The strikers proudly stood next to the shallow pond of soda flowing among large chunks of broken glass.

"Get away from the truck!" I yelled.

"You didn't know what you were in for, did you?" The beanie man, satisfied with the result, folded his arms and waited for my answer.

"Just stand back." I continued to look down at the shattered glass.

"Well, let this be a lesson to you, young man. When we said, 'Don't shop here,' we meant it."

"I can't help it." I felt the need to explain myself, but I knew I'd never get through to him. "I need the money."

"Don't get smart, or we'll make sure you never get out of here." He moved his arms around in the air and pointed toward the other striker. "How old did you say you were?"

"I didn't."

"You look young enough to be in high school. Your parents must not care about you. I've got a son your age, but I'd never send him out to some picket line. I'd be afraid of what would happen." He moved closer toward the remaining cargo. His counterpart kept an eye on me.

"Come on, man," I could feel him getting ready to do something else. "Just stay away from the truck, or I'll have to report you. We're leaving soon, and I guarantee you, we won't come back. We just had to deliver these sodas." I took my eyes off him and surveyed the truck's remaining cargo. The damage was significant, meaning we'd have to go back to the plant and reload.

"I know what you were doing." He leaned against the truck. "You should have never stopped here."

The squeaking wheels on Gibson's hand truck signaled his return, and I turned my head to see him there with his mouth barely open, tugging at the bill of his baseball cap. I felt bad that I hadn't been able to keep up my side of the bargain, but the strikers had moved faster than I'd expected. They'd vandalized the truck before I knew what to do. I didn't have a weapon, and I was too young to fight grown men. Sure, I'd get my licks in, but that fight with Dad months ago had made me a little more cautious.

"Fucking assholes!" Mr. Gibson looked at the strikers and accessed the damage. "You satisfied now?" He had let the hand truck go so that it rested in front of his body, but I could tell by the way he was sucking in air that he could have turned the heavy object into a battering ram.

"Yeah." The strikers looked down proudly at the wet ground. "We just thought we'd show you guys something." The beanie man did all the talking now.

"We get the message." Mr. Gibson's hands were deep inside his pockets. He rattled some keys. "We won't be back. Now get out of the way—we've got another stop to make."

Mr. Gibson grabbed the handle to the dolly and pushed it rapidly toward one of the strikers, as if he weren't going to stop. When the striker stepped back, he threw the hand truck in an empty compartment, secured it, and pulled himself into the driver's seat. He opened my door, and I hopped inside as fast as I could. By the time I pulled myself up, he was shaking his head back and forth. I wondered how this event compared with all the other strikes he'd been through.

"I thought I told you to watch the truck? You hard of hearing or something?"

"There were two of them, and they were moving too fast. I couldn't keep up."

He closed his eyes and put his hands over his ears, a clear indication that there was nothing I could say that would satisfy him. I'd failed a crucial test, but at that moment, Tee's death was weighing heavily on my mind.

I quickly told him the story of what happened to Tee, a story one of the boys who frequented the playground had told me on the way to work. Tee had gotten in an argument with another Party member, a true believer, over Tee's shaky method of fund-raising.

I told Gibson that if Tee had still been alive, I wouldn't have had any problems keeping track of the strikers because I'd have focused on what I was supposed to be doing. The moment I'd taken my mind off of my job, all hell broke loose.

He listened, but he looked at me like I was crazy and then drove off.

LAST RITES

Tee's funeral was held at New Jerusalem Baptist Church. I sat in the pew next to my father with my head bowed and my face hidden in my hands, trying to fathom what the future would be like. My palms were wet from the tears that gathered between the folds of the lifelines, and my throat was raw from coughing.

Attending funerals had never been a favorite activity. As a small child, I'd shied away from viewing dead bodies. The eerie music and the smell of embalming fluid inside the mortuary gave me nightmares. For Tee's funeral, I sat as close as I could to the casket. I'd lost my fear. It was the first time I'd seen him in a suit. He looked like he was asleep, and I wanted to wake him and tell him that things weren't supposed to end like this.

The minister wore a white robe trimmed in red and warned us during the eulogy that an early death would be our fate if we didn't use good judgment. "You hold the key to your own future," he said, moving back and forth across the pulpit.

The adrenaline pumped through my veins like oil through a pipeline and before he spoke again, I pulled Frank's letter from my pocket and held it in my hand. I began to wipe away tears and sit straight. An image of Tee's girlfriend and unborn son flashed across my mind. Tee would never see him grow up. How would they fare now that he was gone? What was my responsibility, if any, to look after them? How could I make things right?

I didn't hear much else after the sermon, and I stayed in my seat during the viewing, preferring to watch the steady procession of friends and family walk by. It seemed as if everyone was there, even Cottonfoot. I was surprised by his appearance. He wasn't the killer, but he'd played a large role in Tee's warped thinking, and I wanted him to disappear. Maybe he'd change his ways after hearing the minister's message. Reverend Greenway's message had certainly made me change my thinking; it had made me regret the garage incident and all the other stupid things I'd done to get myself kicked out of school. But he'd said there was time to turn things around if I acted immediately, even after all that.

His sermon was about a foolish man, who had built his house upon the sand, and a wise man, who built his house upon a rock. When it rained, the foolish man lost his home because he'd erected his home on unstable ground. The wise man's house survived. I wanted to be like that wise man and build myself a better foundation this time. I was ready to take advantage of another boarding-school opportunity if the Proctor deal could be worked out.

When the service finally ended, Dad placed his hand on my shoulder and led me outside to the hearse that would take us to the cemetery.

"It's going to be all right, son," he said, reaching for the door handle and letting me inside. "I've lost friends, too. It'll get better, I promise you."

"I hope so," I said, wiping away more tears. The words of the minister were still fresh in my mind.

Dad put his arms around me.

"I'm turning over a new leaf," I said into his chest.

"You're what?" Dad sounded surprised.

"Turning over a new leaf." I repeated.

"What does that mean?"

"I was listening to the minister, and the things he said about wise men and foolish men made me think about Chadwick. I know you said you didn't think anyone would accept me at another boarding school because of what happened, but I'd like to try it again. I think we should at least call that coach and see what he says."

"Does that mean that if you get accepted, and your mom and I decide to send you to Proctor, you wouldn't blow it?" His tone was skeptical.

"That's precisely what I mean," I said, looking at him and hoping my answer meant he'd tell me to give the coach a call.

"Well, Isaiah, we've talked about this before, and all this looks to me like too much, too late. Of course, the first time around I was a little more gung ho about private school. It was a good opportunity for you then, but I'm not going through this again. It's a nice gesture, but if we decided to let you go and something didn't quite sit right, you'd end up doing something you didn't have any business doing. I know it."

"You won't have to worry about that anymore," I said. "That was in the past. That was before Tee got killed. I think I'm ready now."

Tee's death had scared me. Reports about the search for his killer were in the news daily, and I didn't feel safe anymore. I wasn't a target, but the real truth was that I saw Proctor as my way out of the madness.

"Now you listen, as far as I'm concerned you might as well get this idea out of your mind. What you gonna tell that new coach about the damage bill you're responsible for? What are you going to say when that surfaces?"

"I'll just say I'm working on it. I'll tell them about my job at RC Cola."

Dad placed his hand over his forehead like he was tiring of my repeated requests for another chance. "Somehow, I don't think that's going to fly. Frank was certainly nice to write this letter for you, but I think you should write him back and tell him that we're going to call Coach Goodham and tell him that we're not interested. And while you're at it, I'd like to talk to him, too. I'm convinced, and I think you should be, too, that McClymonds is the best place for you now. Since you've been back, I've seen a marked improvement in your attitude and schoolwork. I haven't been able to put my finger on it, but I've concluded that forcing you to go to Chadwick was quite selfish of me. Making you go was about us, your mom and me, more than you, and it's been an expensive lesson." The hearse driver turned into the cemetery. "Let's just bury everything right here. It's not going to work."

"If you say so."

An array of headstones towered over a freshly dug grave. I'd been selected as a pallbearer. I stretched the muscles in my arms as I watched the thinly framed funeral director slip on his tight-fitting white gloves and open the back door to the car carrying Tee's body.

There had to be a way to get that damage bill paid; I just hadn't figured it out yet. The proceeds certainly weren't going to come from my delivery job. One day of the strike was enough. I was seriously considering not going back and looking for something safer. Knowing Tee, he would have had a plan by now, and that was exactly what got him where he ended up. Looking at his casket, and awaiting the signal from the funeral director to grab the handle, I realized that I wasn't through crying.

SECOND CHANCE

"Mr. Goodham?" I held the receiver tightly in my wet palms.

"Speaking," he said.

"This is Isaiah Issacson. I'm not sure if you remember me—"

"Oh, Isaiah," he said quickly, "of course I know who you are. When we played Chadwick the first time, you really handled us. I knew then that you'd be a better fit at Proctor. I'm sure you didn't feel that way, but I have a sixth sense about stuff like this. Now you're at a public school. Frank told me everything." His voice was high-pitched, barely masculine.

"Really?" I thought about the graffiti and felt embarrassed. I hoped he didn't know about the bill. I decided not to go into it any further. I'd leave his response right where it was.

"Yeah, I made some phone calls on my own. I know about your problems, but we can work around them. So are you interested? Do you think you'd like Proctor? We're not McClymonds High, but we're not Chadwick, either. With you on our team, we'd be fantastic. Don't get me wrong. It won't be *all* basketball, but you'll be fine."

Goodham's enthusiasm was evident. I twisted the phone cord to the receiver around in my hand and waited. I was interested in the idea, I just didn't know how to tell him there would have to be a trade-off, and that he had to be willing to talk to Mom and Dad to seal the deal.

"Of course I'm interested. It's my dad and mom you'll need to convince. They don't want me going to another boarding school. My behavior at Chadwick left a bitter taste in their mouths ..."

"Well, Isaiah, we can work around just about anything, if you know what I mean. Academics? Money? You name it. I'm in the business of helping people."

"You are?" I was puzzled by his generosity. Nothing like this had ever happened to me. He didn't seem like a wealthy or nerdy man, but my parents always said that you never could tell about white people. A lot of them never made their wealth or their knowledge obvious.

"What if I talk to your parents and to the people at Chadwick about you? We could always arrange a meeting here. You haven't seen our campus. I can't tell you how many parents want to enroll their kids once they've seen the place. The trees and the ocean here on the Monterey Peninsula have amazing powers of persuasion." Goodham put a positive spin on everything.

"That sounds good," I said, imagining the look and the feel of new surroundings. "It would certainly help if they heard you talk about that place."

"I'll talk to your parents first, and then I'll see what I can do. Are they around?"

"Not right now," I said, afraid to tell him that the real purpose for my call was to relay the message from my father that we weren't interested. Before I knew it, I'd gotten caught up in the sound of his voice. "But when they come back, I'll let them know I talked to you and that you want to talk to them." I hunted for a piece of paper to write down a note. "So you really think you can persuade them?"

"Just give me a little time, Isaiah. I know we'll work this out."

*   *   *

From the backseat of the car, I sniffed at the foggy smell of the forest and caught glimpses of dried bark hanging from the trunks of redwoods. As Dad drove the car down the narrow, two-lane road toward the Proctor School, the periodic dips and intermittent potholes made it difficult to focus. Outside the window, rays of sunlight cut through the dense fog and between tree limbs searching for the ground.

Wooden signs painted in bold white letters pointed the way to the campus, and I couldn't help thinking that Goodham's favorable descriptions of the place were accurate.

The meeting had been arranged between my parents and Goodham for the first day of summer vacation. Goodham greeted us in golf pants and a bright shirt. He took us around the campus and then to dinner. He talked at length about the new opportunity, but Dad's expression was muted until the coach mentioned paying off the damage bill.

"So what do you think?" asked Goodham at the dinner table. It was the first time during our visit that he'd really paused to take a break from his relentless sales job or offered anyone the chance to speak. His crooked-toothed smile came across as naïve, but contagious, as he sat across from me, holding the fork above his plate. He moved his head back and forth, staring at Mom, Dad, and then at me.

"I don't know," said Dad, still sounding noncommittal. He had worn a dark suit jacket and had removed his tie after the campus tour. "I've been through all of this once before. Like I told Isaiah, it sounds like a good opportunity, but I just don't know what to do. You understand my dilemma, don't you?"

He pushed himself back from the table and ran his right hand over his bushy eyebrows and carefully clipped mustache. Without waiting for Goodham's answer, he kept talking. "I don't want to be the only one making the decision this time. Isaiah doesn't know about this, but my wife and I have decided to get his input." He looked over at Mom, who had removed her glasses and was nodding her head in agreement. The tight curls in her hair moved with the rocking of her body. We'd been here before, but the circumstances were different. "Now, it's gonna be his call, and you're here to witness it." He folded his hands across his chest. "Isaiah?"

"I'm ready." The words came out quickly and without hesitation.

"Oh, boy. That's what I like to hear. I can't wait to tell your new teammates." Goodham dropped the fork and rubbed his hands together. I'd never seen a grown man act so crazy, but that was what I liked about him. I gobbled down the rest of my pizza and waited for my parents to finish talking so that we could take the ride home. I'd have a whole summer to get ready for my new school. It was the first time I could ever remember being really happy about going somewhere new.

I'd finally met a private school representative who felt the same way I did about sports. The new team sounded as if it was going to be good. I could feel it. But that wasn't all. Proctor offered me the chance to make a fresh start. Princess Victoria had set the stage for my transformation on the bus back home, telling me about her fall from grace and that the only constant in life was change. Tee's death and Reverend Greenway's sermon at the funeral made me think about the importance of making good decisions, and I'd promised myself that I was going to change. I knew that no boot camp, black history, or militant attitude alone could help me in my quest for a quality education and a sense of purpose. I'd have to accept change and make good decisions if I were going to make it at my new school. Proctor sounded like a place where I could try out all of these things.

This time, I'd have no one else to blame if my schooling at Proctor didn't work out. This time it was my choice. There was no place to go but up.

June 1, 1974

Dear Isaiah:

Sorry to hear about your friend Tee. I couldn't imagine what I'd do if that were one of my own friends. I'm hoping that one day when this all blows over we'll be able to sit down and really talk about everything. Maybe I can help.
Jenaye

RECONCILIATION

Driving my car up the paved and winding path to Chadwick, I held the steering wheel tightly. Revisiting the place that had caused me so much angst was making my muscles taut. Deciding whether or not the new multimillion-dollar building proposal Chadwick had submitted to American Capital would work was going to be difficult. They'd embarked on a massive rebuilding campaign to expand the campus and fix some old buildings. I'd have to be objective in deciding whether to approve the funds and not let getting kicked out interfere in any way.

Beads of sweat gathered on my face. Was I dressed right? Where was Negley? Had the campus changed? Were there a lot of black kids now? Would anyone ask me about my dismissal? Was Jenaye already here? My marriage had made it impossible to see her. Geneva, my ex-wife, was the jealous type. Trying to stay in touch with Jenaye would have only made things worse. Her invitation was perfect timing.

It felt strange traveling to mingle with classmates and the alumni who had willingly embraced Chadwick. I felt out of place but confident that I'd be well received once some of my former classmates learned of my real purpose. I had to admit that showing up for a reunion to a place I'd been kicked out of would have been more difficult if I'd not been presented with the loan request.

Proctor had ended up being the best place for me—better than Chadwick and McClymonds combined—but part of my success was because I'd committed myself to no longer behaving like an outsider. My transformation into a willing member of another boarding-school community was a story I couldn't wait to tell, which was another reason why it was good I'd come back. Jenaye's invitation to the reunion and the loan request was one thing, but the time and distance had given me a lot more insight into who I'd been when I'd blown things so badly at Chadwick. I was more mature and ready to put the past firmly behind me.

For my first gesture of reconciliation, I parked my car near Negley's house and retraced my steps to the scene of the garage incident to see what, if anything, had changed. Did he still keep the Lamborghini in tip-top shape? I stood there for a moment, looking at the refurbished facade of the garage, breathing in the warm air, and looking through the windows of his house. I felt the urge to walk up, knock on the door, and explain myself, but decided to wait. Why not let sleeping dogs lie? I turned around and headed to the center of campus, where the invitation said the festivities would convene.

I recognized her immediately. Jenaye's long hair rested on her shoulders, her honey-colored skin smooth just like I'd remembered from our first encounter. Standing near the dining room, she grasped a glass of champagne, the sunlight brightening her face. Next to her were people laughing, congratulating her, and grabbing at her left hand. I couldn't help but notice an engagement ring on her finger.

Seeing those hands again reminded me how easily they'd moved all over my body when we'd nearly made love. I was locked in an unforgettable fantasy. I wanted to believe that she'd saved herself for me after all this time, and as unrealistic as that sounded, I had silently convinced myself that was the case. I preferred the illusion of everlasting love. The sun at my back, I moved closer to the silhouette in the distance, hoping that somehow, when her image had become clearer, the ring, the sign she'd committed herself to someone else, would be gone.

"Isaiah?" The sound of her voice broke my concentration. "It's about time you got here. I almost didn't recognize you with that full beard. As usual, you're late."

"My plane was delayed. Plus, it's a long drive from the airport. You should know that," I said, smiling. "I almost forgot how to get here." I adjusted my brand-new pin-striped suit and looked down at my thick-soled shoes to make sure everything was in place. She hadn't mentioned the weight I'd gained, a good sign. "It's good to see you, Jenaye."

"It's been fifteen years," she said. "I just love that suit on you." She moved close enough for me to hug her, and I felt the soft fabric of her loose fitting gown. The hem barely touched her ankles. "Where are your glasses?"

"I wear contacts now," I said, stepping back a bit to get a better look at her. Her hair touched her narrow shoulders. I hugged her again, holding her tightly, as I'd done when we'd danced. She had my undivided attention.

"You have no idea what just happened," she said in her still raspy voice. The braces that had once held her teeth in place had been removed.

"I guess not," I said.

"We just announced our engagement."

"We?" My heart sank even further. The response was barely audible.

"I'll give you a hint," she said, smiling. "It's someone you know pretty well. He went to school here."

"That could be a lot of people, you know. How many guesses do I get? Is he a white boy?" The last part of the question came out in a whisper, but without the slightest bit of hesitation.

"No. No. Turn around and look over there." She pointed to the far side of the platform. "It's Richard Bonar."

I couldn't believe it, but then again considering Richard was the only other black kid left, there wasn't much of a choice.

"Richard?" I said loudly.

"Yeah, we're getting hitched."

"Wow." Seeing his face again reminded me of our final confrontation, but the heat of that moment had long dissipated.

"We've become real good friends. Did you know that Richard is a big music producer now? It was announced in one of the newsletters." She spoke slowly and then stepped back to see the look on my face. "And he works behind the scenes with a lot of big stars. He's on the road a lot, so we've been dating long distance. We were searching for the right place to make the announcement, and since we met here and have kept close ties with the school, this reunion seemed perfect. Now you know why my invitation was so secretive, and why I insisted that you get your butt down here." She took another sip of the champagne, taking her time swallowing. Through the long silence, she waited for me to say something. "I'm not sure if you want to go over and congratulate him. I'll leave that up to you."

"I guess so," I said. "But I'll be back. We're not finished talking yet." I walked through the crowd, trying to remember the names of people I'd only known for a short time. Richard stood in the distance, holding court with members of the crowd. He was still tall and slender, but now he looked as if he paid better attention to his wardrobe. He sported a crisp, blue pin-striped suit, a neatly pressed open-collar shirt, and tan dress shoes. I guess that's what the music business does for you, makes you aware of your appearance.

"Congratulations, Richard," I said. "I just heard the news."

He stood motionless for a moment as the words left my mouth, and then he reached for the lapel to touch my new suit. "This is a surprise. I didn't expect to see you. You're pretty sharp."

"I received an invitation, too," I said. "I wanted to see if there were any changes and make peace with everybody."

"As you can see, there have been lots of changes, but it seems like the biggest change is in you. I can already hear it," he said.

"You might be right. I certainly look at things differently."

"Oh, really?" He stepped back. "How so? We didn't exactly part on good terms."

"I know. I've forgotten about the past. I hope you have forgiven me for what happened here. I know it's been some time, but since then, I've turned things around."

He smiled, as if bygones were bygones. Truthfully, I expected something colder, but he seemed relaxed, almost unfazed by the whole incident. "If it's any consolation, Negley's had his share of trouble since that time, too. He left here a few years ago under less-than-favorable conditions."

Hearing this, I wanted to thrust my fists in the air triumphantly, but held myself in check. "I didn't know that."

"Yeah, he was dismissed for sexual misconduct with a female student," said Richard. "I don't know all the details, but someone told on him, too. I hear he's a reformed man now. Better late than never, right?"

It was hard for me to picture Negley, the bookworm professor, as a sexual predator, but what did I know? "Is that what you said about Jenaye?" I asked.

"To my surprise, things just kinda took off." He looked down. "I know you two had something going at one time, but I had no way of knowing my continued involvement here would result in this engagement. We're helping Chadwick recruit other black kids now. Do you know any that would fit?"

I thought about Tee's son, Rodney, and the opportunity the school could provide. He was fourteen, nearly the same age as I'd been when I attended Chadwick. His grades were exceptional. Getting him in here was the least I could do, especially with his father long gone.

"I've got the perfect candidate," I said. "What do I need to do?"

"We don't have to talk about it now, but just make sure you give me all his information before you leave here. You can submit the application and complete the testing process later. Of course, there are a few more black kids here now, but there's room for plenty more."

"I can't wait to tell him," I said. I was smiling now. "You're a lucky man, Richard. At one time, I thought it would be me marrying Jenaye, but ... well, you two will be all right. You've got a lot in common." They were linked by their love of music, but I didn't believe a word of what I was saying. Telling Richard that he had a lot in common with Jenaye just felt appropriate for the moment.

"You'll be okay, too, Isaiah. Before you know it, you'll find the right person again. Just keep yourself busy. What kind of work you doing now?"

"I'm the chief financial officer at American Capital." My dreams of playing pro ball and becoming the next Bill Russell had ended after a successful college career at Cal. I'd been drafted by Lakers but didn't make the final roster. Disappointed, I'd given up on hoops completely and poured all my energy into becoming an executive.

"Sounds impressive," said Richard with raised eyebrows. "You ought to start sending in your accomplishments to the alumni newsletter."

"Jenaye told me about your work as a music producer. I never thought you'd be involved with music. Do you think you'll come up with a big hit?"

"I hope so," he said. "But it's harder than you think."

Given Richard's love of art, it wasn't surprising that he'd finally found his calling. He told me the story of how drawing superheroes as a teenager had led him into the world of creating music. It was all art, he said. There was more to the story, but we needed more time to talk about it. If we kept talking, I'd never get back to Jenaye. We could cover more ground later.

I shook his hand again and excused myself. Jenaye had moved to the other side of the platform since our opening discussion, and I took the long walk in her direction so that we could finish where we'd left off.

"That was a long congratulation," she said. "What'd you tell him?"

"That I'm happy for the both of you," I said. "But that I still wish it was me."

"You were married, Isaiah."

"*Was* … that's the operative word," I replied.

"I'm sorry things didn't work out in your marriage. At one time, you seemed like you were happy."

"Things changed," I said, referring to the gradual transformation of my marriage into an unbearable union. Geneva had fallen in love with the church, and I'd done the same with my career. Going in opposite directions, she attended church daily, and I stayed at work, causing a strain in our relationship. The good thing was that I'd arrived at a point where I was about to decide on the fate of an important construction project at my old school.

"That seems to be the story of your life so far, isn't it?" She grasped the glass tighter and waited for my reaction. It seemed as if she had been waiting years to deliver that observation.

"What do you mean by that?" I fired back, wanting her to explain herself fully. She could have been talking about a litany of past failures, including my attempt to make it through Chadwick.

"You know what I'm driving at," she said. "I expected to see you on television playing for the Lakers or telling me you became an activist."

"Yeah, I wasn't good enough to make it to the pros, and as for activism, my dreams ended with the death of a friend. After your help in geometry, I think I got more confident in math." I had to laugh at the comment that was intended to lighten things up. "And what about you? I never thought you'd be announcing your engagement to Richard at an alumni function or that he'd be a music producer."

"I'm sorry about your friend. I remember the story from a while back. How could I forget? Anyway, careers are hard to predict." She wasn't interested in continuing that train of thought. "So what else is going on with you? Fill me in. I'm waiting."

"You already know that I got promoted to chief financial officer at American Capital ..." I paused a moment to gauge her reaction. It was my turn. "I'm glad you sent me the invitation, but I'm here to do a little work, too. I've got to do some due diligence for the company."

"Due diligence?" she asked. "Is that accounting talk?"

"Yeah, I'm just checking things out around the campus before I make a loan decision. That's my big announcement."

She blushed. "Okay, okay. Good for you. I knew you had it in you." She took a sip. "I guess my math tutoring really helped, didn't it?" She didn't wait for an answer. She smiled briefly and continued. "Me, I started my own public relations company, and so far, business has been going well. If things stay like they are, I won't have to go back to corporate America."

"You don't need to worry about much. You've got the drive." I moved closer, so that only Jenaye could hear me. "It's strange, but I still feel like I owe you an explanation. After I got kicked out, things happened so quickly that I never got a chance to explain myself. It's probably wasted breath now."

"I couldn't believe you did it."

"It was foolish," I said. "I didn't know what I was doing. I stopped by Negley's old house on the way here. They've repainted the garage and everything. Richard told me what happened to him."

"And Breedlove is the headmaster at another school."

"What happened to him?" I asked.

"He couldn't raise enough money from the alumni. Hagman's the new leader here."

I knew that from the financing package, but I played along anyway. I wondered about his reaction when he'd found out that I'd be the one deciding the fate of the proposal. "I should have known that was coming. Hagman always had his pulse on this place. He was on the fast track."

"So are you," she said.

"I'm on the fast track for a different reason. Since Tee died, I've been trying to set the example for his son. He's almost ready for high school, and

I've got to keep him on the right path. I've already told Richard about him. Since you're both working with the school, maybe you can get him admitted. It'll be good for him. If he makes it, it'll teach him he can thrive in any situation."

"That's what I was trying to tell you all along," said Jenaye, waving her finger in my direction. "Richard and I will make sure Rodney gets adequate consideration. Just don't forget to donate money to the school when you get another big promotion. At the rate you're going, you'll be on the cover of *Business Week* in no time."

"Don't worry, you'll get a check from me." I moved toward one of the tables so that I could pick up a glass of the champagne. I felt like making a toast. "You and this place will forever remain imprinted on my brain." I picked up the champagne and sipped it. The taste was bittersweet, like the moment. "I think your engagement and us getting together after all this time deserves a toast."

"I'll say."

I lifted the glass. Through the clear liquid and the bubbles, Dofi's face was visible. What was she doing here? Did she recall our dance? Was she available? I lowered the flute to get a clear view. We'd hit it off beautifully at that first dance, but the Hello Dance had ended in disaster. Had she heard the announcement?

"Is something wrong?" Jenaye could see that I was distracted.

"I just saw someone else I haven't seen in a while."

"Is it someone I know?"

"Maybe," I said, quickly changing the subject.

"Well, let's finish this toast."

Suddenly, the disappointment I'd felt from the engagement bombshell felt a little easier to handle. We clicked our glasses together, and the sound rung in my ears like a bell. Maybe that tone signaled that it was finally time to move on.

Printed in the United States
146780LV00008B/29/P